STUCK IN SECOND GEAR

CARMEN REID

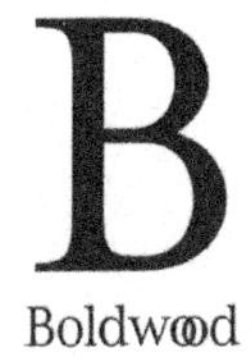

Boldwood

First published in Great Britain in 2024 by Boldwood Books Ltd.

Cover Design by Cherie Chapman

Cover Images: Shutterstock

A CIP catalogue record for this book is available from the British Library.

Paperback ISBN 978-1-83751-712-1

Large Print ISBN 978-1-83751-711-4

Hardback ISBN 978-1-83751-710-7

Ebook ISBN 978-1-83751-713-8

Kindle ISBN 978-1-83751-714-5

Audio CD ISBN 978-1-83751-705-3

MP3 CD ISBN 978-1-83751-706-0

Digital audio download ISBN 978-1-83751-707-7

This book is printed on certified sustainable paper. Boldwood Books is dedicated to putting sustainability at the heart of our business. For more information please visit https://www.boldwoodbooks.com/about-us/sustainability/

Boldwood Books Ltd, 23 Bowerdean Street, London, SW6 3TN

www.boldwoodbooks.com

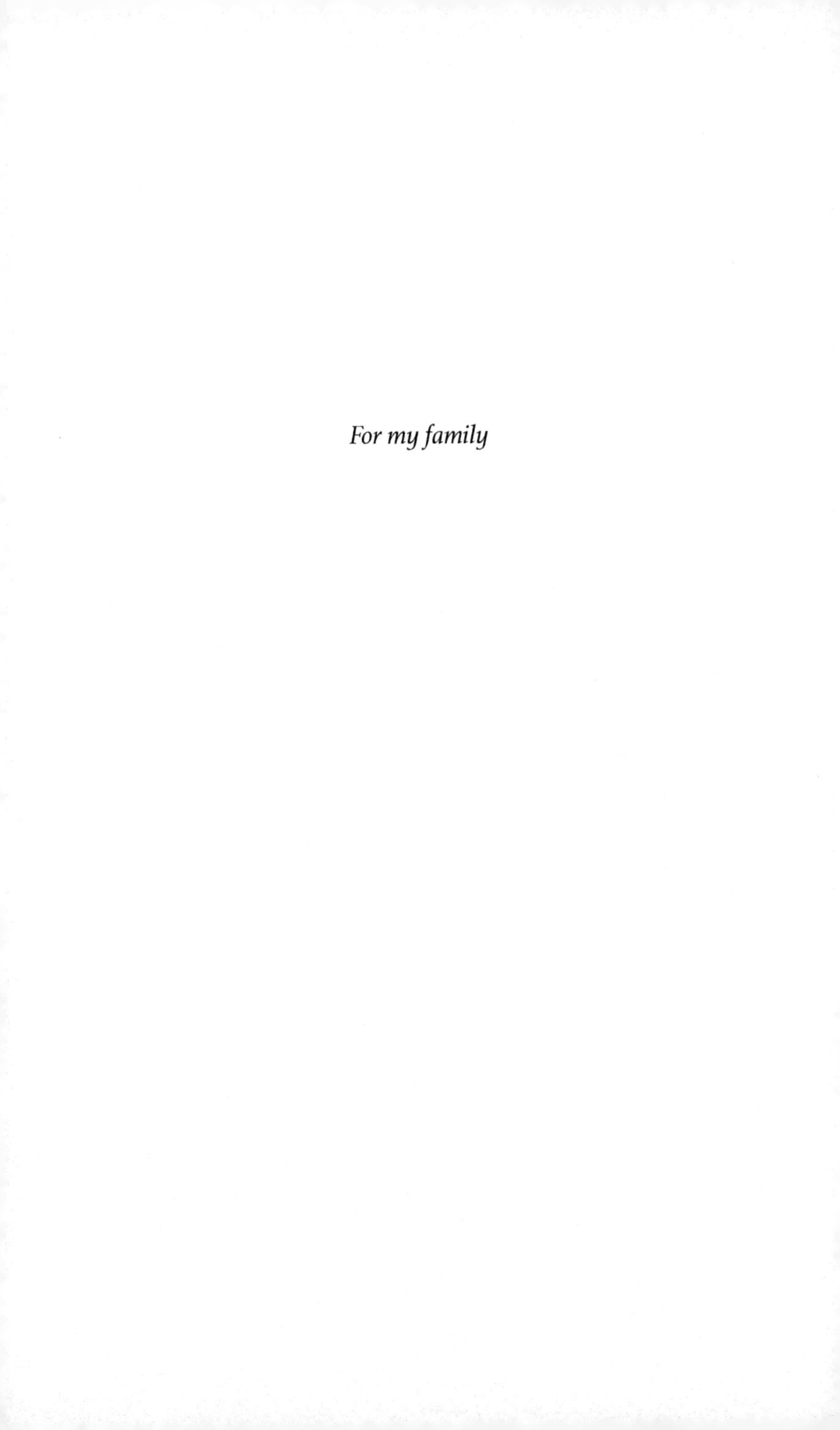

For my family

1

'Hello, is that Mrs Marshal?'

'Yes, but it's *Ms* Marshal,' Lucie replied, emphasising the Ms heavily. Honestly, more than twenty years into the twenty-first century, you'd think garage mechanics could cope with divorced women who did not want to be reminded that they were once married to berks like Miles Marshal.

Not for the first time, she wondered if she should revert to her maiden name and become Miss Lucie Chilvers all over again. But she'd been a Marshal for more than half her life, she realised with a shudder, and her daughter, Zoe, was a Marshal too, of course, unless she was going to marry that man and take on his surname, now that they were having a baby.

What was his surname? It occurred to Lucie with a burst of regret that she didn't know. Since her divorce from Miles, there was a distance between her and Zoe that had never existed before and although it made her deeply sad, Lucie felt as if she didn't know where to begin with repairing it.

'So, it's about this car,' the mechanic said, interrupting her thoughts.

'Yes, well, how is it doing?' As the car was eleven years old, had broken down and had been stretchered to the garage on the back of an AA lorry, she wasn't exactly looking forward to the patient update.

'Well...' He sighed and she could picture him shaking his head sadly. 'It needs a lot of work.'

She braced herself and wondered how much 'mechanic' she would be required to speak here.

'The exhaust has to be replaced,' he began. OK, exhaust, yup, she knew that was the pipe sticking out the back.

'Along with the brake pads, one brake disc and the wheel struts.'

Lucie tried to keep up. This was something to do with braking and wheels.

'We need to look at the power steering as something isn't right there,' he went on. 'And you broke down because the clutch cable has gone, so that needs to be replaced.'

Clutch cable? What in the freak was that? Did anyone really know?

'Two of the tyres are bald, so they'll have to be changed.'

Oh God, tyres were always bad news. They were made of rubber but seemed to cost more than kryptonite or uranium.

'So, altogether, I'm afraid you're looking at about £2,400 worth of work including labour.'

'How much?' she asked, hoping that maybe she hadn't heard this correctly. Good freaking grief, this was bad. The bloody car had only cost her £5000 and now she realised why.

'£2,400,' he repeated. 'Power steering, wheel struts and the clutch cable involve quite a bit of work. And to be honest, there are some other things needing doing too, but this would be the bare minimum to get it back on the road and through its MOT in June.'

Lucie did a mental run-through on the current state of her bank accounts. It was nearly the end of May, so only a few hundred pounds were left in her current account and she needed all of that for groceries, bills and any other expenses before payday. Her precious 'rainy day' savings account, carefully scrimped and saved over the past two post-divorce years, stood at exactly £2,867. And then there were the two credit cards. One was hers and was about £500 in the red, due to some of the unexpected expenses incurred as she set herself up in her extremely modest post-divorce rental flat.

The other... Oh dear God, that bloody other card, with a debt of almost £9,000. That other card had been racked up by Miles but had been landed on her as part of their acrimonious divorce agreement, when she'd slowly come to realise that there weren't any 'assets' to split between them – only enormous debts caused by all the terrible business decisions her ex-husband had made. Too late, she'd realised that this particular card which had been used to pay *his* expenses had been in *her* name.

The full divorce revelations had totalled to absolutely not one penny of equity left in their beautiful home, a credit card £9,000 in the red in her name, plus being legally obliged to sign half of her pension savings over to him and having to wind up her own interior design business because it was too interconnected with his company. The only slight positive amidst all the calamity that had struck almost exactly two years ago now was that she'd never been a director in Miles's company. Otherwise, she would now be liable for half of the £470,000 he still owed banks, other lenders and the tax authorities. And he'd offered her a directorship several times. She shuddered at the thought.

'So...' The mechanic broke the long pause. 'Do you want us to go ahead with the work?'

Now it was her turn to sigh. What choice did she have? She couldn't ask them to tow it to another garage for a second opinion. Selling the car wasn't an option as it wasn't worth much and she needed it for all the regular visits to her dad. And she certainly didn't have the money for a new one. So, that preciously scrimped rainy-day account would have to be raided. And then there would only be £467 left. Not enough for any kind of rainy day at all.

She felt a jag of self-pity. Mrs Lucie Marshal used to drive a two-year-old white Mercedes with leather seats and personalised plates: LUC 13M. Mrs Lucie Marshal used to live in a fabulous architect-designed house with a wow-factor kitchen and marble-clad bathrooms; plus, she had enjoyed the gorgeous wardrobe, the holidays and the lifestyle to match. So it was hard to now be struggling to pay for repairs on a tatty old Nissan that she knew could not last much longer, even if it did get new brake discs and bloody wheel struts.

Still, moping about and dwelling on what had been and gone wasn't going to help. So, she took a breath and tried to sound brisk and together as she said, 'Yes, please go ahead.'

'No problem. It'll be ready for you tomorrow afternoon,' the mechanic added.

So that meant taking the bus to go and see Dad today.

* * *

Before she left the flat, Lucie checked herself over in the mirror. *Not too bad* was her first thought. Thanks to her beautiful mother, she had the kind of strong, olive skin that held wrinkles at bay for longer, and today she had enhanced it with a touch of blusher, brown pencil round her coffee-coloured eyes and a swipe of plum lipstick. Her brunette hair, home-coloured, was just above shoulder-length with a thick blunt fringe, which she trimmed herself between hairdresser visits. She thought she could still pass for a woman in her forties despite turning fifty the Year of The Divorce. Talk about two major calamities happening at once. Her stars had definitely not aligned that year. Oh no.

I'm maintaining, she thought to herself, *in spite of it all.*

As she had a day off work today, she was in jeans and a nice shirt instead of her office clothes. She still carried an expensive handbag and wore a good watch and gold earrings – all left over from her previous life. But this cheap and practical hooded anorak she was pulling on now, bought at the supermarket and designed to cope with ordinary life – walking to the station, popping out to the garage for milk – wasn't something that the former Mrs Lucie Marshal would have wanted or even needed.

I used to wear Chanel... came the vicious little thought to torment her. Followed by *I used to run my own very successful interior design business. And now I wear a Tesco anorak and work in admin and catch the bus.* But it never helped to think like this. She knew it didn't help. So she sighed, shook her head and tried to think about something, anything, else.

With yet another sigh, she scooped up the assortment of envelopes that had arrived in the post, stuffed them into her handbag without much of a glance, and hurried off to the bus stop.

After a fifteen-minute wait in this bland part of town, she caught the bus, took a seat, and spent several minutes looking out of the window. For late May in the south of England, it was a cool and gloomy day, so everything looked duller and greyer than usual. She remembered the unopened mail and brought the envelopes out of her handbag.

Turning them over in her hands, she could see that two

were obviously junk mail, so she pushed those back into her bag. Of the remaining two envelopes, one looked like a bill or a bank statement; the other was a silver envelope with a large white label on the front, her name and address handwritten in black, elaborate, curled handwriting. She had an ominous feeling about that envelope, so she turned to the much more boring white one with that unmistakable financial communication vibe. Ripping it, she brought out the pages and unfolded them.

Oh, for crying out loud. It was a statement for that bloody credit card. She stared for several moments at the balance outstanding: £8,775. Next month's minimum payment was going to be £263. Infuriatingly, she didn't even know what Miles had spent this money on. To find out, she'd have to dig back through stacks of old statements, assuming she'd kept them. In fact, how could she have kept them when she didn't even think she'd seen them? Miles had kept his use of her card hidden from her and must have jumped on the statement every month as soon as it arrived because she'd not known about this bill until the divorce, and now, here she was facing a payment of £263 a month for at least the next four years, and she didn't even know what for.

Impulsively, she took out her phone and dialled the customer contact number. When she finally managed to get through to a human, she asked, without much hope, if she could get copies of the statements that showed what the original transactions were.

'There haven't been any purchases for two years, so is it possible to look back before then?' she asked.

'Certainly,' came the chirpy reply. 'We'll be happy to help you with that.'

After a pause, the voice gave some company names that meant nothing to Lucie.

'In July 2022, there are payments to NuLife Co and Rejooven8 Ltd... Then in August, there's a £2,500 payment to the Inland Revenue.'

That sounded like Miles... spend now and worry about the tax bill later.

'Are you able to send me those statements please?'

'Of course, they'll be with you within five working days.'

Once she'd hung up, she was left holding the shiny silver envelope with the elaborate handwriting. She stared at it for several moments. Already, she had a horrible suspicion and felt that she would like to spend just a few more moments holding it, and not knowing the exact, awful details. But, glancing out of the window, she could see that the stop for her father's house wasn't far away now, so maybe it was best to just get this over with.

She pushed her finger under the envelope flap and tore the silver paper, then she pulled out the thick card and accompanying slips of paper.

Reluctantly, and with a pain in the pit of her stomach, she read the words 'To Lucie and her guest', handwritten at the top of the thick and luxurious invitation, followed by:

Jacasta Fletcher
and
Miles Marshal
request the pleasure of your company
at their wedding
and
ceremony of love amidst the peonies
#peoniesandlavender

Maison Violette, near Perpignan, France
on Saturday, 16 July, from 3 p.m.
Ceremony – drinks – dinner – dancing
Please RSVP by 16 June
www.peoniesandlavenderwed.com
#Jacastasweddingstory

It wasn't possible, as Lucie sat on a bus in a Tesco anorak, not to feel stunned by this, even though she had known it was coming. Well, she'd known her ex-husband was engaged to this beautiful Jacasta person, fifteen years his junior. But Lucie hadn't known until now that they were getting married in July, in a *ceremony of love amidst the peonies,* whatever the heck that was, and *in France,* and that they were going to invite her, along with that sad 'plus one' request.

Good freaking grief.

She wouldn't go.

Of course she wouldn't go!

Why on earth had they asked her? Only to make themselves look good, look magnanimous, of course.

Maison Violette, near Perpignan, France... She resisted the temptation to google it straightaway, but had visions of a gorgeous French mansion house with a marquee in the garden on a hot summer evening near the Med.

Her first furious thought was how could Miles even afford a wedding like this when he was still supposed to be in so much debt from his disastrous business fail, which had pulled their marriage down with it?

She looked through the other papers that had come with the invitation – a list of accommodation options with 'some rooms are available at Maison Violette for family; please contact us to arrange', then there was an RSVP card, plus a page with instructions on how to access the gift registry, the wedding website, the wedding venue and plenty of encouragement to follow Jacasta's daily updates on Instagram.

Feeling a flare of anger, she crumpled the pages up, folded the invitation in half and stuffed all of it back into her handbag.

Just leave me out of it! I don't want to know! she thought to herself.

Bloody Miles... How dare he land on his feet like this when she was now living such a totally different life.

Bloody Miles and his gorgeous young girlfriend and their glam French wedding. All so very different from when they got married all those years ago.

2

It had been years since she'd thought about *their* wedding, but now with her ex-husband's wedding invitation scrunched up in her handbag, Lucie found she couldn't help herself.

Their wedding had been low-key – a trip to the registry office and afterwards, a sit-down hotel dinner for about thirty guests. It had been a struggle to winnow down the family and friends on both sides to get to the limit imposed by her dad's wedding budget. Her dad was very well-off now, of course, but back then, he'd still been building up his business and there hadn't been much money to spare for lavish wedding events. Especially when they were unplanned.

At the age of twenty-five, Lucie had married Miles, six months after she'd first met him and two months after she'd discovered she was pregnant. A hurry, a rush, a whirlwind even. But that was handsome, ever-energetic Miles, always pushing on to the next thing, determined to get on with life, make his fortune, build his empire. And she'd been caught up in it all; plus, it had seemed like the right thing to do – marry him, have their baby, grow up and start creating their family and their future together.

Until she'd met Miles, she'd been quite a different person. She'd thought of herself as arty, creative, and just a little bit cool. She had an architecture degree under her belt and a slightly 'wild child' past. She'd studied in London and had sought out the cool crowd, snagging invites to the most fashionable gigs, clubs and parties. She had plenty of colourful stories to tell about sneaking celebrities and singers in and out of clubs and gigs to avoid fans, photographers, or even people they owed money to. She had been a regular at the kind of house parties where the models and the bands of the moment dropped in. Somewhere, someone had a photo of her lighting Kate Moss's cigarette. Yes, back in the 1990s, Lucie had counted several pretty famous stars as casual friends.

But when she'd met Miles, she had been impressed with his 'let's work hard and get on' philosophy. Until she'd met him, she'd been working, yes, but she'd been coasting along, hovering, waiting on the sidelines for her life to begin. But once Miles arrived, she was quickly married, living in a house with a garden in commuter-belt Bromley, waiting for her first baby to arrive. 'Where is being cool and arty going to get you?' she remembered him asking. 'It's time to toughen up and knuckle down.'

Together, they had worked relentlessly, deciding early on that one child was enough because they were full of plans and ambition and wanted to give their daughter, Zoe, a wonderful life. So Miles had carried on his day job as an estate agent for several years, but they'd started building Miles's property business and Lucie's interior design service on the side until those companies were big enough to work in full-time.

And so much success had come their way, pushing them on

to dream bigger, aim higher, earn... and borrow... more and more. Looking back, of course she knew she should have concerned herself more not just with her own business, but also with Miles's. She should have asked far more questions and she should have regularly poked about in his profit and loss spreadsheets herself.

But he'd always assured her that everything was fine: 'Don't worry about it. I've got it all under control with the accountants. Clever people – they're keeping me right. You concentrate on what you're good at – picking paint colours, choosing fabrics, making your customers' houses and my offices look fantastic. There is tonnes of money rolling in, *Lucie-Lu*.'

And that was how it had felt, for years. Current accounts stuffed with tens of thousands of pounds, beautiful cars, beautiful clothes, wonderful holidays, lavish nights out, the very best schools for Zoe. A relentless whirl of more properties, more projects, more clients and more success.

Until, about five years ago now, when she'd first felt just the hint of an uneasy undertow... That was the way she thought of it. As if something unsuspected and dangerous was lurking beneath the calm waters. Letters from the tax office arrived on the doormat too often. Miles developed a late-night whisky-drinking habit, seemed to lose his relentless optimism, and then came phone calls that he would leave the room to answer.

'Nothing to worry about. Honestly, darling, trust me.'

'Oh, some cashflow issues, it will all be sorted next month when that big payment comes in.'

When she thought back now, she realised she had let the undertow exist in the background, on the edge of her thoughts, for far too long. So when it had all finally come to the surface, it was far too late for her to be able to do anything about the situation.

In the end, it wasn't the debts, it was the deception that had strained their marriage to breaking point. She'd still thought she'd been in love with him until the sheer scale of how much he'd hidden from her and how much he'd risked, without ever consulting her, had finally become clear. Desperate, but sure everything would come round soon, he'd borrowed from far too many lenders, including high-interest, short-term loans. He'd left huge tax bills unpaid, until their remaining assets, even bank accounts, had all been frozen, and he hadn't told her anything about any of it. Worst of all, he'd bet their home by *forging her signature...* and he'd left her to imagine that everything was just carrying on as usual when, in fact, it was all crashing to the ground.

The uneasy undertow, the feeling that things weren't as they should be; that's what she should have paid attention to, not just about the finances, but even all those years ago when she'd first been introduced to Miles and made her choice.

At their wedding, she'd worn a lovely cream dress, not expensive, an off-the-peg bridesmaid dress from a high-street shop. Her dark hair, long then, had been piled onto her head then adorned with a gold band and a scattering of small, cream roses. She'd carried a bouquet of cream, white and green and she'd worn her mother's drop pearl earrings.

Just starting her third month of pregnancy, she'd thrown up before the ceremony, but apart from a fuller cleavage, she'd still looked girlish and slim. Looking back now, twenty-five seemed young to get married, but back then, she'd felt grown up and determined. She'd made her decision. She'd been completely convinced she was in love with Miles, wanted to marry him, have their baby, and start building their fabulous lives together.

But right at the back of her mind, she'd known even then that there was an undertow. She hadn't admitted it to herself at the time, but she could take it out from her memory and examine it a little more closely now. The truth was – she'd never been certain that Miles was the man she should be spending her life with. She'd just tried hard to convince herself, to make it work.

The year before she met Miles, there had been a work colleague she'd been so powerfully attracted to, convinced that something was going to develop between them, certain that this man was The One for her. But somehow, despite all the talking, laughing, confiding, longing looks and growing sense that a fire was building between them, the relationship never got started. Either he was seeing someone, or she was with someone, or one of them was sent off on a work project. The timing had never worked for them. Convinced she was in love, Lucie had pined for him, but never told him.

What could you do when you were twenty-four and desperate to have love, and for your grown-up future to begin? You couldn't just sit around and pine and hope that your unavailable love would suddenly become available. No, you had to get out there and meet a man like Miles, full of charm, enthusiasm and energy, be dazzled and believe that you wanted to get caught up in his whirlwind and be carried along. '*Toughen up and knuckle down.*'

All the time she'd been married, she'd tried not to dwell on the decision she'd made back then to give up on the other man and actively choose Miles. But now, she found herself wondering how different things could have been.

* * *

From the window of the bus, Lucie could now see her stop coming into view on this beautiful, leafy street with its generous, comfortable houses, so she reached over and pressed the bell to alert the bus driver. This street had never been her home. Her parents had moved here long after she and her older brother, Richard, had grown up and moved away. The charming, spacious house with its luxurious garden had been chosen just a few years before her father's planned retirement, with her parents brushing off all suggestions that it was too big, as they insisted they would need the spare bedrooms for family visits and the generous flower beds, lawns and vegetable patch to 'keep us from disappearing into the couch'.

Alighting from the bus, Lucie walked to the front gate of the house and paused, not able to resist a smile. The front garden was full of cheerful, colourful flowers – hollyhocks, delphiniums, tulips and stocks – as well as three busy bird tables and a stone bird bath where a cluster of sparrows was lined up to take a dip. The bright flowers and the bird playground had been her dad's idea. All part of his 'this place needs cheering up' philosophy after the sudden death of her mother eight years ago.

So, with Lucie's help, the awful period of grieving had been followed by busy weeks of decorating when they had both been so relieved to have a project and all the distraction of making the house over with bright flowers and colourful garden furniture outside and, inside, yellow walls, dazzling white and blue walls, vibrant modern paintings, bright curtains and sofas and, on her dad's insistence, surround sound, so he could play jazz, Elvis, Classic FM and The Beatles in his sitting room, kitchen, bedroom and sunroom.

'Life is so precious and short,' he'd said to her so often after her mother's death. 'You've got to remember to live every single day.' So, even now, when he was facing a terminal illness himself, he was relentlessly cheerful and optimistic, and Lucie was so grateful for his positive energy because the thought of losing him too was never far away. Over the years since her mother's death and in the wake of Lucie's divorce, they'd become very close. Her dad had become her mentor, her sounding board, her constant, and she wasn't ready to think about life without him. He was 'seriously' ill. That was all she could admit to. She wasn't ready to deal with the word 'terminally' yet.

* * *

Moments after she'd rung the bell, her father's carer, Domenica, opened the door with a wide smile.

'Hello, Lucie, good to see you. How are you today?' she asked.

'Good, good,' she insisted, 'and how is the reluctant patient?'

'Good grief! Never call me that!' she heard her dad shout out from the sitting room. 'Patient? Never! I'm the *im*patient!'

Lucie and Domenica exchanged a smile.

'He's doing just fine,' Domenica said. 'Go on in. I will be in the kitchen fixing you a sandwich.'

'No, really, I'm...' Lucie began, but she already knew it was hopeless. Domenica would make her the sandwich and insist she ate it, and that sandwich would be so beautifully assembled and delicious looking that Lucie would not be able to resist. So, she said, 'Thank you very much.'

'Here comes Lucie,' her dad greeted her, arms out wide for a hug from his spot on the sofa, blanket over his knees, his trusty copy of *The Telegraph* open on the crossword page. Yes, he was terribly skinny, but he was already nut brown because he spent every available moment chasing rays in the garden, and his lean and craggy face only made his smile all the wider and his bright eyes more vibrant.

'Hello, darling girl,' he said as she leaned in for a hug, trying not to notice how thin his back and shoulders were now, how light the arms were around her, because then she would have to think about how little precious time was left with him.

'Hello, Dad.'

'Pull up a pew' – he gestured to the space on the sofa beside his feet – 'and give me another word for pessimistic, begins with "g", six letters.'

She considered.

'Pessimism... should be right up your street.' He gave her a cheeky wink.

'Ha ha,' But she thought about her current mood and the matching weather, and came out with, 'Gloomy?'

'That's the one!' he exclaimed, writing it into the squares. 'You're the expert. So, what are you gloomy about today, my darling?'

'Are you asking because I look gloomy, or because there's always something?'

'Both, I suppose,' he said.

She sighed and leaned back into the comfortable cushions behind her.

'Guess what arrived in the post today?' she began.

'Your invitation to Miles's wedding in the south of France,' her dad replied, to her astonishment.

'How do you know? Don't tell me the bloody man has sent you one as well?'

'Ha! That would be a bit much even for Miles. No. No invitation for the ex-wife's father, who is possibly going to have pegged it by July. No, Zoe messaged, even sent me a photo of the thing. Perpignan, eh? That's a very nice part of the world. You should go.'

'Dad!' Lucie snorted. 'Of course I'm not going to go. I'm not going to sit at his wedding like some sad spare part, clapping while he does the first dance with his nubile new wife. Bloody hell, no, never!'

'Lovely part of the world though... and July. It'll be hot. Plus, you can get your money's worth, eat a huge dinner and drink all the drinks at his expense,' he smiled and waggled his eyebrows at her.

Despite her outrage, Lucie did have to think about that for a moment. It was three whole years since she'd last been abroad and too long to mention since someone had last bought her dinner.

With a glance at her dad, Lucie had to ask, 'So, how has he got the money to pay for a lovely French wedding, two years after very narrowly avoiding bankruptcy not just for himself but for me too?'

Her dad shook his head and looked back down at the crossword. 'Damned if I know. Maybe something has turned around for him again. He always had the luck of the devil. Or maybe she's paying. He has very good taste in wives, or he did have when he married you.'

'Thank you.' She smiled at her dad but suddenly felt that small shudder of fear. How could it be true that he wasn't going to be here for much longer? And how on earth was she going to cope with that?

Domenica came back into the room just then to deliver the kind of luscious sandwich Lucie had come to be very grateful for, along with a glass of water, and a small milky drink for her dad.

'What flavour are we going with today, Domenica?' her dad asked.

'Vanilla and strawberry,' she replied.

'Absolutely delicious,' he said, picking the glass up and

taking a sip. 'No one tells you that the best part about being ill is that you get to have milkshakes instead of meals,' he added. 'Another childhood dream fulfilled!'

'OK, I'll leave you two to gossip and finish the crossword,' Domenica said as she began to head out of the room again.

'Perfect, and thank you. Now, Lucie,' her father began, 'an inconvenient tax, begins with an "I", eleven letters.'

'Dad, that isn't in the crossword,' she said, telling him off.

'No, but I know you don't want to talk about these things, but we have to, well ahead of HQ and D-Day.'

'D-Day' was what her dad, with his dark and irrepressible humour, had nicknamed his impending death, while 'HQ' was the hospice that he would be going into when carers, Domenica and Jacqui, could no longer manage looking after him at home. Lucie suspected this inconvenient eleven-lettered tax was 'inheritance'. And even though thinking about him dead filled her with dread, her dad, ever the businessman, was going to want to talk through some financials.

'I've had Eric, my lawyer, over, and we are all tidied up and good to go, which is a great relief, I can tell you.'

'Dad...' Lucie warned; she really didn't want to talk about it. Talking about what would happen to the house, how his savings would be shared out, who would get his beloved paintings, or record collection... it was horrible, morbid, awful. It felt as if it was bringing his death closer. And the idea of gaining from his death, which she knew she would, was terrible. It made her feel incredibly guilty.

'Now, just listen and I'll go over the basics,' he said. 'Then I'll get Eric to send you and Ritchie a copy of the latest will. Does that sound OK?'

'I suppose so.'

'OK, here we go.'

Then, quite cheerfully, as if he was running through a new project, or a planting scheme for the garden, he gave her the outline. The house would not be sold until after his death, because that was more 'tax-efficient', and the money was to be split between her and Ritchie, with a generous sum also going to Zoe, and Ritchie's two children. There were pension plans and investment accounts that she and Ritchie would inherit between them and there was also a healthy savings account, which would pay for Domenica and Jacqui for as long as needed and give them a severance lump sum.

'You and Ritchie used to squabble to the death when you were little, but you're civilised grown-ups now, so I trust you to sort out what you want to take from the house between you. See if the grandchildren want anything too – especially Zoe, as she'll be setting up home – then flog the rest, and do it cheerfully, my darling. There will be a healthy old sum in the bank for you when it's all done and dusted. And you don't have to share any of it with the ex-Mr Marshal, so that's good news.'

For a long moment, as she imagined her beloved, endlessly optimistic dad no longer being here and the horrible task of emptying, packing up and selling this lovely house, she swallowed the hard lump in her throat and didn't have any words for him.

But finally, she managed, 'Thank you, Dad, for giving it all so much thought. For looking after us and thinking of us all. And now, please can we talk about something else?'

She quickly wiped a stray tear from her cheek as her dad sat up straight, patted her on the knee and replied, 'Of course, let's get back to Miles's wedding and why you should definitely go!'

3

Even at Lucie's next visit, her father wasn't ready to give up on trying to persuade her to say yes to Jacasta and Miles's invitation.

'We'll make a list,' he said, snatching up his pen and the little notebook that he liked to keep to hand. 'Pros and cons.'

'Dad, there are literally no pros,' she insisted, pouring herself a fresh glass of water from the jug set out on the garden table. Today, he was stretched out on a comfortable lounger in the full glare of May's sunshine, but still had a tartan rug over his legs because he was so frail now that he rarely felt warm enough.

'Cons,' she began. 'I don't want to go to France even for a weekend because you'll be even more unwell by then and I want to be here with you.'

'It's one weekend,' her father said. 'And maybe I'd like the peace and quiet,' he added, but gave her a wink.

'Well, next thing – surely people don't usually go to their ex's weddings, do they? I don't want to have the other guests wondering "what's *she* doing here?" Miles's family will be there, his disapproving mother and that snippy sister, Melissa. And it's not as if I have some gorgeous toyboy to take with me to make myself look good.'

'You could hire one,' her dad suggested. 'I'm sure I've seen that in a film.'

She just pulled a face at this before adding, 'And I can't think of anything to wear... and I'm definitely not buying something new just so I can stare at it in the wardrobe for ever afterwards, thinking of their bloody wedding. And it's a huge expense to go to the south of France to their "destination" wedding for a weekend, hashtag-love-in-the-lavender or whatever it is, and, just, no!' she exclaimed. 'I don't want to go! And you can't make me!'

They caught one another's eyes at these words and both had to laugh because she sounded like her petulant six-year-old self having a meltdown.

'OK, we've heard the cons, now consider the pros,' her dad said calmly. 'Number one: it's only six weeks away, so I will still be here under Domenica and Jacqui's care. Hopefully, no need to move to HQ before the end of July at the earliest. I know you're likely to be on "compassionate leave" by then, or whatever they're calling it these days – and very generous of employers to let their staff wander off and hang about geriatric death beds for weeks on end—'

'Dad!' she exclaimed. 'You think my mind will be on work while you're busy... pegging it?'

'Still, you'll be on leave. You've got some grim weeks ahead of you, so why not enjoy a little holiday?'

'Holiday? We're calling being frog-marched to my ex-husband's wedding a "holiday" now, are we?'

'Plus, *your* family will be there, not just Miles's family. Zoe and her partner, Zoe's cousins, who you never spent much time with. You are still their auntie. And as for nothing to wear...' He scoffed. 'Your fabulous clothes are all boxed up in one of the spare bedrooms upstairs and you can't tell me there isn't something glamorous up there that would be perfect for this occasion. And, yes, you're single, but why not show that you're still standing? You're unbroken, undaunted, undiminished.'

'Too many crosswords, Dad.'

'My darling girl, you could go and have some fun,' he added. 'Drink champagne, kick off your heels, dance on the grass, and remember that life is to be lived. You don't ever do that any more. You used to be full of fun as a girl – so much fun. Too much fun...' he teased.

Her response to this was a sigh and a roll of the eyes before she said, 'I think you can guess why I've not been having much fun lately... what with the near-bankruptcy, the divorce, Miles re-marrying, you getting ill. It's not exactly been a picnic.'

'All the more reason to put your best foot forward and enjoy life again,' her dad insisted. 'And who knows? Maybe you'll meet someone interesting at the wedding. Have a fling.' He chuckled. 'And wouldn't that be a wonderful revenge?'

Lucie cracked a smile at this. She felt all his love and care for her in these words. She suspected he was worried about her: divorced, living alone, Zoe all grown up and working in London, Ritchie and his family in Australia, Miles remarried, her mother gone and probably, by the autumn, her beloved dad would be gone too.

She felt the familiar stab of sadness and tried to stop it in its tracks.

'You're only fifty,' her dad went on.

'Fifty-two,' she reminded him.

'So young, in your prime! So much life to live – decades if you're lucky.'

'This is the advantage of hanging out with old people.' She gave him a wink.

'And Zoe is able to go, isn't she? She won't be too far gone to travel?'

'Zoe said she was going. She'll be thirty-four weeks. Her baby's due the last week of August.'

Even as Lucie said these words, she still couldn't believe them. Zoe's baby... How could her baby, Zoe, possibly be having a baby of her own? With a man Lucie had yet to meet. And no doubt everyone would tell her that was her own fault. No quicker way to fall out with your adult daughter than to tell her maybe she shouldn't be rushing into the lifelong commitment of a baby with a new boyfriend so soon after the upheaval of her parents' divorce. But she couldn't unsay what she'd said, and what upset her so much was that she and Zoe had always been so open and honest with one another. Was that just supposed to stop now? Was Lucie supposed to say only what Zoe wanted to hear for the rest of their lives?

'Lovely time of year to have a baby,' her father said. 'I'll definitely try to hang about for the baby. But if I'm rambling and dribbling, you are to make sure they whack up the morphine pump and finish me off.'

'Dad, please!'

'And Zoe's man – Rafi, isn't it? Is he going to the wedding too? And have you met him yet?' he added.

'No... you know I haven't met him yet, I would have told you. And I don't know if he's going,' Lucie admitted. And for a moment, she wondered if she should confide more fully in her dad – about how she'd aired all her doubts and anxieties about the boyfriend and the baby to Zoe at the start of this pregnancy, and it had been a big argument that still didn't feel as if it had been repaired. Of course, they'd seen each other since, they spoke and messaged... but it had caused a coolness. Zoe was guarded with her mother in a way she'd never been before. And Lucie worried about it, wondering how it could be repaired. She was also fretting about her daughter becoming a mother in her twenties, in London, with her very busy job, and wondering how Zoe was going to manage.

'No doubt you're in a frenzy of anxiety about it all, you old worrywart,' her dad said, guessing at her thoughts.

'Well... do you blame me?' Lucie asked, and then she couldn't stop some of her angst from spilling out. 'No word of marrying, no word of even moving in together. Zoe is six months pregnant. She's going to be a single-mum nurse. That is not an easy life. And she's only twenty-seven.'

'Older than you were,' her dad reminded her.

'You never regret having your baby, of course you don't. But it would have been easier if I'd left that till I was older,' Lucie said.

'You made it work,' her dad insisted. 'And so will she.'

'She is so clever, so capable. She could easily have done medicine. Life in London would be a lot easier on a doctor's salary than a nurse's.'

There; now Lucie had gone and blurted it. The other thing that continued to annoy her, had annoyed her for almost ten years now: why had Zoe picked nursing rather than full-blown medicine? She still didn't understand it. So bright, so capable, so together and independent... she still didn't understand her daughter's choice.

And yes, Lucie worried that this Rafi guy wasn't committed and her daughter was going to be left to bring up the baby alone. But suggesting this to Zoe had completely upset her and that was why Lucie and Rafi still hadn't met.

'You know, Zoe seems very happy and not worried at all

about everything that you're busy fretting about,' her dad pointed out. 'She's very busy, of course, but she loves her work. And take it from me, no one ever thinks the man their daughter chooses is good enough.' He gave a little chuckle at this.

'Turned out you were right,' Lucie said. 'And can I just say, you never mentioned anything at the time.'

'Well, would you have thanked me?' her dad retorted. 'You were expecting his baby and everything seemed to go pretty well for twenty-odd years. So, I'm glad I kept my thoughts to myself, as all parents should.'

Ouch.

And maybe she *should* have kept her thoughts to herself. But that's not how it had once been between her and Zoe. They'd always been able to be completely honest and open before. But the relationship with Rafi... and, yes, Lucie and Miles's divorce too, these things had changed the mother–daughter bond.

There was a pause in the conversation. Her dad leaned back against the lounger headrest and closed his eyes. They'd been talking for some time now and he was probably very tired.

'I should shut up and let you have a snooze,' she suggested.

'I'm not snoozing,' he insisted, 'I'm closing my eyes to better appreciate the song that the very clever blackbird is singing from the top of the cherry tree.'

'Ah.'

His eyes still closed, he added: 'Lucie, you should go to the wedding and enjoy the heck out of your still-young self. Go upstairs to the back bedroom, look through your boxes for an outfit, and at least think about it. You can thank me later.'

'Right...' Lucie said, getting up. She wasn't going to the wedding and that was final. But she did need to get out of her dad's hair for a bit, so maybe she would go upstairs and face the things lurking in those upstairs boxes – out of sight, but not entirely out of mind, ever since she had packed up and left the marital home.

* * *

Pulling a big cream-coloured cardboard box out from under the bed, Lucie felt completely half-hearted. Now that she was up here, really, the last thing she wanted to do was look through prized treasures from her old wardrobe and get upset about the life she didn't lead any more.

She made great efforts every day, as she went about her daily routines – visiting her dad, commuting to her admin job, working, buying her groceries, tidying her flat – not to think about what had been and gone. She tried to focus on the present, the here and now, and was that so bad? She'd been divorced for two years and her dad was dying. The present was challenging enough without torturing herself about how life was once. And as for the future, there were only two points in the future that she was focused on right now – her dad's death and the arrival of Zoe's baby. She didn't have any spare capacity to think about what the future held for her beyond these two momentous events.

She looked under the bed again. The big, smooth, cream-coloured cardboard boxes were full of beautiful clothes from her former, glamorous life. She didn't want to open them and revisit all that pain and regret. In all honesty, she didn't even know why she was hanging on to these things. She was never going to wear them again and really she should just sell them and enjoy having some extra money.

She didn't want to look back. Looking forward was not easy because it was going to bring a lot of sadness and she didn't know where she was heading after that. But she definitely did not want to look back. She wasn't going to Miles's wedding and that was final. She had put the 'no thanks' RSVP in the post today.

She was just about to get up from looking under the bed when she saw that at the back behind the cream boxes was a smaller, older cardboard box. She couldn't think what was in there, so she put her arm and her head under the bed, stretched out, got hold of it and part-slid, part-wiggled it out into the open. This box was dusty, and the thick Sellotape was dried out and curling up at the edges. This hadn't been part of the big pack up from when she had moved out of the marital home – now sold, of course. No, this box looked as if it had been here for years, maybe even left over from her childhood bedroom.

She easily peeled away the old, dried-out tape, then she opened the flaps. Right at the top was a fat envelope full of old photographs. She slid them out and had to stifle something of a gasp as her eyes fell on the top image.

It was years and years since she'd seen this photo... taken just before she'd met Miles. Now, vivid memories of that work night out so many years ago flashed into her mind. A big crowd of them enjoying a well-deserved dinner at one of London's swankiest restaurants. There she was, twenty-four years old, in that lovely silver and gold dress with the wide shoulder straps. Her arms were bare, her hair loose, a delighted smile across her face. And there *he* was, Clark, sitting right beside her, the kindred spirit, the man she'd worked with, laughed with, fallen so completely in love with all those years ago. She still couldn't quite explain why nothing had developed between them. Somehow, although it had felt so possible, so almost inevitable that they were going to get together, they'd never been available at the same time and at the height of the time when something could have happened.

What struck her now, as she looked at this photo all these years later, was the obvious answer to the question that had tormented her back then. *Does he have these feelings about me too?* Looking at his face now, objectively, as a true grown up, the only sensible answer was – *oh yes, he does, he really does.*

Sitting side by side, turned to face one another, oblivious to the photographer, they looked exactly like a couple. Their eyes were locked. They were deep in conversation, smiling widely, and totally captivated.

He was such a handsome man – fit, cared about his clothes to the right extent – not too much (like Miles), not too little – and always smelled so good, she remembered. They had worked together for the year before she'd met Miles. Clark, a few years older, a rung or two ahead of her at the architecture firm, helping her to learn, appraising her work, encouraging her efforts, telling her all about the buildings that had inspired him. Yes, work hours, he was all seriousness and ambition, determined to get better every day. But out of hours... he had been fun and funny. Loved her clubby, finger-on-the-pulse knowledge, so together with other colleagues, they had gone out and spent most weekends immersing themselves in every kind of music. Her wrangling them tickets to the hottest bands, the exclusive clubs, getting them onto the guest-lists and into those roped-off VIP areas.

It had been more than a little intoxicating to be standing next to him at work, concentrating and learning from him, knowing that later that night, she would be brushing up against him on the dancefloor.

No doubt their colleagues had thought they were going to end up as an item. And Lucie had thought about it often enough too. But something always got in the way... She had a boyfriend when he was free, he was seeing someone when she was available; maybe that had only added to the attraction building up between them. But then he was sent to the US with work for five months. And in those five months, she had met and married Miles, moved and left her job, and she hadn't seen Clark since.

All this time later, looking at the photo, seeing the obvious delight in their eyes as they laughed together, Lucie had no idea what to do with the knowledge that she might have missed the very thing that she should have been running after. And now it was all too late. Far too late. She pushed the photo back into the envelope, put the envelope back in the box, closed it up and shoved it under the bed again.

4

Zoe Marshal glanced up over the top of her face mask at the Intensive Care Unit nurse who had just arrived at the patient's bedside to take her place and allow her to go on a long-overdue break.

'Sorry you've had to hang on... it's been chaos all morning,' her colleague apologised.

'I know, not your fault,' Zoe replied. 'But, oh my God, I am prepared to literally kill and step over the bodies for coffee if I have to.'

The two colleagues spent several moments handing over and making sure the patient's notes were right up to date, then Zoe got up and headed for the exit of the critical care ward. Out in the corridor, she lowered her mask, freed her hair from the surgical cap, untied her plastic apron and ran her hands over her tired face and her obvious pregnancy bump.

'Hello, baby girl,' she murmured as her hands went over the blue scrubs material at the side of her belly. 'Let's go and get ourselves some water, a sandwich and a big, milky cappuccino. Then let's try and get Daddy on the phone, hmmm?'

After washing her hands and face, and re-tying her long, dark ponytail with the help of the bathroom mirror, Zoe made her way to one of the hospital's cafés. Once her sandwich, banana and coffee had been purchased, she settled down at a table and prepared to call Rafi.

As he worked from his tiny flat as a cyber security expert, it was usually easy enough to get hold of him on her breaks, unless he was in a meeting or caught up with some particularly tricky task. She looked at her phone... nearly noon. She'd been sitting at Mr Williamson's bedside monitoring his care for nearly five hours straight without a break. No wonder she felt tired.

Hitting Rafi's number, she could feel the twinge of tension in her system. Surely by now, twelve o'clock, he would have done what he'd said he would?

She listened to the dial tone for just a few moments before she heard his voice.

'Hey, Zoe, how are you doing?'

'Hi, babe, not too bad,' she replied. 'Long morning, but that's nothing new. We're hanging in there.'

'I hope you're looking after yourself—'

'Of course I am,' she assured him. 'We'll power on through the next few weeks and then I'll be on a lovely, long leave. I'm so looking forward to it.'

'Yeah.'

In just that one word, she heard the kindness, the warmth, in his voice and knew she loved him. It was so exciting to be planning a baby with him... and planning a new home together, the three of them. Please...

Pause.

She waited.

Maybe he could go first. Maybe he could tell her that he'd

spoken to the estate agent this morning and the flat was going to be theirs. Maybe he'd even have a provisional moving-in date... Could it even possibly be before the baby's due date?

She let the pause go on for as long as she could stand, then had to break it with a questioning: 'So...?'

Silence.

'So, have you been in touch with the estate agent?' she asked. 'Have you put our offer in?'

Zoe could feel herself holding her breath as she waited for Rafi's answer. She pictured him sitting at his desk with those enormous screens in front of him, his huge headphones over his ears and those impossibly long eye lashes brushing against the deep olive skin of his face. She found herself thinking about how beautiful their daughter would be, raven-haired like both her parents with skin somewhere between Zoe's light olive and Rafi's much deeper tones. What colour would her eyes turn? Deepest brown like her father's or with some of the mossy green flecks that Zoe saw in her own hazel irises?

'Zoe...' Rafi began. 'I just... I realised that I don't like it enough.'

Her heart dropped and she waited for the list of niggles to begin.

'It's a twenty-minute walk to the Tube,' he went on, 'and a thirty-minute walk to the park. The second bedroom is very small and I'm going to have to fit my desk and all my work stuff in there... and where will that go when our daughter needs her own room? The living room is open to the kitchen, so I can't have my desk there. So, I just don't think it's right for us. We can't rush into this. It's a very big, very expensive decision.'

'Jesus, Rafi...' Zoe whispered. Her head was bent down low, so that no passing colleague could see that she was in danger of crying. Everyone at work knew her as strong, determined and completely capable. No one here needed to know that she couldn't persuade her boyfriend to buy a home with her just three months from the imminent arrival of their baby.

'This is the third time that you've changed your mind at the last minute,' she rounded on him. 'The third time! The first place was too close to the Tube station; the second place was too north-facing and gloomy. And I agree, yes, we ideally need three bedrooms, so you can have an office. But we can't afford anything that isn't in Outer Mongolia with three bedrooms, so we have to compromise.' Angrily, she added, 'My God, can't you get that into your head?'

'But we can't be looking for another new place in two years' time,' he insisted. 'There's stamp duty, lawyer's fees, moving costs – that would just be a huge amount of money wasted.'

'Maybe you could go and work in your company's office when our baby needs her own room,' Zoe snapped. 'Did you think of that?'

'I work very long hours and so do you. Me doing a long commute to the office and back isn't any help to us,' he replied. 'Working from home is the best option.'

Plus, she knew it was what he preferred. Rafi was quiet, happiest in his own space, and almost painfully shy. If they hadn't been the first people on the scene when a cyclist was knocked from his bike two years ago, she had no idea how she might ever have met him. He rarely went out, had only a couple of close male friends, and few interests outside his work. But none of this detracted from him being the kindest, most interesting, most handsome man she'd ever met. She really did love him. Even if they were the proverbial opposites who attract. At work, she was surrounded by far too many of those arrogant, alpha-type pricks, and Rafi was the perfect, completely refreshing antidote to all that.

But they needed to move. There was a healthy deposit stacked in both their bank accounts, ready and waiting. There was a budding baby, who would be here by the end of August, and she had to have a home for their little family, or she was going to... explode!

She was desperate to be that heavily pregnant lady picking out paint colours, assembling a cot, buying her very own pots, pans and crockery. She'd spent almost ten years moving from student rentals to shabby flat shares, and she was done. She would honestly settle for somewhere in Outer Mongolia if that was what was required. Outer Mongolia was probably a lovely country, much maligned.

'Are you sure it's the flat?' she asked him now. 'Are you sure it's because this flat isn't right and the other ones weren't right either?'

'What do you mean?' he asked.

'Well, here we are with you backing out at the last minute again. Maybe you don't want to move. Maybe you don't want to live with me and our daughter.'

She took a steadying breath in and out as she listened to him protest that this wasn't the case at all.

As calmly as she could, she added, 'If you don't want to be a dad, if you're thinking about breaking up with me and getting out of all this, I need to know now, OK? Not when our girl is one month old or six months old. You just tell me right now, so that I can buy my own place and get on with my life. OK?'

'Zoe! Please don't say that!' he exclaimed. 'It's not that. Of course it's not that! I just don't want to buy this flat. That's all. I've been on the website and I've booked us a viewing for the weekend. It's really promising, only ten minutes from the Tube...'

The Tube he didn't even want to take to work. Why was this

such a big deal for him? She wiped at the tear that had slipped down on to her cheek. She just didn't want to do this any more, spend the weekends trudging through unfamiliar streets, peering at other people's decorating mistakes and untidy belongings, and all the time wishing and wishing that housing in London was much cheaper and they could afford the place with three bedrooms and a garden that they really needed. The kind of home that you would want to bring a baby into. Instead, *everything* was a bloody compromise. That was the truth. And this flat had been fine, honestly, she would have made it lovely for them all. So why was he being so bloody stubborn and so bloody reluctant?

He doesn't want to live with us... the voice in her head kept insisting. *He's thirty-four, he's been on his own too long.*

Even now, they planned their time together and apart every week, according to her work rota. Usually, she spent two or three nights in his cramped, one-bedroomed place and he only came to her busy flat-share for one night. Three nights a week, they were apart.

'I'm working really late and you need your sleep,' was his standard reason. But maybe he just couldn't imagine a time when he wouldn't have his own space, and his own time to himself. What kind of father would that make him? *Maybe you're better off on your own... You could find someone else, in time,* her inner voice suggested. But this just prompted further tears to slip down her face.

'Rafi, living together is going to be fine,' she said. 'We'll make it work. We'll enjoy it.'

'I know! Of course it is,' he insisted. 'But we need to find the right place – a good place.'

'Are you sure?' she asked. 'Are you totally sure that's what you want?'

'Yes, Zoe, it is,' he insisted.

But somehow, she just couldn't trust herself to fully believe him right now. She was tired of looking. And she was so tired of men who told you one thing, what you wanted to hear, when all the time they meant something else quite different. Right up until today, she'd believed that Rafi was not one of those guys, but now she couldn't be sure.

'OK, OK,' she conceded. 'Send me the link to this place we're going to visit. And I'll look on the websites for anything else that looks promising. But, damn, Rafi, I really liked this flat. And next time, we have to go through with it.'

'I'm sorry,' he said. 'We will find somewhere just right.'

She gave a long, exasperated sigh.

'And what about my dad's wedding?' she remembered. 'I have to reply to them. The sixteenth of July, remember? Are you going to come? Have you booked the time off? I need to get our flights sorted.'

'Um... yeah... thanks for the reminder. I'll find out about time off...'

'You'll need to take the Thursday and the Friday before. Dad's got some events and a big family dinner planned for Friday. He's really looking forward to meeting you,' Zoe added. 'So, you are going to come?' she asked again.

'Yeah... of course, if I can get the time off.'

'Can you let me know by the weekend?'

Rafi's 'Yeah... sure...' in response to this was far too vague for her liking.

Once again, she wondered if he was just telling her what she wanted to hear.

5

Deva Nadar squirmed uncomfortably in his seat, wishing he hadn't put on this tight grey suit, let alone the white shirt with the stiff, constricting collar and this noose of a tie. No matter how many times he ran his finger around the tie to loosen it, it seemed to creep back up into place, threatening to cut off the circulation to his brain. No, it was no good, he would have to take it off, stuff it into his jacket pocket and undo his collar buttons. No matter what the rest of them thought.

In the dim light of the theatre, just before curtains up on the second act, he glanced across at the group of guys from his class. They had won this trip to one of London's biggest musicals in a uni competition. He was the one who'd seen the uni advert for the competition to analyse an entertainment business. He'd organised the group, taken charge of the project and been the perfectionist who'd made sure it was good enough to win, all so they could get these premium seats to one of his absolute favourites – Andrew Lloyd Webber's *Phantom of the Opera.* But he could tell the other guys were starting to get bored.

While he was mouthing the words to every song, and trying

to lose himself in the perfection and sheer gorgeousness of the performances, his appreciation of every detail of this show kept being interrupted by a whisper from Nate, or a giggle from Greg, and as for Will's suggestion that they all turn up suited and booted – why had he listened to that? He glanced over at them again, this group of five ambitious lads; to be honest, they all looked like candidates from *The Apprentice.* Something the others would no doubt be delighted to hear, but Deva felt out of place and oddly disappointed.

He wished he'd just saved up, bought a cheaper ticket and come on his own, dressed exactly the way he wanted. The feeling that he wasn't really part of this group, and that the others had just gone along with the competition as something else to put on their CVs, stole over him. Once again, he'd tried to be part of the gang, tried to 'get' them, make jokes like them, use the same phrases, even put on a suit and tie like they'd wanted to, but all of this trying to be like them made him feel even more of an outsider and a fraud. The feeling that nothing about them was really like him began to grow and now it was triggering that familiar, but unwelcome, nervy, anxious feeling.

He was in the third term of his first year on a very prestigious business degree in London. But he knew he didn't fit in. There was no module that he'd really enjoyed yet, no classmate that he'd really connected with. *Shut up*, he told himself. *Business is a huge field. Just learn the stuff you need to and then you'll graduate and find the business that works for you.* Maybe he would become an accountant for a huge theatre like this one. Maybe that would work for him.

But as the lavish red velvet curtain was pulled back to reveal the set for act two, and as the orchestra broke into those achingly familiar opening bars, he felt the flutter of anticipation in the pit of his stomach at the song he knew was coming. He didn't want to be an accountant for a business like this... Oh no. He looked with deep, heart-felt longing at the stage. Yes, he wanted to work here, but definitely not as an accountant...

* * *

Deva clapped and clapped and clapped after the final curtain came down. He stood up, whistled and even cheered. There was a tear on his face and he quickly brushed it away before any of his fellow students saw. How could they possibly know how important this show had been to him? Or how many times he must have played this music over and over in his little bedroom at home in Glasgow, dreaming of Paris, dreaming of stage shows and music and costumes and a life far away from the one he was living? *I'm in London,* he reminded himself. *I'm here, in the theatre, watching, listening – I'm right here, a part of this.*

'Deva, we're going to go to this cool bar not far from here. You coming with us?' Nate asked as they made their way out of the row of seats and into the packed aisle to slowly follow the crowd out of the theatre.

For a few moments, Deva considered. He pictured a crowded, noisy place, having to shout to be heard, not being able to follow the conversations over the hubbub, not hearing the jokes, laughing at the wrong time, chipping in with the wrong comments, gulping at beer to drown his growing anxiety. He didn't want to go, but he saw Nate's friendly encouraging grin.

'Go on, it'll be a laugh,' Nate said.

And Deva was on the brink of accepting because it felt so good to be asked, to be invited, wanted, part of the gang, after what felt like a lifetime of being cold-shouldered at school, and never getting the invitations, never being able to join in with the

Monday post-mortems of what everyone else had got up to over the weekend.

But Deva already knew what he really wanted to do. He wanted to get back to his room, where he would change out of this awful suit immediately, where he would play tonight's music all over again, where he would close his eyes and remember all the best moments from tonight's performance.

'No, you're alright,' he told Nate. 'I'm going to push on home.'

After saying his goodbyes to the rest of the group quickly, before they tried to convince him to go with them, Deva headed to the underground station, took the Tube to his part of the city, then made the short walk to the anonymous block where he had a tiny student bedsit. Soon, he'd navigated the reception, the lift and his corridor without having to say more than a quick hello to one or two familiar faces and then, at last, he was in the quiet, blissful solitude of his own room.

The relief when he closed and locked the door on the outside world and finally felt that he was home, alone, himself, un-judged, not trying to be anything for anyone, was physical. His shoulders dropped, his hands unclenched, and his face relaxed from the tense mask put on for the world outside into a much softer expression.

He went to his bedside table and switched on the lamp there, instead of the harsh overhead lights. The creamy low-watt bulb lit up Deva's little haven. It was immaculately tidy, as always. His narrow bed had a duvet in a cream cotton cover pulled ruler straight and sharp; on his desk, where all the pens were herded into two neat pots, a laptop was placed bang centre beside a notebook with a smart black cover. On the walls was an unusual choice of artwork for a business studies student. There were three large framed posters, all famous portraits of the legendary fashion designer, Coco Chanel. They were striking – Coco's jet-black bob, her pale skin, white pearls and black dress all set the monochrome theme for Deva's room.

He loved being here, in this space that, for the first time in his life, looked exactly as he wanted it to. No need to impress anyone else with this room, no need to conform to anyone's expectations. Here, in his own little cocoon, he could fully indulge in his love of France's most famous fashion designer, the music of the seventies, and songs from the greatest musicals. The classic *Phantom* poster was also framed on the wall, and taking pride of place on the bookcase were five Chanel biographies, all read several times over, and several lavishly illustrated books about his favourite musicals. On the shelf above the books were two small, prized bottles of scent – Chanel's Pour Monsieur and the classic, No 5.

Deva took off the suit and shirt, then pulled on his pyjamas and wrapped himself tightly in his beloved, well-worn dressing gown. Lying down on the bed, he checked his phone and saw a rash of messages newly in from his mum. It was late, but she was never one to spend much time sleeping.

> Hello Deva, did you get my email about Uncle Miles's wedding? I know he will want us to be there. So I will RSVP for us all.

Followed by:

> Your sisters and me will all fly from Glasgow. But if you're working in London over the summer, it makes sense for you to fly/take the train from there. Can you book your ticket please? And I'll pay you back. Wedding is 16 July, but M wants us there on 15 – big dinner and stuff planned.

Followed by:

Does that sound OK? I know you will enjoy being in France again. Love you, Mxxx

Followed by:

How was the musical? As good as you hoped? Xxx

Deva got up from the bed and went over to his artfully arranged shelf. He picked up the little bottle of No 5, bought in Duty Free, secretly, on the way home from a family holiday. He pulled off the glass lid and directed a short blast onto his inner wrist. Then he breathed in that sharp-sweet, powdery, utterly distinctive scent that evoked so much. His mother, yes, but also many other glamorous women he'd known and admired. This was the smell of theatre lobbies, cocktail bars and, of course, Coco herself. Fashion designer, muse, style icon, business-woman extraordinaire, who'd gone from being a child abandoned in a convent orphanage to become one of the richest, most famous women in the world. Her essence was available to everyone, anyone, by taking the lid off this bottle and squirting her unique formula into the air.

Deva sat down on the bed and picked up his phone to reply to his mother.

Hey Mum, excited about Uncle M's wedding. France! I'll book time off and take train. Perpignan! So close to Aubazine, Brive La Gaillarde and other places connected to Coco that I'm desperate to visit. I want to stop in Paris too.

His mum was the one person who knew about his Chanel

obsession, and he wasn't surprised to get a reply from her almost straightaway.

This trip is about the wedding, D, not rushing about France chasing your ideas. But if we can fit something in, maybe.

Now there was something else Deva was wondering about... but he knew just what his mother would think of this. Still, if you don't ask, you don't get... and all that. And after tonight, he definitely wanted to ask.

Do you think Uncle M would like me to sing at the wedding? Maybe at the ceremony or afterwards? Should I message him and ask?

He crossed his fingers and hit send.

Oh Deva, I thought you were putting singing to the side to concentrate on your studies.

This will be in the summer holidays

You'll be working, remember

I can still practise singing in my spare time

Fine, you message him and ask. But don't be surprised if you get a no. Jacasta wants everything to be perfect.

I'll be perfect!

Well, send a message and see what they say

OK, goodnight, Mum xxx

Love you xxx

Deva slumped back on his bed now. It didn't matter what his mum said, or even thought. He was going to find a way to stop in Paris so he could follow in Chanel's footsteps. He would stand in the Place Vendôme, gazing at the Ritz Hotel where she once lived. Then he would cross the square to the iconic Chanel shop on the other side of the street and stroll down Rue Cambon to gaze in the windows of her other stores. Brive La Gaillarde was maybe optional, but *nothing* was going to stop him from going to Aubazine, to visit the convent where Chanel spent the formative years of her youth.

For Deva, Chanel represented the spirit of independence and determination. She'd been small, like him, and overlooked, like him, and had plenty of 'issues', like him too, but somehow through sheer belief and stubborn determination, Chanel had created a fabulous life for herself. The life she knew she was destined to lead. She'd worked very hard, but it had given her freedom to live the life she wanted – and now images from his favourite Chanel photos came to mind: Chanel in pearls, Chanel in black, Chanel on a yacht, by the beach, Chanel wearing the one item guaranteed to cause a scandal in the 1920s – trousers!

Independence, determination, the willingness to defy convention – that was what Deva loved about his heroine. This was what inspired him.

And it was crazy... but whenever Deva daydreamed about stepping through the imposing limestone arch of the Abbey, where Chanel had spent her youth, he pictured himself wearing something that bore the legendary Chanel label, and he was carrying the iconic 2.55 quilted handbag.

6

TWO MONTHS LATER – 12 JULY

Lucie lay back on the sun lounger in her dad's garden trying to relax and enjoy the warmth of this beautiful morning. She closed her eyes and took a slow breath in and out.

It was the start of her 'compassionate leave' absence from work, which would allow her several weeks of fully paid absence, followed by as much unpaid leave as she needed.

'Take your time,' her manager had insisted. 'We'll miss you, of course, but don't come back until you are ready.'

Thinking ahead to when her father would be gone was awful, so she tried not to do much of that. Next week, her brother and his family were arriving from Australia and the move to the hospice would be coming soon. Her dad, ever practical, had already made all the funeral arrangements, right down to the choice of sandwiches, and had even organised a survey of the house and chosen the estate agent.

'All you and Ritchie will need to do post-D-Day is pack the place up, call the lawyer and liaise with the estate agent. A hassle, I know, but it will keep you busy and stop you dwelling on what's been and gone,' her father had told her in his usual upbeat tone.

It was strange, but the frailer he grew, the more cheerful he seemed to become. Lucie was beginning to wonder if this wasn't something to do with the drugs he was on. He'd always been an energetic optimist, but now, his happiness was on an even higher plane, edging towards euphoria.

She glanced over to the sun lounger set at a little distance from hers, where her dad, almost skeletally thin now, was determinedly puzzling his way through the daily crossword.

'Eight letters, "m" blank, blank, "r", ceremony to join two together in wedded bliss,' he said, but there was a crafty edge to these words.

'Dad!' she complained gently. 'That is not in the crossword! If you want to bring up the fact that Miles's *marriage* is this weekend, you can just say so, but I've got no comment.'

'Are you regretting your decision yet?' he asked.

'No! I want to be here with you, enjoying this gorgeous weather and the daily crossword challenge.'

'I have no idea why,' he said. 'Not when you could be in the south of France with your family... drinking, dancing...'

'Laughing at Miles's hair plugs and Jacasta's over-the-top gown,' she added sourly.

This made her father laugh.

'Really, he's been mucking about with his hair?' he asked.

'From the photo Zoe showed me, his hair and his teeth look suspiciously different. But if you've got a young wife who's an "influencer"' – Lucie couldn't resist a snort – 'then you've got to keep up.'

'What in the heck is an "influencer"?' her dad asked. 'One of those social media types that flogs their wares to their "followers", I suppose.'

'You've got it – apparently clothes and cookware are her areas of expertise.' Lucie tried to sound casual about it, but in truth, she had spent more hours than she would care to admit following the gilded, carefully 'curated' online presence of beautiful Jacasta Fletcher. Yes, she was following #Jacastasweddingstory on Instagram and had snooped about the wedding website.

Honestly, she'd always known Miles was vain, but she didn't know how he could stand this level of scrutiny on his every move – those endless photos of the 'happy couple' strewn all over Jacasta's feeds tagged #mygorgeousfiancé #bridetobe #myeternallove #abouttobeyourwife. It was nauseating.

'Zoe is very excited about going,' her dad added.

'Yes, well, Zoe loves her daddy. So much easier to love someone who didn't completely rip you off.' She heard exactly how bitter that sounded, but once in a while, she had to let the darkness out.

Her father turned his head to look at her. 'Do you think that's what happened?' he asked.

'Well... I thought I'd divorced a nearly bankrupt man. I left with hardly anything. I left with *his* debt on *my* credit card, which I'm still paying off, by the way. But here he is, just two years later, having some big, lavish, south of France wedding. Is that not a bit suspicious?' she fired back.

'Did he fold up all the companies?' her dad asked.

'Well, according to Miles's lawyer,' Lucie began, because that was how she'd managed to weasel out this nugget of information, 'there may have been one commercial property, registered overseas, that he managed to hang on to, so maybe it—'

'Has turned around,' her father said, finishing the thought.

'And if that's the case, then don't you think I should be entitled to a share of it?'

Her father let out a sigh. 'Hard to say, my darling. The important thing is not to stoke up your bitterness about it all. Keep moving forward, keep looking forward. You will be very comfortable once I've popped my clogs. You can make big plans... or just sit around and enjoy life for a change... like I am trying to.'

He brought the paper up to his face again.

'Sorry,' she said. 'I didn't mean to bring all that up.'

'No time to be bitter, keep moving forwards,' he told her again. 'There's a lot of life left to live – for you, anyway.'

'Dad...' she warned.

'Sorry. Right... Unworldly, eight letters, ends in "nt".'

But thoughts as to what this word could be were interrupted for them both by the trill of Lucie's phone. She picked it up and looked at the screen.

'It's Zoe,' she said before she answered. 'Hello, darling, how are you doing?'

'Mum, have you seen the news?' Zoe blurted out, sounding totally upset.

'No, what's the matter?'

'It's the trains! Eurostar has just announced a three-day strike, starting tomorrow!'

It took a few moments for Lucie to piece it together – Eurostar, the Channel Tunnel, the train to France... Miles's bloody wedding.

'Oh, Zoe, were you going by train? I thought you would be flying.'

'The train was going to be fine,' she replied. 'I thought it would be much more comfortable, easy access to the loo – but a three-day strike!'

'Oh hell. Can you get a flight?'

'No! I've been trying for two hours solid. Everything is

booked. The only option is a car ferry crossing tomorrow night. So I've booked that, but...'

Again, it took Lucie a few moments to join the dots – Zoe didn't have a car, and maybe Rafi didn't have a car either.

'Can you hire a car?' she asked her daughter.

'Yes, of course I could hire a car! But it's a bloody long drive for a woman who can't get comfortable, needs to wee every hour, and takes a regular daily nap,' her daughter snapped back.

'So can Rafi drive?' Lucie asked.

She heard the long and angry sigh. 'There are two problems with that' – she heard her daughter's angry tone – 'one, Rafi can't drive, and two, Rafi isn't coming.'

'Oh... but why not?'

'Couldn't get the time off work, apparently.'

Lucie knew her daughter well enough to hear the underlying fury in those words. Now was not the time to launch into any kind of motherly 'are you sure he's really committed' line of questioning.

'So what are you going to do?' Lucie asked, genuinely not knowing what the solution was here. Maybe her seven and a half months pregnant daughter would have to stay at home and join in with the lavish, influencer-themed celebrations on Zoom, like in the Covid days.

'Oh my God!' Zoe stormed. 'Is that all you can say? What am I going to do? I thought, Mum, I thought you'd at least offer...'

'Offer what?' Lucie asked, totally caught off guard.

'To drive me!' Zoe's voice had now moved into a high-pitched mix of fury and upset.

'Drive you?' Lucie repeated, completely astonished. 'All the way to Perpignan... when Dad is so ill and to *My Ex-husband's Wedding*?'

'It's Dad's wedding!' Zoe exclaimed. 'And I have to go. I absolutely have to be there!'

'No, you don't!' Lucie's voice was raised too now. Really, what planet was her daughter on? How could Lucie leave her dad? And drive to Perpignan in what exactly? Her ancient old Nissan? All the way down there? Good grief, that journey couldn't even be done in one day. They'd have to make an overnight stop... No, no, no, it was out of the question.

'My car would struggle to make it to Dover,' Lucie added, 'let alone the south of bloody France. You'll have to think of something else.'

To her surprise, Zoe hung up.

'Oh, for goodness' sake!' Lucie exclaimed, looking at her phone in dismay.

'Oh dear me,' came her dad's calm and unruffled response.

Lucie suspected the hurt, the surprise and the dismay was written all over her face, but nonetheless, her dad was now smiling at her. Yes, that euphoric 'all is right with the world' smile was growing wider and wider, as if he'd just had the most wonderful idea.

'Well, my dear, this is fate playing its hand,' he began. 'This is meant to be!'

'What on earth are you talking about?' she snapped.

'From what I could gather, Zoe can't get to the wedding without a car and a driver. So, if you agree to be the driver, dear Lucie, well then, I have the car!' He looked completely delighted at the idea.

'Oh no, Dad,' Lucie said straightaway, 'I am not driving Zoe to France and I am absolutely not driving Zoe to France in your enormous Jag.'

In Lucie's opinion, the swanky Jaguar XJS, bought as her father's retirement present to himself, was a ridiculous car. It had cost a fortune to buy. It cost a further fortune to run and maintain, but if her father wanted to swan about in this showy monster on the fifty or so miles he drove every month, well, that was his business.

'But the old girl hasn't had a proper adventure for years,' her dad added.

'I hope you're referring to the car.'

'Of course...' He laughed. 'But that's exactly what she needs – the open road, the wind in her hair, the bright sunshine on her face...'

'Still talking about the car?'

'Well, maybe you and the car,' he admitted. 'Look, if I could go on this one last glorious journey with the Jag, I bloody well would. So, why don't you do it for me?' With a wink, he added, 'Call it my dying wish.'

'Dad, that is emotional blackmail and completely unfair!' she protested.

'Would I have driven a heavily pregnant you to the south of France if you absolutely had to go?' he asked, fixing his clear blue eyes onto hers.

She swallowed. And felt the prickle as tears formed in her own eyes.

Her dad, who had always, always been there for her. Who was still there for her. What would she do without him? Dear God, it was just cruel.

'I don't want you to... leave us,' she heard herself say in a low voice. 'I keep thinking that it can't happen if I'm here with you.'

He smiled. 'Look, I promise, I am not going to die this weekend.' He slapped his thigh vigorously. 'Plenty of life left in this stringy old bean. Now, I want you to go. I want you to take my beautiful car and drive your daughter to the wedding. Don't go to the thing if you don't want to. Book a hotel, drink wine, eat cheese, swim in the sea, and when it's all over, drive her safely back home again. I will still be here. I promise. Ritchie and his family arrive on Thursday and I'm not missing that!'

When her expression still hadn't changed, he threw in, 'I'll pay the petrol because she's a thirsty old girl, and your hotel, my treat. So, you have no reason to say no, Lucie. None. Plus, it will be good for you and Zoe to spend some time together. You'll have time to talk. Time to find out all about this Rafi. Reconnect with your girl and put your worries to rest before the baby arrives.'

Lucie was sitting straight up on the lounger now and her arms were folded.

Her overriding feeling was that she didn't want to go, but still, she had to admit, some of what her dad had said was true. It wouldn't be easy having a fourteen-hour conversation with Zoe, or however long this journey was going to take. It really would not be easy. And it *might* do them good... or they *might* fall out forever – that was a definite risk.

But still, she didn't want to go.

She didn't want to be anywhere near bloody Miles and his bloody wedding.

Her phone burst into life again and although she expected it to be Zoe, when she looked at the caller ID, she was very surprised to see the name of Miles's sister, Melissa.

Melissa?

They hadn't spoken since well before the divorce. And Lucie hadn't liked Melissa all that much to begin with. All that fussing over her three girls and her, quite frankly, weird and totally indulged little boy, Deva. Deva had allergies and couldn't eat x, y and z. Deva had asthma and needed a room with fresh air and no carpeting. Deva turned out to be neurodiverse, so was allowed to wear headphones and trainers and jogging bottoms to every family event. Maybe he'd wear them to the wedding.

He would be a teenager now, of course, or maybe older. As her father had pointed out, they'd never seen much of Melissa's family, Zoe's cousins.

'Hello, Melissa, it's Lucie,' she said, answering the call.

'Oh, Lucie, thank goodness I still have your number,' Melissa gushed. 'How are you?'

'I'm fine. How about you?'

'We're all well... very well, thanks. I'm sorry we haven't been in touch...'

'Yes... well...'

Awkward pause.

'So...' Melissa went on. 'It's about Miles's wedding.'

'Oh, right... well, it may come as a surprise, but I won't be going to this one,' Lucie said, wondering what on earth Melissa could possibly be calling her about, two years since she'd ceased to be Miles's wife.

'No, of course. I understand. Yes...' Melissa hesitated. 'It's just, um, I don't have a number for Zoe and I was wondering how she was planning to travel, because Deva, he's in London now. And he was going to go on the Eurostar. Why he didn't book a plane, I've no idea. Oh good grief...' she exclaimed, voice rising. 'This is such a mess!'

'And the Eurostar has just announced a three-day strike.' Lucie was catching on – Deva was now in the same situation as Zoe.

'Exactly. What a disaster!' Melissa continued. 'And Deva gets so completely stressed when there's an unexpected change of plan. We're all flying from Glasgow. I've tried to get him booked onto a flight from London, or a flight from Glasgow, but there's absolutely nothing. So then I thought about Zoe. How is she travelling?'

'She was booked onto the train too,' Lucie began with a strange sinking feeling. 'But she's managed to get a ferry crossing for a car tomorrow evening.'

'Oh?'

Lucie heard the little note of hope in Melissa's voice. And the sinking feeling grew.

Then she looked up at her father, who was smiling and raising his hands. 'The fates have intervened,' he said.

'So...' Lucie took a breath. 'I'm going to drive Zoe all the way there,' she heard herself say, though she could hardly believe it. Then, even more unbelievably, she added: 'Deva is very welcome to join us.'

'Oh! Oh, my goodness, that's amazing!' Melissa sounded almost tearful. 'Thank you, thank you so much! This is so kind of you. We'll chip in for some of the cost, of course. But thank you, Lucie. Deva will be so relieved.'

Lucie could hardly believe it. What on earth was she signing up to now?

Bloody Miles and his *bloody wedding*!

7

The following afternoon, Zoe arrived at her grandfather's house via a taxi from the train station. Lucie hadn't seen her daughter for weeks, so she hurried to the front door to greet her when she heard the bell.

'Oh, Zoe! Hello! And look at you, blooming and beautiful!' she exclaimed, pulling Zoe and her sizeable bump in for a hug.

Her daughter was tall, capable and strong – a gym regular with squared shoulders, strong arms and legs and a ready smile. Zoe's dark hair was tied up in a no-nonsense ponytail; she wore a touch of makeup, and she was dressed in a lovely summer maternity shirtdress in her favourite shade of bright blue with a white pattern. She really did look beautiful and also a little thoughtful and serious, Lucie recognised.

'Hello, Mum.' Zoe, even taller today in wedge-heeled espadrilles, bent down to kiss her mother on the cheek.

'How are you feeling?' Lucie asked as she guided Zoe and her trolley bag into the hallway.

'Apart from all the peeing, I'm good,' Zoe replied. 'Really

good, in fact. Work can get a bit tiring, but not too much longer to go. How about Gramps, how's he doing?'

Dropping her voice, so there wasn't any danger of being overheard by her father, Lucie warned her, 'You've not been for a little while, so you'll notice quite a change. He's very thin and a bit yellow, gets tired, but still so cheerful. I think it's the drugs.'

Zoe's eyebrows went up. 'Is the doctor up to date on the yellowing and the cheerfulness?'

'Yes, totally up to date. She was here this morning.'

'Good. Don't want him getting an overdose at this stage. Not when we're about to head off.'

The immediate look of concern on Lucie's face caused Zoe to add, 'Honestly, if the doctor's happy, let's not worry. Sorry, Mum, I shouldn't have said that.'

'OK... right. Head to the loo if you need to and then come out to the garden where I've put out some cakes and things, and would you like a cup of tea?'

'Coffee, please, Mum. And a big glass of water.'

Lucie watched admiringly as her girl still found the energy to bounce up the staircase, taking the steps two at a time.

* * *

'Hello, Grampa!'

'Ah, there she is!'

Lucie thought it was lovely to see the delighted smiles pass between these two as Zoe came out into the garden.

'Don't get up!' Zoe insisted, but her grampa stubbornly sat up on the sun lounger, then swung his legs round, prised himself upwards and stood, a little wobbly, waiting for her hug.

'Can't have you bending over me in your condition,' he insisted as she put her arms around him and squeezed tight.

'Are you sure this baby is still two months away? You look fit to pop,' he told her.

'Six weeks to go,' she said, then, pointing at her stomach, told it sternly, 'You stay in there, baby girl. I'll let you know when I'm ready.'

'Good luck with having a child that does what you tell it – I never had any success with that,' was her grampa's comment.

'Very funny,' Lucie replied. 'Now, come and sit over here at the table, Zoe, and pick something nice to eat. Dad, I'll bring yours over – scone, coffee cake or a piece of sponge? I've bought out the bakery.'

'Well, maybe a little piece of sponge,' he decided. 'No doubt Domenica is mixing up my shake to help wash this down.'

'Oh yes... Let me go to the kitchen and find out and I'll make Zoe her coffee,' Lucie remembered.

'Thanks, Mum. I'm going to quiz Gramps about his health and his meds.'

'I can't wait,' came his wry response.

But Lucie smiled, because it was lovely to have her little family together.

When she returned with the protein shake, a big cup of coffee with milk, and glasses of water for them all, she took her seat at the garden table, ate her slice of cake, and everything was calm and civilised for a good ten minutes or so. Her father answered some more health questions, Zoe seemed satisfied with the answers, and she cheerfully answered their questions about how she was getting on with her pregnancy.

She even entertained them with some funny stories from the ward.

'Not that there are many hilarious anecdotes from ICU,' she added. 'So we have to take our laughs where we can get them.'

There was a relaxed, comfortable silence, when they all seemed to enjoy looking out over the flowers, listening to the rustle of the trees and the buzz of insects toiling away in the heat of the afternoon.

Then Lucie seemed to spoil it all by asking Zoe how it was going with finding a new home.

'Here we go with the interfering questions,' Zoe said with a roll of her eyes.

'Zoe, it's only because I care very much,' Lucie countered.

'No, we haven't found a place to buy yet. It's London and it's complicated,' Zoe said, still sounding as if her hackles were up.

'So... are you going to move in with Rafi?' Lucie ventured.

'Nope.'

'Are you going to move somewhere else on your own?'

'Nope.'

'So...' Lucie paused, hoping Zoe would explain where she was planning to be when her baby arrived.

Zoe crossed her arms and the scowl across her face was a serious warning. But still Lucie had to ask, 'You're not going to carry on living in your flat share with the baby, are you?'

'You just can't let it rest, can you?' Zoe snapped, as if it was all Lucie's fault.

But then Lucie had been a mum for twenty-seven years, so by now, she knew perfectly well that this was fairly typical – just mention a problem, because you want to help solve it, and don't be surprised if your child acts like you're somehow to blame for the whole thing.

'I don't think I should "just let it rest",' Lucie said as calmly as she could. 'I know you have a deposit. I know you've wanted to put in offers... What I don't understand is the hold up. And, no, I don't think it's a great idea to bring a baby into a flat share while the baby's father lives somewhere else. You probably don't think it's a great idea either.'

Zoe's scowl deepened and her foot began to tap in that way it did when she was particularly annoyed.

'And I might as well tell you that I don't understand why the baby's father...' – Lucie couldn't bring herself to say 'Rafi' because that was a casual, friendly nickname that you couldn't use when you were absolutely furious with someone for letting your daughter down – 'isn't coming with you to the wedding, to meet your dad and the rest of your family.'

'Look, he couldn't get the time off work, OK?' came Zoe's angry response. 'He's planning to take lots of time off once our daughter is here, so he's saving it up.'

'And what about moving? And buying a place together? Is that still going to happen?' Lucie couldn't help herself from asking.

'I think you need to keep your nose out of other people's business, OK?' Zoe snapped.

Lucie looked at her daughter. It didn't matter how strong, capable and together Zoe was, that great big baby bump made her look vulnerable; no, it actually *made* her vulnerable. Everyone who'd ever had a baby knew what Zoe was in for, but no one would be able to warn her or prepare her for the full extent of it – least of all her mother.

'You'll need all the support you can get,' Lucie warned. 'And with a sleepless, crying baby, you'll need your own space.'

'What did I just say?' Zoe warned.

'Zoe, I'm worried about you,' Lucie admitted. 'I've never met this guy. He's not buying a home with you or moving in with you. He's not coming to the wedding. Is he as committed as he should be?'

There; she'd said it, even if she knew she was pouring petrol onto the flames. At least it was off her chest and out in the open between them.

'Mum, for God's sake, will you give it a rest?' Zoe asked angrily. 'I am a grown up. I can run my own show and I don't appreciate you butting in.'

She stood up and turned to her grandfather. 'Sorry, Grampa,' she began. 'I thought this would be a nice afternoon and a chance to catch up with you, but Mum has to make everything horrible. So I'm going to go and have a little lie down on the sofa inside until she's calmed the F down – sorry, Grampa,' she repeated.

And with that Zoe went into the house, treating her mother to another furious glare on the way.

Lucie took a mouthful of her tea, but it had cooled to lukewarm and didn't bring any of the comfort she required.

'That went well...' she said to her dad, before giving a long sigh. She seemed to be sighing a lot these days. Well, bloody hell, there was a lot to sigh about.

'I worried about you too when you were in that condition,' came his reply.

'I had a husband and a mortgage,' she pointed out.

'Would that make it better?' he asked.

'Yes, I think it would. Say what you like about him now, but Miles is a good father and he was always there for Zoe. I mean, this is so woolly!' she exclaimed. 'Honestly, I don't think this Rafi guy will be around for long, do you?'

'How on earth should I know? I've never met the guy and neither have you,' her dad replied. 'But if Zoe thinks he's a good guy, maybe we'll have to trust her. She's a very sensible girl.'

'Do you think? Sensible enough to be a single-mother nurse in London? That is a huge task.'

'One of the very disagreeable things about getting older, my girl, is that you have all the experience; you think you know all the answers, but none of these blasted youngsters will ever listen to you!' he warned. 'Nothing you can do about it. You have to let people make their own way – even your beloved children.'

'Is there absolutely nothing I can do then?' Lucie asked, pained at the thought.

'I think you must have been in your mid-thirties when I finally decided that I would only offer my advice if you asked for it. I thought it was a good decision.'

'Right, but she's still in her twenties,' Lucie protested.

'Which only means she'll listen even less,' her dad delivered the brutal truth.

'So I just have to "be there for her" then?' Lucie scowled.

'Well, that sounds a bit Californian, but I suppose so,' said her dad.

'Pick up the pieces when it all goes wrong?'

'Or stand on the side lines and clap when it all goes right.'

'Do I even know you any more?' She managed a laugh. 'You sound a bit Californian yourself.'

'Oh God, what are they putting in my medicine?' he asked, shaking his head.

'Exactly what I've been wondering.'

There was a loud ring on the doorbell.

'Is that the time?' Lucie glanced at her watch. And yes, it was 4.45 p.m., almost exactly when their next visitor had said he would arrive.

'So that will be your nephew?' her dad asked.

'Yes...' Lucie stood up and felt a bit flustered. She hadn't seen Melissa's boy, Deva, for years.

Heading out to go and open the door, she told her father, 'I'm not sure what to expect.'

8

Lucie opened the door, smiled, and took a long look at this young man on the doorstep, much more grown-up than she'd expected, who was saying hello enthusiastically, calling her Aunt Lucie and holding out his hand to shake hers.

He was on the short side and slim with chestnut skin and a short bob of dark, faintly curly hair. He'd obviously inherited much of his looks from his dad – Selvi. Lucie cast her mind back and came up with the memory that Selvi was a Tamil refugee from Sri Lanka, who'd come to the UK in the 1980s. He and Melissa had met at university, had three children and divorced around ten years ago or so.

'Never liked him much, she's probably better off without him,' had been Miles's take on it, while Lucie had quietly thought to herself, *Never liked her much, he's probably better off without her.*

Deva was casually dressed in jeans and a t-shirt with bright white, bouncy-soled trainers and a big set of white headphones round his neck. There was a messenger bag slung over his shoulder and a sizeable, wheeled suitcase beside him.

He looked nervy, a little twitchy almost, but smiley and eager to please.

'Hello, Deva,' she said as she shook his hand, 'how nice to see you again – all grown up. Please come in.'

She showed him where to park his bag and then ushered him through the house.

'We were having some tea and cake in the garden, with my dad. I was trying to think if you'd met him before... maybe at a family get-together, but you might not remember him. I'm afraid he's not very well.'

'Yes, Mum told me. Very sorry to hear about that. I'm afraid I don't remember meeting him.'

So the introductions were made, both to Lucie's dad and to Zoe, who'd come back out to the garden. Then Deva settled into a chair, answered 'tea please, no milk' to Lucie's question about something to drink and brought out what looked like a stack of buttered rice cakes from his messenger bag. 'The joy of being gluten free,' he explained.

'Oh dear,' Lucie's dad sympathised. 'Off to France and no baguette or croissants for you.'

'I'm used to it,' Deva said amiably, taking a sip of tea and a small bite from a rice cake.

Then Domenica appeared to usher Lucie's father in for 'rest-time'.

'I'm definitely not allowed to call it a nap.' She smiled at them as she led her patient away, leaving Lucie, Zoe and Deva outside together.

Lucie led the conversation, sticking strictly to topics that wouldn't rile Zoe all over again. She asked after Deva's mother, father and sisters. She asked when they were arriving in France for the wedding, where they were staying and the usual kind of things.

She couldn't help noticing that it was a little heavy weather trying to chat with Deva. His answers were very brief. He never seemed to pick up the conversational ball and run with it, so she would be left in the silence to come up with more and more questions of the small-talk variety. He also kept touching the headphones, which were still around his neck, as if he longed to pull them back over his ears.

Meanwhile, Zoe was saying very little and not exactly helping her out. If this kept up, it was going to be a very long drive to Perpignan. She pictured Deva in the back of the car with his headphones on and Zoe sitting in stony silence beside her for mile after mile after mile. But it was too late to back out now.

'What time do we leave here?' Deva asked her suddenly. Before she could reply, he followed up with, 'And what time does the ferry set off across the Channel? And what time are we due to arrive in Calais?' All the questions sounded a little nervy.

'Well, the ferry doesn't leave till 10.30 p.m., so I thought we'd have a light supper and set off at about seven-thirty,' Lucie told him. 'That gives us loads of time to get there, check in and get on board. The crossing takes about two hours, but because of the time difference, it will be about 1.30 a.m. when we arrive. My plan is we park at a service station and have a bit of a sleep. It's a big, comfortable car, so we should manage a nap. Then we set off again when it gets light. After about seven hours of driving, we'll break the journey with an overnight stop in a little town about halfway down France and set off the next morning. We should be at the venue by early afternoon on Friday.'

Deva was nodding his head vigorously at all these details. Then he surprised her by launching into a long monologue about the route, explaining that there were two directions they could go along the ring road around Paris – to the east or to the west – and then the various options that would take them down towards Perpignan.

'You've given this a lot of thought,' Lucie told him with a smile. 'Sounds like I won't need to rely too heavily on Google Maps then.'

'No!' Deva looked anxious. 'The Massif Central of France is quite sparsely populated, so Wi-Fi coverage can be patchy. Do you have a road map of France? We should bring one with us.'

'That's a good idea. I bet Dad has one lying around and if it looks too old, we'll buy a new one at the ferry port,' Lucie said, hoping to reassure him.

This didn't seem to put Deva's mind entirely at rest and he began to suggest a route through the mountains of the Auvergne.

'Smaller roads, but it might save some distance,' he explained. 'And there are some interesting towns on the way.'

'Right... well, maybe we can look at the map on the ferry and see what we think looks best?' Lucie suggested. A long conversation about routes was what she really did not want right now. She needed to head upstairs, check over her luggage and make sure she'd packed everything.

'Did you know that Coco Chanel grew up in the Auvergne region?' Deva asked now. 'I'm doing a project on the evolution of the Chanel brand, but to be honest, I've been obsess— fascinated,' he corrected himself, 'by her for years.'

'Oh really?' Lucie smiled. This was unexpected. Deva in his plain t-shirt, jeans and trainers didn't exactly look like a young man with a Chanel fascination.

'Yes... I know just about everything about her. I could probably go on *Mastermind*,' he joked. 'And if we drove through the Auvergne, we could go to Brive la Gaillarde and Aubazine, which were both very important places in her childhood and early years.'

'Oh, well, I'm not sure there will be much time for sightseeing,' Lucie replied.

'No,' Zoe added, 'we're on a pretty tight schedule. Maybe you could go when you're heading back?'

'Mum's booked me on a flight,' Deva said gloomily.

There was a pause. Lucie felt as if she'd offered quite enough with the lift to Perpignan; she wasn't going to make any rash promises about visiting obscure little towns on the way. Even if Coco Chanel had grown up there.

Chanel... Just the name sent her on an unwanted trip back down memory lane, towards her past glories. Yes, believe it or not, there was a time in her past when she had been a Chanel customer. She tried to nip those thoughts in the bud, because it honestly seemed like a dream now, so long ago, but then Deva took her by surprise.

'One of my first encounters with a real Chanel item was seeing you carry a beige 2.55 handbag when you came to Granny Marshal's birthday party, Aunt Lucie.'

'Really? My goodness!' Lucie was astonished that Deva, who must have been eleven or twelve at the time, would remember a detail like that.

'That's what got me started,' Deva said with a smile that looked as if he was remembering happier times. 'Everyone was so impressed by that bag, talking about it, wanting to feel it, open it – and I just had to find out why. Then the story of this incredible woman in France began to unfold. Have you still got that bag? Or any of your Chanel things?' he asked, closely followed by the painfully blunt, 'My mum said you might have had to sell all your expensive things when you and Uncle Miles went bust.'

Lucie nearly squirted her tea and Zoe couldn't help giving a snort of suppressed laughter.

'Oh, that's quite a personal question, Deva,' Lucie said gently.

A look of surprise mixed with embarrassment came over Deva's face. 'I'm very sorry,' he began. 'Sometimes, I forget what I'm allowed to ask and what I'm not allowed to ask. My mum said she told you quite a long time ago that I'm on the autism spectrum, but she thought I might need to remind you.'

Now it was Lucie's turn to feel embarrassed. Here she was wondering why Deva didn't know what the right thing to say was, and now she was in exactly the same situation.

'Oh, I'm sorry,' she began. 'I don't think I really know what that means... or what I'm supposed to...'

Now Deva was smiling at her. 'Then that makes two of us,' he said.

'Mum!' Lucie had earned herself another glare from Zoe. 'You can't say you've *never heard of* autism or the autism spectrum?' she blurted.

'Well, not really, not in detail, not in person. Sorry, Deva.'

'It's fine, honestly, just be yourself,' Deva said, 'and I'll try not to be myself,' he added with a shrug.

'No, Deva,' Zoe protested. 'You do you and we'll be fine with that, honestly. I know we don't know each other well, but we're family.' She gave him a smile. But now they were all somewhat stranded in an awkward silence.

After several interminable moments, Lucie suddenly had a bright idea to help some of the time pass before their light supper and departure. 'You know,' she began, 'I didn't sell any of my Chanel things. They're in boxes here at Dad's house in the spare bedroom. Would you like to come and have a look, Deva?'

'Oh! My goodness! Of course,' Deva replied, jumping up from his chair with such excitement that he knocked over his empty teacup.

* * *

It had been a full two years since Lucie had looked inside these precious cream cardboard boxes. She had quite deliberately packed them up and stored them here at her dad's, hoping that out of sight would also mean out of mind.

If she had been on her own opening the lids and delving into the tissue paper for her most treasured possessions, she would be instantly sad. She would be raking over the ashes of the glory years – when maybe she had turned a blind eye to the fact that she and Miles were drifting apart because both of their businesses were so time-consuming and so successful and there was so much money floating around. Enough to be an occasional visitor to the New Bond Street Chanel store, enough to be able to drop £400 on a pair of sunglasses and thousands of pounds on handbags and dresses, without even thinking too much about it.

But with Deva sitting on the floor beside her, gasping with astonishment as each item was revealed and showcasing his incredible depth of knowledge, it was a different experience altogether. She put her feelings about the past to one side and felt as if she was seeing these items properly, not just as flashy possessions that underlined her previous success, but as works of art in their own right.

He was clearly thrilled and, giving her a running commentary, he pointed out all kinds of things she hadn't known about these clothes and bags.

'Look at this armhole!' he gasped. 'Look at the craftsmanship here.' He picked up the soft, camel-coloured jacket and examined the stitching where the sleeve met the body. 'She was obsessed with armholes. Did you know that? She thought that the placing of the armhole was the most important element in the fit. If the armhole is right, you can swing your arms and be comfortable, plus the armhole dictates how much fabric is available to cover the body, without the need for a bust dart. Genius, right?'

'If you say so.' Lucie smiled. 'I've never thought about it like that.'

'Oh my!' Deva picked up the beige quilted handbag with a look of awe on his face. 'Here it is, here's the bag where it all began for me!'

He ran his hand along the glossy surface and lifted the flap to reveal the distinctive red leather lining.

'She was a very good rider,' he added, making it sound almost as if he knew Coco Chanel personally, 'absolutely loved horses, and the saddles and bridles and all the workmanship that went into them – the design of this handbag was testament to that, carefully quilted and padded leather. And it was revolutionary because it was based on a soldier's haversack, and it had straps, which let women put it over their shoulder or dangle it from the crook of their arm, so they could have their hands free – to dance, to smoke, to drink a cocktail. Before this bag, a lady had to carry her purse in her hands.'

'I did not know that,' Lucie admitted.

Deva was already pulling back the tissue paper to see what else he could find.

'No!' he gasped. 'Not a black lace evening dress! I can't believe you have one of these!'

Tenderly, he lifted the dress up from the box in all its slinky, lacey glory.

'I bought it for an awards ceremony,' she said, remembering the occasion, 'it was a big, important, glittery event. Miles was on the shortlist, but he didn't win.'

'This is breathtaking!' Deva exclaimed, standing up to unfold the dress to its full length. 'I need to take some photos of all of these things.'

'Of course,' she agreed, and she was glad she was seeing him like this – his excitement, enthusiasm and obvious knowledge allowing him to forget his nervy awkwardness.

'And, Aunt Lucie, will you be taking these things with you to France?'

'Oh no, they're in storage here. They're safe here.'

'But you should wear Chanel to the wedding,' he insisted.

'Oh!'

Lucie realised he didn't know about her plan to drop them both at the venue and get away as quickly as possible to the little hotel beside the sea that she'd booked for herself for two nights, a full hour and a half's drive away from the wedding venue. She'd booked a room with a terrace overlooking the beach. Because she had decided she would drink the wine, eat the cheese and swim in the sea, just as her dad had suggested.

'I'm taking you and Zoe there, Deva. I'm not going to the wedding.'

'My mum said you were invited but you probably didn't want to go.' Tipping his head to the side, he added in a gentle and sympathetic voice, 'Chanel had a lot of hard times with men in her life. The love of her life died in a car crash when she was thirty-six.'

'Oh...' Lucie hadn't known this tragic fact.

'And the man she was in love with for a decade married

someone else, because he needed an heir and Coco couldn't have children.'

'Oh... I didn't know that either,' she said.

'Her clothes are soft and wearable, but they are also made to protect you and help you to be strong. So, if you did decide to come to the wedding, you should wear your Chanel.'

9

Lucie was trying to pay close attention to the directions of the man in the high-vis vest, who was guiding them out of the depths of the ferry's parking deck and into the queue of cars heading towards the enormous metal ramps and dry land.

The Jag, despite her practice drive around town and the time spent on the motorway to the ferry port at Dover, still felt like a beast to handle on tricky manoeuvres like this. Yes, she'd once driven a sleek saloon car almost as long and as wide as this, but she was now used to driving her little Nissan. Parking, even turning a corner, all felt like major operations. Everything about the Jag was bigger, stiffer and more difficult. Honestly, it was like driving a bus.

Calm down, she told herself as she drove hesitantly forward. *You'll get the hang of it.* Zoe, however, did not look so sure. From the passenger's seat, she glanced over with a look of concern as Lucie struggled to move the gearstick from first up to second.

'I'm just not used to it,' Lucie said.

'That's kind of obvious,' Zoe replied.

'I'll get there,' Lucie insisted.

'Here's hoping.'

Lucie glanced in the rear-view mirror at Deva. He had his headphones on, was bouncing slightly to his music and mouthing the words to whatever song he was listening to. Although it was dark, he seemed to be looking out of the window with enthusiasm at everything. On the ferry crossing, while Lucie and Zoe had looked for quiet window seats and even spent some time out on deck, queasy at the motion of the ship, Deva had rushed around exploring and wanting to experience everything.

He'd drunk volumes of Coke and only come back to them now and then to exclaim: 'The onboard shop has all this fantastic stuff!' or 'There's a movie room!' and 'I am loving the slot machines! Pinball!'

Yes, on the ferry, Deva had been the human equivalent of a pinball, batting about from deck to deck, restlessly rushing from one thing to the next.

Lucie manoeuvred the car into the queue and then laboriously onwards through the checkpoints. Finally, when their passports had all been checked and stamped, she nudged the beast out onto the road, self-consciously keeping to the right-hand lane as they began to follow the directions from the satnav and the road signs to Paris.

'Next stop, Paris!' Deva exclaimed from the back seat.

'Next stop, a quiet snooze,' Lucie told him, glancing at the new French time in the corner of the satnav screen – 1.44 a.m.

After negotiating two roundabouts that required all her concentration, then spending another twenty minutes on the road, Lucie saw a turnoff for a service station ahead and decided to take it.

'We can use the loos, wash our faces, then park up for a bit of a sleep,' she told her passengers.

'Good idea,' was Zoe's response, and she waved at Deva, who slid his headphones down so that Zoe could explain where they were going.

'Sleep?' he exclaimed, eyes shining as he took in the lorries, the cars, the bright neon lights of the service station. He made it sound as if sleep was a totally impossible idea, which was possibly the effect of all those Cokes on board the ship.

But the funny thing was, once they'd all used the loos, bought bottles of water and settled back down into the car, Deva was the first to fall asleep, nestled up against the pillow he'd made from a comfortable-looking sweatshirt, headphones down around his neck.

'He looks sweet and much younger asleep,' Lucie whispered. 'And how are you doing?' she asked Zoe, who had wound the big leather passenger's chair down as far as it would go and was trying to get comfortable.

'Not too bad,' Zoe replied, also keeping her voice low. 'One advantage of a huge car, the seats are very nice.'

'Maybe we should have got a hotel for tonight too?' Lucie fretted.

'No, we're fine. A few hours' nap now, followed by a good long drive, and then we'll sleep well at the hotel tonight.'

'The hotel did look nice, on the website anyway. It's in a little village, in the hills,' Lucie told her.

'Sounds good...'

Then there was a long pause and Lucie hoped Zoe was managing to drift off, but out of the dim darkness in the car came the unexpected question, 'Mum? Do you miss being married to Dad?'

'Oh... right...' was Lucie's first and rather startled response.

This felt as if it was coming at her out of the blue and she really did not want to re-hash any of the long, fraught divorce conversations she'd had with her daughter back when it had become inevitable that this was what was going to happen between her parents.

All that time Lucie had spent reading online advice about 'how to handle divorce with your grown-up children'. It turned out to be not much easier, and no less of a shock, than if you divorced when your children were young. In fact, if anything, some articles had warned about the resentfulness of grown-up children, the deep-seated worry that their childhoods had been built on a lie, and they could no longer trust their happy memories.

'I loved Miles very much, for years,' she began.

'I know that and I believe that,' Zoe said. 'But what about now when you're on your own in that little place? Do you miss him? Are you lonely?'

Those felt like two very separate questions.

'I miss a lot of what I used to have, Zoe. I miss our lovely house. I miss the security, the luxury even, of when our businesses were going great guns and there was plenty of money to go round,' Lucie admitted, feeling a wave of the sadness that she was always working to keep at bay. 'And then there are those normal, empty-nest feelings. I miss you being small, you being at school, even you and all your friends landing on us in between university terms and eating the fridge bare. I miss those gorgeous holidays...'

'Oh yeah, me too,' Zoe added.

'Life seems very quiet now.'

'Oh dear, Mum,' Zoe sympathised.

'And...' – Lucie struggled for the best way to put this – 'I miss the version of your dad that I was in love with. But the person he turned into for me – and I'm not saying it was the same for you, and of course there was all the stress to blame – but how he behaved to me in those last few years... It was very disappointing. Too disappointing,' she added. 'I can't forgive him. I will probably never forgive him. And I'm sorry if that's hard for you to hear.'

'OK,' was all the reply Zoe made.

Lucie paused before adding, 'I don't miss all that drama from our final year. It was too hard. No one should put their wife through that. And yes, I'm sure my life now looks small and pretty dull to you – with my little flat and commuting to my little job, but at least it's all mine. I'm in charge of it. No one can come in and pull the rug from under me. It feels safe,' she said. That was the word. It wasn't exciting. It wasn't glamorous, but yes, it was very safe.

'After everything I've been though, safe is fine with me.' Smiling at Zoe, Lucie added: 'I'm really looking forward to your baby girl arriving. I'll want to be very involved with her. I hope that's OK with you.'

'Totally fine with me,' Zoe said. She'd turned onto her side and her voice sounded sleepy. Whatever she thought about her mother's reply to her question, she wasn't telling. But at least the air seemed to have cleared a little between them. Lucie hadn't mentioned Rafi and thought that it was better not to for now.

In the hour that followed, Lucie wound her seat back a little, but not enough to intrude on Deva's space. She closed her eyes, she tried to count backwards from one hundred, she worried about how tired she would be if she didn't sleep now, but sleep would not come.

Instead, she found herself thinking about that other cardboard box under the spare bed at her father's house. Not the one with the tissue paper and the Chanel clothes, but the smaller, older one that she'd seen again when she'd pulled the cream boxes out for Deva.

That box was the one disturbing any chance for her to rest now. That dress... that photograph that she'd found after all those years... that man. How could something that had happened so long ago be suddenly taking up all this space in her head all over again?

It was her age, she thought, classic mid-life crisis territory. Or it was the fact that she was alone after so many years of being married. That was why she'd got all wistful and nostalgic and was now going over and over the feelings she'd had back then. Endlessly wondering if she should have waited for Clark to come back from the States instead of rushing into her relationship with Miles – as if there was anything she could do about it now.

She tried to tell herself off, tell herself to get it together. She was trying to be content with the flat and the job and the life she'd rebuilt from the shambles of the divorce and the closure of her business. And there must have been good reasons that she had barely thought of Clark in all this time. *Maybe I was too busy,* she thought now. *Maybe I was suppressing it. Maybe I was determined to convince myself and everyone else that Miles was the right decision. A good decision.*

For goodness' sake Lucie, pull yourself together. But she could feel tears sliding down her face.

He wasn't available, she reminded herself. But here came the hard, smooth pebble of regret. *But I never let him know how I felt.*

Maybe if she'd been brave enough to do that – then everything would have been different.

10

Lucie must have drifted off at some point because she was aware of waking up at the first glimmer of daylight. Her eyes opened and for a moment, she struggled to work out where she was. In a car... which car? Then she looked around and saw her passengers, realised what a crick she had in her neck and remembered exactly where she was and what she was doing.

She also remembered last night and having that little cry in the small hours. She brushed all those thoughts to the side now. Wasn't everything always so much worse in the small hours? In the daylight, you could pick yourself up and get back on with the business, and even the welcome busy-ness, of creating another day.

Beside her, Zoe was stirring, and even Deva seemed to be coming round from his deep slumber.

'Morning everyone, how does coffee and a French pastry sound?' she asked in brightest mumsy tones. 'Shall we go in and see what they've got?'

So the little trio headed for the services building where loos and sinks were used, and steaming cups of coffee and crispy apricot and chocolate pastries were bought. And then Lucie remembered that Deva was gluten-free, so she went back to the counter and managed to find him a packaged chocolate-coated rice cake.

Deva had brought the map book along with him and as they ate and drank and started to come back to life watching the sun come up and the sky lighten, he studied the route they would take today.

'So...' he began. 'I know the satnav is going to guide us round to the east of Paris, on the ring road, the Périphérique, but I've just plotted the route that goes around on the west side and it only takes twenty minutes longer.'

Zoe was quick to ask the obvious question. 'And why would we want to go west and take a route that's twenty minutes longer?'

Deva propped his face up on his hands, his eyes began to scan out of the big glass windows and something of a dreamy expression came over his face. 'Because if we take the western route, then we would be able to make just a very small detour down the Avenue de la Grande Armée and into the Place Vendôme.'

Lucie and Zoe stared at him, desperate for some further explanation as to why they would drive into a busy city, no doubt absolutely jam-packed with traffic, and make today's long drive even longer.

'If we went to the Place Vendôme,' Deva continued, 'we could actually stand outside the Ritz Hotel where Coco Chanel lived for thirty-four years. Then we could walk down the Rue Cambon' – his voice seemed to go both quieter and higher – 'and we could go into Chanel's original Paris boutique. And this would honestly make several of my dreams come true in just twenty minutes or so. It's just a tiny little detour. And it will be completely amazing and totally worth it.'

Zoe picked up her coffee cup and said, 'Deva, if you can convince my mum to drive the Beast the long way round Paris and stop off in the city centre, I will need to take some lessons from you.'

'I don't think it would be very sensible...' Lucie began.

'And I rest my case,' Zoe said. Then she drained her coffee cup and put it down on the table with a harsh tap.

Lucie felt riled by this. Really, was this how Zoe saw her now? Just a boring, middle-aged mum, who never did anything remotely interesting ever? Mrs Totally Safe and Staid?

She wanted to say something like: *Do you know I used to party with all the London cool people?* Or, *I once helped Jarvis Cocker sneak out the back of a nightclub to avoid the press...* But she realised, with something of a jolt, how long ago that was. And how mildly desperate she would sound.

So instead, she asked Deva, 'Have you ever been to Paris?'

'No, never, but I am desperate, *desperate*, to go. Please, even just fifteen minutes in the Place Vendôme and you will be my favourite auntie forever,' Deva wheedled.

This made Lucie laugh.

'And what about us, Zoe... We went to Paris when you were about ten, didn't we?'

'I only remember Notre Dame and Disneyland,' Zoe replied, 'and literally begging you to get me a Mickey Mouse balloon, which I held in the car all the way home.'

Lucie laughed again: 'Disneyland! Oh my God, I hated that place so much. I swear I saw French Minnie Mouse smoking a cigarette. And it rained relentlessly all day long. The entire day, not one single break in the rain. Everyone was wearing those yellow capes they had for sale there.'

'Yeah, even I remember that,' Zoe chimed in. 'Dad loved it though. He went on every single ride – even the teacups that were obviously for babies.'

'Yes, he did,' Lucie recalled.

'Always up for an adventure,' Zoe said.

'Always taking the risks,' Lucie countered. But she felt jolted by this comment too, and wondered if those were the roles that she and Miles had fallen into over the years – the risk-taker and the wife who played it safe. But if you'd built a life with someone who was always taking risks, was it so surprising that you would be the one who was dotting i's, crossing t's and paying attention to the details – checking the insurance policies, making sure the household bills were paid, setting the budgets, reining him in? If only she'd done more of it, she couldn't help thinking. If only she'd asked to comb through the accounts of his many different businesses – dotting those i's, doing the sums, checking repayments and interest rates. Maybe it wouldn't all have gone so badly wrong.

But she wasn't Mrs Miles any more, so her decisions didn't all need to be safe and sensible to counterbalance his. No, she could decide for herself. For the first time in years, she could ask herself, '*What does Lucie want?*' and act on the answer.

'Look, I don't want to promise we can stop in Paris,' Lucie began, 'but if we make good time on this part of the journey' – she registered the excited hopefulness on Deva's face, not to mention the surprise on Zoe's – 'then maybe we can take the detour.'

'That is amazing!' Deva exclaimed.

'Really?' Zoe asked.

'Maybe…' Lucie clarified, 'if we make good time.'

Zoe gave some sort of raised eyebrow, smirk expression at

Deva that Lucie understood immediately. Obviously, Zoe didn't think she would, so maybe Lucie needed to prove her wrong.

Deva got to his feet, coffee cup in hand, and urged them up. 'C'mon, no time to lose. Time to get a shift on.'

As they walked out of the station and climbed into the Jag, Deva regaled them with a volley of facts and information.

'Coco Chanel opened her first boutique on Rue Cambon in 1910 when she was twenty-seven years old. The first thing she designed was hats and they were hugely popular. Then came comfortable jersey tunics, then the radical trousers, bathing suits, jackets with pockets and handbags with straps. I mean, she was wearing trousers and bathing suits when both were considered a scandal,' Deva told them.

'And what about No 5?' Zoe asked as Lucie pulled the Jag with a huge new tank of petrol back out onto the main road. 'When did that arrive on the scene?'

'First created in 1921,' Deva replied. 'It's probably fair to say that it only went mass market after the Second World War though, due to the involvement of the Wertheimers, who were her business partners. She gave the perfume out free to the American GIs liberating Paris. She was a revolutionary designer, no doubt about that, but she also had a genius for marketing. All those legendary quotes she gave to newspapers and magazines, building her brand. And the perfume – that was so that everyone could have a piece of Chanel, even if they couldn't afford couture, and it was the perfume that made her so incredibly rich, fabulously rich.'

After a little pause, he added: 'She was the Duke of Westminster's girlfriend for ten years.'

'Really?' Lucie was surprised that she didn't know this.

'Yes, and maybe, if she'd been able to have children, they

would have married. But, in the end, he left her for a much younger woman who gave him an heir.'

Lucie felt her hands grip the steering wheel a little tighter. Those words had led her thoughts to Miles and Jacasta, and now she was wondering, would Jacasta want a baby? Was Zoe facing the prospect of a sibling twenty-eight years her junior? And how would Lucie feel about that? Probably even more middle-aged and cast aside and irrelevant.

'So, are you planning to work in fashion when you graduate, Deva?' Zoe asked. 'It sounds like you should, sounds like you know so much about it.'

'Uh, well...' Deva began, and both Lucie and Zoe couldn't help noticing that at this question, all the enthusiastic energy seemed to drain from him and once again nervy, uncertain Deva was back. 'I-I don't know about that,' he said. 'I mean, I know almost everything about Coco, but fashion...' He glanced down at his sweatshirt. 'Not sure about that. I'd like to work for one of the big production companies that puts on musicals, but I know just what my mum and dad will think...' He trailed off.

'Oh, never mind that,' was Zoe's robust response, 'you've got to do what you want to do and not worry about what your parents think.'

Lucie glanced at her daughter, stung by yet another warning not to interfere in her life, but Zoe just kept her eyes ahead on the road. When she looked back at Deva, he was giving a non-committal shrug, and then his headphones went back on.

The miles ticked by. There was another stop near Amiens, dictated by Zoe's small bladder and the Jag's thirsty engine, but then they were back on the road with less than an hour to go till Paris. Looking at the time, Lucie guessed they would be there by 11 a.m., and this was earlier than she'd expected.

As the signs for the Périphérique began to appear, signalling the choice between going west or going east, she was still undecided. This was a very big, ungainly car. She tried to imagine driving down narrow streets or reversing into a parking space. Really, it would be so much easier to stick to the motorway, bypass Paris and carry on south towards the village in the hills where they were stopping for the night.

Adventures always come with difficulties, unforeseen snags, extra costs, headaches, even tummy bugs. You remembered the highlights, though – the view, the meal, the moment – and hopefully, you would forget the extra effort or any troubles. If she was standing in the Place Vendôme, would she still be replaying the effort of weaving through the traffic, finding a parking space, or working out how to put euro coins into the meter?

'Do we have any euro coins?' she wondered out loud.

'What for?' Zoe asked.

'Parking.'

'Are you serious?' Zoe turned to her. 'Are we going to do this? Are we going to go into Paris, Mum? In this beast?'

Lucie smiled and pushed down the indicator decisively. 'Yes!'

'Deva!' Zoe leaned over and tapped her cousin on the arm. 'Aunt Lucie is heading west! Coco Chanel here we come!'

Deva swiped off his headphones and let out a yelp of excitement.

11

It was only slightly less horrific than Lucie had imagined to crawl around the Périphérique's multiple lanes of slow-moving traffic, then peel off into a traffic-packed boulevard and be guided by the haughty female voice of the satnav into a multi-storey car park just a few streets away from Deva's holy grail.

Finally, the beast was at rest and its stiff and crumpled passengers stepped out. Lucie tried to smooth out her blouse as best she could and ran her hands over the deep creases in her cotton trousers from sitting in the driver's seat so long. Zoe stretched her arms up over her head and shook out the tension in her shoulders.

Meanwhile, Deva looked down at his t-shirt and jeans.

'I don't feel ready,' he said with a note of anxiety. 'I'm not dressed for this. Just give me a minute to change.' Then he dived back into the car.

When he re-emerged, a well-cut cream-coloured shirt, ironed and only a little creased from being in his suitcase, had taken the place of the t-shirt.

'Very smart,' Lucie told him, but this didn't seem to provide him with enough reassurance.

'Sorry... sorry to keep you both, but I'm going to change my shoes too.' And back into the car he went.

'He's getting so nervous,' Zoe told her mum quietly. 'I think there's a risk he might not go through with this. We'll have to help him.'

'What can we do to help?' Lucie asked.

Deva emerged from the car once again and now the big white trainers had been replaced with smart black leather lace-ups, no doubt brought to wear to the wedding.

'You look great,' Zoe said with a smile. 'And black and white, very Chanel. So...' She started to walk away from the car, hoping Deva would follow her. 'What music are you going to play when you walk down the Rue Cambon and stand in front of The Ritz? Have you got a Chanel playlist?'

Deva's face seemed to brighten at the thought of this.

'Music?' he blurted. 'I hadn't even thought about that. But you're right, you're right! I need to pick the perfect music.'

The headphones went back on and as he looked at his phone, Zoe looped her arm through his and told him as she steered him forwards, 'You concentrate on the tunes and I'll keep us right on the pavement.'

And so, the little party of three made their way out onto the street, the sunshine and the busy throng of a summer's day. It was only a ten-minute walk before they were first of all on the Rue Cambon, where Deva's thrill to be at this legendary destination was infectious.

He made them take a photo of him outside the Chanel shop. Then he took a group photo of the three of them. Then Lucie, to her own surprise, took a firm grip on the door handle and said,

'Come on, I'm sure they'd love such a dedicated fan to come inside.'

Then, despite the look of fear that flashed over Deva's face, they were in, feeling the cool blast of aircon, breathing in the powdery, lavender-musk of the world-famous perfume and surrounded by beautiful items displayed in an almost museum-like way.

An assistant appeared at their side immediately to welcome them in French and English. It had been some years since Lucie was in a boutique as exclusive as this one. And she felt just that slight shrinking of her soul as it occurred to her that she would never be shopping in Chanel again. That chapter of her life was closed. And maybe she hadn't even appreciated it enough when she'd been living it. But, nevertheless, she didn't want Deva to feel that he couldn't stay and enjoy at least a little moment of time at the shrine of his muse.

So she took a breath and said that she would like to look at the shoes, and meanwhile, could her family just have a little look around? At this, the assistant focused on her and took her to the wall of gorgeous high-heeled, low-heeled, two-tone shoes of utter perfection, and Lucie went through the rigmarole of trying on two pairs in order to give Zoe, and especially Deva, time to wander through the space, savouring it to the full.

When Lucie had made her polite excuse along the lines of 'They are so beautiful, but I think I'm going to see what else is available elsewhere' then it was time for them all to exit the hallowed hall and get back out onto the hot sunshine of the street once again.

'That was amazing,' Deva told them. 'Amazing! Even better than I could have ever imagined.'

Then they turned the corner and were standing in the Place Vendôme, with the splendour of The Ritz hotel ahead of them.

There was a beautiful café in the square with tables and chairs set out on the broad pavement and an awning above to keep customers in the shade. Without liking to think too much about the cost of even a sparkling water here, Lucie suggested, 'Deva, would it work for you if Zoe and I take a seat and have a drink here? And you can go and look around the square and the streets by yourself?'

'Perfect!' Deva enthused, almost bouncing on the balls of his feet. 'Perfect... I'll be back here in about half an hour?'

'Yes, go on then. And take plenty of selfies!'

'Are you doing OK, not too exhausted with the travelling?' Lucie asked her daughter, looking over the café table at her and wondering how someone she remembered vividly as three years old in a fluffy headband and tiny denim pinafore dress could possibly be pregnant with a baby of her own.

'I'm tired, but I'm doing OK,' Zoe admitted. 'And I'm glad we drove into the city. It's beautiful, it's lovely to be here and we've made Deva very happy. Plus, for once I'll have something nice to post on Instagram. I'm guessing you've been sneaking a peek at Jacasta's wedding posts?'

Lucie glanced at her daughter, wondering if it was OK to confess how much those posts had made her snort with laughter.

'They might be a little guilty pleasure of mine...'

Zoe was smiling, 'Yeah, OK, they might be a slightly guilty

pleasure of mine too. Ohmigod, she is obsessed with the details.'

'That's putting it mildly.'

Their drinks arrived and it seemed natural to talk about their visit to Paris all those years ago, and other past family holidays to France. *Yes,* Lucie thought back with some relief as they reminisced, *we were a happy family. We were good parents who loved and still love our daughter.* Because sometimes she had worried that the divorce had spoiled it all – the past, the present and the future.

'I really loved all our family holidays,' Zoe told her. 'And I'm fine with you going your separate ways, but it is sad that there won't be any more times with the three of us.'

'No...' And Lucie could see it from Zoe's point of view. No quick weekend visit to the parents, but having to see her and then Miles, separately, with all the added time and complication this brought. No future invitations to hang out with Mum and Dad at their sunny villa rental, reminiscing about the fun they'd once had in the past. It must feel to Zoe that she had lost the future of her original family.

Well, maybe Miles should have taken some time to think of her and his daughter and how this was going to play out for them. But she had to face it, men like Miles rarely wasted any time worrying about the effect of what they were doing on others. They thought of themselves, they pressed ahead, and they let everyone else tidy the mess up afterwards.

The world idealised the risk takers, but where would they be without the lieutenants who pinned the visions down and got stuff done? Not one of Miles's office developments would have been such a success without her attention to detail. She was the one who had picked out sofa colours, wall coverings, artwork, light fittings, giving this location a pastel 'ski chalet' vibe and that one a 'luxe artist studio' look.

'I'm not ready to play happy families with Miles yet. But maybe in the future,' she told Zoe now. 'There's always hope we can morph into one of those Californian-style families and get together for Christmas Day or on your baby's birthday and be genuinely pleased to see one another.'

'Sounds nice,' Zoe said, 'let's hope we can get to that.'

'Well, when I'm not still paying off your dad's spending on my credit card, maybe I'll feel a little more positive about him then.'

'Oh no,' Zoe's eyes widened. 'How did that happen?'

'Things got divided out and I got stuck with £9,000 on my card that I didn't spend.'

'You should tell him, Mum. He might not even know. What did he spend it on?'

'I only recently found out,' Lucie couldn't help the brusque note in her voice. When the information had arrived from the credit card company, she'd looked up the companies online and been astonished at her discovery.

Looking at her daughter now, she said, 'It turns out that I'm still paying for his hair transplant and his new teeth!'

12

Deva could have stayed in the square for the rest of the day, taking photos, darting from one important address to the next, spitting out one fact more fascinating than the next: 'Did you know that Chanel was a Leo and she placed a lot of importance on astrology, tarot cards and her lucky number, five? Her gravestone features five lion heads carved into white stone.'

But Lucie finally had to round him up, as the prospect of straying into a third hour of car parking at €25 an hour was not appealing. Especially after the damage done to her budget by the coffee and sparkling water at the café on this very elite pavement.

When they were finally back in the car, out of the city streets and back on the Périphérique, it was as if the entire car population of Paris, or maybe the entire north of France, had descended. Bumper to tail as far as the eye could see.

'What's happened?' Zoe asked. 'Is it rush hour?'

But this seemed unlikely as it was only 2.30 p.m.

'Maybe it's something to do with the holiday,' Deva offered from the back seat.

'What holiday?' Lucie wondered.

'It's July fourteenth today – it's a big celebration of the French revolution... I heard this tourist talking about it,' Deva explained.

Lucie could have kicked herself. 'Oh God! Of course, July fourteenth is Bastille Day. It's a national holiday. I'm surprised the Chanel store was open. So, good grief, we're completely stuck in the holiday exodus on Bastille Day. What is the satnav telling us?' Her eyes went to the screen. 'Any shortcut suggestions? How long till we get to our village?'

'Looks like five and a half hours,' Zoe groaned, 'with an hour and a half spent covering the next ten miles or so.'

'Thank goodness you went to the bathroom recently,' Lucie offered.

'OK, no one is allowed to mention bathrooms, toilets or anything to do with weeing or water because it will just set me off.'

'How about a blast of Abba to raise the spirits?' Deva offered.

'Maybe later,' Lucie suggested. 'I'm not sure that's quite the soothing traffic jam music I need right now.' She had enjoyed the detour into Paris, but now she wasn't convinced it was worth sitting in an extra hour or two of traffic.

'You just let me know what you want and when you need it. I am your in-car DJ for today. You gave me Chanel, Aunt Lucie, I can give you whatever sounds you want for the ride.' With that, he slipped his headphones on, checking out of the conversation and leaving Lucie and Zoe to choose silence or chat in the front seat.

The traffic crawled, the bright sun beat down on the car, the tarmacked road, the glinting metal vehicles around them. Lucie had the aircon on low, so as not to make the Jag gulp down any more fuel than was necessary, and she checked all the dials over again. The petrol gauge showed the tank was half full, the oil was fine, and the temperature gauges showed the car was running a little hot, but that was to be expected. It was about twenty-seven degrees out there, maybe more.

Zoe's phone buzzed and she pulled it out of her bag. She read the message, typed a reply at speed and then, buzz, another reply arrived. This went on for several moments. Buzz, type, send, buzz, and repeat. Finally, she sighed and tossed the phone back into her bag.

'Rafi?' Lucie asked, keeping her voice the bright side of neutral, wondering if she could open up a conversation about this man without igniting another burst of Zoe's anger.

'Yes, Rafi,' Zoe said.

'I'd love you to tell me a bit about him...' Lucie ventured carefully. 'I hardly know anything. And I know that's because I've not really given you the chance to tell me,' she added quickly.

Zoe looked at her mother and Lucie could see the expression of caution on her face.

'I don't want to give you any ammunition,' Zoe said. 'I don't enjoy disagreeing with you about him.'

'Look, I am sorry if I've got it all wrong and upset you. Really, Zoe, I am sorry,' Lucie said, hoping that a full, hands-up apology might go some way to smoothing out things between them. 'If you've picked him, he must have a lot going for him. I know you. You're very special and I hope that means he's very special too.'

'He is special...' Zoe began. 'But he's complicated.'

If Lucie wanted to sigh, she held it in because sighing would make Zoe clam up just when she might be ready to tell her mother a bit more.

'OK... let me try to explain,' Zoe began. 'Rafi is the same age as me. Very tall, dark and handsome, very... I don't want to use the word "shy". I prefer private, or quiet. It takes a long time to get to know him. But when you do, you're allowed into this whole fascinating world that no one else knows about.' Zoe glanced at her mum and Lucie smiled to encourage her. 'And I like that because... well, if you want to be Freudian, I suppose he's very different to Dad,' Zoe went on. 'Dad is open and loud and out there and everyone knows all about Dad. Rafi is quiet and sensitive and it's all going on in the interior. He likes to think and read and go for long walks.'

She paused thoughtfully, then said, 'And my daily life is so loud and busy and full-on that I enjoy being calm when I'm with him. We can be quiet together and I can recover from everything I have to go through. It's hard, Mum,' she said, looking over at Lucie again and catching her eye. 'It's hard to be with people and their families when they are really ill, or when they die... Sometimes it can feel as if we did everything we could, but it wasn't enough.'

Lucie reached over and took hold of her daughter's hand.

She didn't say anything. What could she say? She wondered if she'd been too wrapped up in her own problems to support Zoe as best she could.

She knew Zoe worked too hard on an understaffed ward. Some days when Lucie called her, Zoe's face was marked with the mask she'd worn for so many hours.

A fragment of one conversation came back to Lucie. Zoe, staring at the screen and telling her in an exhausted but still proud voice, 'We're fighting a losing battle out here. We are doing everything we can and I'm so proud of everyone I work with, Mum, but it's a battlefield in there.'

'I don't think I have been there for you as much as I should have been,' Lucie said now. 'I've been very caught up in the businesses going down, the divorce and now Dad being ill.'

Zoe shrugged. 'You've had a tough time... I can hardly blame you.'

'But I'll do better,' Lucie said, 'going forward.'

The car nosed forward.

'Tell me more about Rafi... if you want to,' Lucie said.

'His family is from Iran. He's been in the UK, in London, since he was three. But there's trauma when a family uproots like that. No grandparents, no aunties and uncles around to support you; you become very isolated. If you met him, you'd think classic computer nerd... Doesn't want to talk much, just wants to get back to the screen. But it's more than that... His whole world is on the other side of that screen. His people, his landscapes, his stories. All the things we get from family and friends and connections in the real world, he has had to find it through that screen.'

Zoe smiled then added, 'I like being the person who can bring him out of that. So we talk together and cook food and clean his flat, do some DIY, enjoy time outdoors. I like to take him away from the imaginary world and out into real life.

'When we go out of the flat,' Zoe went on, 'I think he must have low-level agoraphobia, because he wants to wear a hat or a hood and a certain jacket to kind of protect himself against the outside world. And, believe me, I already know what you're thinking...'

'Do you?' Lucie asked. 'You'd hate it if I said that to you.'

'Yes, but you're thinking, hasn't Zoe got enough people to take care of in her life? She works in intensive care, she's about to have a baby, maybe she doesn't need a precious sensitive soul who needs her to look after him as well. You were thinking that, weren't you?'

'Maybe...' Lucie admitted guiltily. 'Well, something along those lines. Yes, I'm worried for you, is that so wrong? Having a baby is not as easy as it looks on Instagram, Zoe. It's hard. It changes your life. Having a baby in London, when you're working as a nurse and your partner has... issues...'

'Mum...' Zoe warned.

But it was true. It did sound like Zoe would be looking after this fragile man just as much as she'd be looking after her baby.

'It's going to be really hard, but I want to help you as much as I can,' Lucie said.

'I just wanted to tell you, and please listen,' Zoe went on, 'that Rafi does look after me. He does really care and I'm sure he's going to be a very good dad. And I didn't want you to meet him until I could explain all of this.'

'Why won't he buy a home with you? Why won't he move in?' Lucie asked, knowing it was blunt, knowing she sounded exasperated, but still having to ask these questions anyway.

'I'm trying to work through that,' Zoe said calmly, but Lucie could hear the undertow of anger. 'It's almost as if he can't seem to imagine it. He can't imagine leaving his flat. He can't picture how we could make a new home ours together. Make it the way we want it. He'll say things like, "I don't like this kitchen" and not seem to get that we can change it, change everything to the way we want it to be.'

None of this was reassuring to Lucie. But she could at least appreciate that Zoe was very committed to Rafi. What she needed was some sign that Rafi felt the same way about Zoe.

'Do you think you'll persuade him to move?' Lucie asked.

'Well... it's baby steps, Mum, baby steps.'

They fell into silence again, because Lucie didn't want to risk another row or outburst. But still, as the traffic finally began to ease and the road opened up so they could begin to cover the distance between Paris and the village where they were stopping for the night, she couldn't help thinking that her daughter needed a grown up, a partner, not another fragile and sensitive soul to look after as she entered this very challenging new phase of her life.

She could have done medicine. She could have married another doctor, Lucie couldn't help thinking. Instead, what is she getting into? Some strange, troubled guy with commitment issues, and scraping together to buy a flat in a dodgy part of town...

Her thoughts tossed on round her head for mile after mile.

* * *

Soon there was another stop at a service station, for coffees, water and toilet breaks. It was not long after 4.30 p.m., so the fiercest heat of the day had passed and now that they were up on higher ground, there even seemed to be something of a breeze.

'Welcome to the Massif Central,' Deva told them as they walked back towards the car, taking in the bare, rocky, mountainous landscape around them, still warm and shimmering in the late heat of the afternoon.

'I feel a Chanel fact coming on,' Zoe teased.

'Oh, of course, this is where she was from. "The volcano from the Auvergne", one of her friends nicknamed her, saying her hair and her eyebrows were as black as lava and her character was as hard as the impervious rock.'

'I like that,' Lucie told him, wondering if there were any geological features she could be named after... craggy old rock of ages, maybe, Vesuvius of repressed fury, more like.

'According to my phone,' Deva continued, 'we have about one and a half more hours on the road before we get to the village. Shall I be DJ? Play some music to keep us all going?'

'Go for it,' Zoe encouraged him. 'Hit us with your playlist.'

So, as they settled into their seats, Deva brought a small speaker out of his rucksack, hooked his phone up to it and then started to fill the car with a bouncy, lively mix of show tunes, Abba, high energy dance music... Anything to make the long miles on the smooth, much quieter road through the mountains go by more quickly.

And finally, as the sky began to take on a more twilight-ish cast, the satnav was guiding them off the main road and towards a village of pale yellow limestone houses perched higher on the hillside above them.

'Oh good grief,' Lucie complained as the road became narrower and more twisty, and she had to slow down considerably. 'If I'd known it would take another twenty minutes to get there from the main road, I would have picked somewhere else. It looked as if it was just five minutes off the route.'

Although, thinking back, had they even passed anywhere else for the last twenty minutes or so?

'It looks very pretty,' Zoe assured her, before adding with a wink, 'Did you pick it so you could show off on your Insta feed?'

'Oh, ha ha.'

'I'm sure it will be worth it once we get there,' Zoe added. 'I am so tired and hungry and in need of a wee. All the wants, all at once.'

Another ten minutes later, they were driving into the small high street of an old-fashioned French mountain town. It seemed bustling, with lots of people out and about, and red, white and blue bunting fluttering over the streets.

'Second on the left,' Lucie instructed, glancing at the satnav.

The turning brought them into a narrow, shaded street, then there was one more turn before they came to a small car park and what looked like the back entrance of the hotel she had booked.

'Here we are, I think,' Lucie told them.

'Brilliant,' Deva declared. He turned off the music and the car fell silent, which, after more than an hour of blasting music, felt a little strange.

'Oh my goodness.' Lucie leaned back in her warm and sticky seat and felt a wave of relief. 'Well done, everyone. I can't believe we've made it all this way. And it's been fun, most of the time.'

'Yeah,' Zoe agreed. 'I hope the loo is very nearby.'

'I hope the beds are comfy... and they better have wine,' Lucie added.

* * *

All the bags were emptied from the car. And was Lucie imagining it, or was there one more bag than she remembered? She was sure Deva had arrived at her dad's with just one pull-along bag. Now he had the pull-along and a duffle bag as well as his rucksack.

But never mind. The three of them hustled through the door and along the corridor to the reception area.

There they were met by an effusive Frenchman who took Lucie's name and then checked everyone's passports with something of a flourish.

'Welcome to my hotel,' he told them cheerfully. 'Your wish is my command, as they say.'

'We've had a very long day of driving,' Lucie told him. 'I think we'd all just like something to eat and then a long sleep.'

It was disconcerting to get a loud laugh in response to this.

'What's wrong?' Lucie asked.

'Dinner, no problem, but sleep?' he asked with a surprised expression. 'It is Bastille Day. There is a big party in the town all night long. We thought you come here for the celebrations!'

13

'What? Oh! I didn't think about that.' Lucie couldn't deny her shock at this news. They'd been driving forever and now the prospect of a sleepless night in what she'd thought would be a calm and tranquil village was not exactly filling her with glee.

'I'm so tired, maybe I'll be able to sleep through the once-a-year party,' she added.

'Once a year, *non*.' The hotel owner shook his head. 'Every three months there is a party here.'

Then he explained where their rooms were and told them to come down in an hour or so for dinner in the dining room.

Upstairs, Lucie and Zoe found they had pretty, adjoining rooms, all pastel colours and flowery curtains, with a shared bathroom, while Deva had a separate, narrow room to himself with his own en-suite.

As soon as Lucie was in her room, she sank onto the bed and stretched herself out full length, so grateful to not be driving and to have a little time to herself. *Must call Dad,* she thought to herself. He would want to hear all about the trip so far and how the Jag was managing. But that could wait; for a moment, she was going to stretch, rest her eyes and try to unclench her shoulders from the driving position.

Dinner in the hotel was the three of them round a table, while a handful of locals congregated in the bar area. It was a properly leisurely French meal with homemade quiche and salad to start, then a leg of duck each, served with vegetables and, for dessert, small pots of chocolate mousse. There was a half bottle of white wine, which Lucie polished off a little too rapidly, while Zoe and Deva drank water and Cokes.

When the wine had made a mellowing effect, Lucie couldn't help asking if there had been any update on the Jacasta wedding Instagram feed.

'Oooh...' Zoe brought out her phone and scrolled to the relevant account. 'Let's see what today has brought... Flower decorations, check. Photo captions says: "It just has to be pink peonies, white roses and lavender for me... The heart and soul of a wedding is its flowers." Favours... also check,' Zoe went on, 'She tells us, "I've created these pink heart-shaped macarons, filled with white and iced in purple with J&M to match the flower theme."'

Zoe showed them photographs of the little pink gauze bags of macarons, tied with gold string and bearing a label, hand-written with the words 'macarons of love... from our hearts to yours'.

Maybe it was the wine, but Lucie had to give an undignified snigger. 'Macarons of love... Macaron off, you precious little princess. When she says "created" these macarons, I take it she means she went online and ordered them from www.pernickety-precious-wedding-favours.com. What an utter pantomime. Please tell me there is more?'

'Mum… is this so you can laugh at it?'

'Of course! Good grief, Zoe, I'm sure Jacasta is a perfectly nice human being. I'm sure their French wedding will be delightful, but surely I can have a little tiny laugh to myself about this? Are you not laughing?'

'Smiling,' Zoe admitted, 'not laughing. She is a nice human being,' Zoe went on. 'She maybe cares just a bit too much about the details, but she is nice and I think she's good for Dad. OK… so.' Zoe scrolled. 'Here we have a photo of "the wedding girls" who have apparently enjoyed "a gorgeous pamper afternoon", according to the caption, "being massaged with organic lavender oil and "rolfed" into a state of "meditative bliss".'

Zoe held out the phone and they all looked at the photo of Jacasta and her three friends in a whole candles-towels-flowers-blue-sky setting.

'Got to admit,' Zoe said, 'I would not mind being rolfed into a state of meditative bliss myself.'

'Not with those ninnies though,' Lucie couldn't help snipping. 'They are too busy worrying about whether their eyebrows are on trend. They're probably having wedding-themed stickers lacquered onto their pink, white and lavender gel nails as we speak.'

'And is that so wrong?' Zoe asked.

Lucie sighed. 'Sometimes I am very glad that I didn't grow up in an era when you don't just paint your nails, you worry about how you're going to decorate your nail gel. It's just all too much. Are boys wasting their time on this stuff?' she said, not meaning Deva in particular, but he felt he had to answer.

'Not typically, but each to their own. Live and let live...' He shrugged.

'I am so tired,' she added, 'I am tempted to order a brandy at the bar, carry it up to my room and not stir again until the morning.'

'Same,' Zoe added, 'just minus the brandy, obviously. How about you, Deva? Bed, or are you considering a stroll around the celebrations outside?' she asked.

'Is that a good idea?' Lucie fretted.

'Mum! Deva is twenty, not pregnant or an old lady.'

'I'm not an old lady,' Lucie protested.

'Still, the night is young. Deva is a handsome young man,' Zoe went on. 'He probably wants to get out there and check out the talent.'

'I don't know about that...' Deva said, sounding shy.

'It's a tiny town,' Zoe added. 'I'm pretty sure you're not going to get lost or into any kind of running street battle. So you should probably get out there, chat up a few old ladies. There might be fireworks; that's a Bastille Day thing.'

'Well... maybe later...' was Deva's non-committal response. 'I think I need to chill on my bed for a bit.'

'Yeah, me too,' Zoe said.

'Agreed. But first, a trip to the bar,' was Lucie's verdict. Those Insta pics... The fact she was going to be dropping Zoe and Deva off at the wedding venue tomorrow. Miles was definitely getting re-married. No doubt about it. He was moving on with breakneck speed, and she... well, she obviously wasn't.

'Bloody macarons of bloody love,' she hissed.

* * *

As soon as Zoe got to her room, she closed the door and sank down gratefully onto her bed, which was a touch saggy and creaky, but she didn't care. She stretched to her full height and let out a long, relieved sigh. The small of her back ached, her shoulders ached, her neck ached, her legs ached, the muscles supporting the weight of her round, pregnant belly ached and her ankles felt fat and puffy, so it was a huge relief to finally stretch out and sink down into a soft mattress.

She could feel her eyelids begin to weigh down and, if she let it, sleep would be quick to follow. Instead, she put a pillow behind her back and reached for her phone to call Rafi.

'Hello, Zoe, how are you doing?' he asked, and it was lovely to hear his soft, calm voice. 'How is the journey so far?'

'Hello, babe... How can sitting in a car for hour after hour be so tiring?' she complained.

'I'm so sorry you couldn't get the train,' he sympathised.

'I'm so sorry you're not making this trip with me.'

'Work has been chaos this week,' he told her. 'I think I'll be up most of tonight trying to make the 7 a.m. deadline. Who sets a project deadline for 7 a.m. on a Saturday?'

'Crazy, mad bosses who want you to work all night,' she suggested.

'Yeah, well, you know all about those people.'

'So true. I am so looking forward to our baby leave,' she added.

'Yeah, me too...'

Now, missing him, knowing that he was going to be working through the night, she had to admit, 'I worry a lot that you're not really going to take the time off. They won't manage without you, they'll guilt trip you into "just a few hours a day" and before you know it, you'll be at your screen, headphones on, doing a full ten hours.'

'No, honestly. I've made it totally clear. They're hiring a very expensive temp in for a month. The handover won't be pretty and the temp will probably call me a lot to start with, but it is going to happen, Zo.'

'Promise me?'

'Promise,' he told her.

And although that was reassuring, now she knew she was going to have to raise her other big worry too, because much as she was trying to be calm and let Rafi go at his own pace, she couldn't stop thinking about it. And she knew perfectly well that her mother had a point – they needed to move.

'So, where are we going to have the maternity leave, Rafs? You, me and the baby in my flat share? Or you, me and the baby in your teeny, tiny flat? She's due in six weeks' time. There is no way we will have found a place to buy and have moved into it by then. Absolutely no way,' she repeated for emphasis.

Rafi let out a sigh.

'Has your mother been...?' he began.

'Yes, she has, and I've got to admit that she has a point. I'm worried, I can't stop thinking about it. Where is home for our baby? And are you going to be there for us? You keep saying you will be... but I need proof, Rafi. I need to believe it.'

There was a long pause and Zoe could feel her fingers gripping the phone tightly. She was putting pressure on him, which she knew he didn't like. But this was serious. They had to decide what to do next. They had to make a move. She needed a big, tangible sign that he was committing to her, to their daughter, to their future. And if he couldn't do it, then... then... in her heart, she felt that this would be the beginning of the end for them as a couple.

'I have been thinking about it,' he began hesitantly. 'What

about if we both move out of our flats and rent a place that's big enough together?'

She was about to protest, list all her reasons why she didn't think that was the right thing to do next, but he went on with, 'Hear me out, Zo. If we rent somewhere together, we can move before the baby is here.'

'Well... if we start looking, like, tomorrow,' she told him.

'And we don't have to find the perfect thing, and we don't have to decorate... or buy furniture... Plus, we can keep saving and in a year's time or so, we'll have more money to get the bigger place that we need.'

'But...' Zoe could feel that painful ache at the back of her throat, but she was determined not to cry. 'It's still so temporary,' she began. 'A rental... We can be asked to move, or you can just get fed up and move out, I can't do any special decorating for our daughter's place. It's not what I want,' she said forcefully now. 'It's not what I want! I need something more from you. I need you to commit to being with us.'

'Zoe... I don't know why you're being so—'

'Don't you dare say emotional!' she warned him.

'I was going to say insecure.'

Pause.

'I am here for you. I am here for our baby. Why can't you believe that?'

'Because you aren't here!' she protested. 'You were supposed to be in France with me, meeting my family and going to my dad's wedding. Is that so much to ask? I've been carrying our baby for almost eight months now and you can't even make one weekend's worth of effort for me. Instead, you're where you always are, where you always want to be – in your little flat, at your screen, with your headphones on at bloody work!'

When there was no reply to this, Zoe hung up.

She stared at the rose-coloured wall ahead of her and could only think that if Rafi had done what she'd suggested back in May, they would already be in their flat together. She would be assembling the cot, painting the bedroom walls, building a home for her fledgling family. Instead, he'd stalled and hesitated and now they were no further on and she still felt that, in his heart of hearts, he didn't want to move in with them. He didn't want to commit. Yes, her parents had recently divorced, but she didn't think what she was asking for was too much, or anything out of the ordinary. Maybe this wasn't going to work out. Maybe he just wasn't going to be able to give her what she needed to feel as loved and as secure as she needed to feel.

For just a moment or two, Zoe allowed several tears to escape, but she hated to cry. What did crying ever solve? So she went into the bathroom, ran the tap and carefully washed and dried her face.

When she got back to London after this wedding, she would have to decide what was best for her and the baby, even if it meant making some hard decisions.

Deva sat on the narrow bed in the narrow room and willed himself to feel calm, but he was jumpy, fizzy with nervous energy and the thought of settling down now for the night seemed like madness. It was far too early. There was so much to see! To do!

He still couldn't get over *the fact* that he had been standing in the Place Vendôme today. He had stood outside The Ritz! He had really, truly, been inside the Chanel boutique on the Rue Cambon and run his hands over intricate lace panels, creamy silk blouses, jackets made of whisper-soft cashmere tweed. The images were still playing inside his mind. It had been so exciting, so unforgettable. He wasn't ready yet for this day to end.

And now he was in the heart of France, in the Massif Central, not even very far from the Auvergne region where Coco herself had been born and spent the earliest years of her life. There was no question of staying in this little room and settling down to sleep. He had to get outside and experience the air, the people, the streets, the hustle, and try to imagine what her life here was like over a hundred years ago.

He turned his attention to the duffle bag on the floor that wasn't his. He had spotted it upstairs in that spare bedroom at Aunt Lucie's dad's house. And, overcome with emotion, he'd made the spur of the moment decision to 'borrow' it. Just as he had 'borrowed' all the items that were inside it.

At some point, of course, he was going to have to tell Aunt Lucie what he had done. And he could hardly expect her to be pleased. But... He felt compelled to rub his hands comfortingly together at the thought, his fingers now itching to touch those things again, his eyes longing to run over them, to try to absorb every single little detail. Soak it all in. Learn from it.

He wasn't sure if he could ever express to Aunt Lucie, or to anyone, in fact, how important this was, just how much it meant to him. This wasn't 'an interest'. This was something he felt compelled to do. He couldn't think about anything else. It was an itch, an urge that had to be satisfied. More powerful than any other one he had experienced before.

So Deva sat on the floor beside the small duffle bag. Slowly, he pulled the zip open, then, holding his breath, he opened the bag. Oh, oh! There they were. And even more beautiful than he'd remembered.

Very carefully, he lifted out the beige-coloured Chanel 2.55 handbag, and then the softest Chanel tweed jacket in that pale, supple wool. Underneath, he knew there was a tweed matching skirt and that very special slinky, black lace dress. But for now, those could wait; for now, the bag and the jacket were enough. He ran his hands very carefully over the soft, quilted leather of the bag. Then he pulled the supple woollen sleeves of the jacket through his fingers. So soft... so beautiful.

Into his mind came this daring, crazy, even quite wild thought.

Really? *Really?* Could he do that? Would he? *Should* he? He had always stopped himself before. But what if he went out tonight, alone? Who was here to stop him? Who would even know?

A big, shiny 'Yes!' formed in his mind. This was possible. This was a plan! This was something he was going to do, just for himself. Well, just for himself and for Coco. She would understand, he thought. She would cheer him on.

Quickly, before he could overthink it, or worry too much about it, or stop himself in his own tracks, Deva peeled off the warm, sweaty clothes he'd worn for most of the day and headed to his bathroom for a quick shower.

When he was dried and back in the bedroom, he pulled on a pair of lightweight linen trousers and a clean, white t-shirt. Then with care and reverence, he slipped his arms into the creamy tweed jacket that bore the legendary label and smoothed it down over the front of his chest. Then he looped the chains of the 2.55 bag over the crook of his elbow. Breathless with nerves, he stood for a long time in front of the bathroom mirror because this was even better than he could ever have imagined. He was here in France, wearing *the* jacket and carrying *the* bag. Staring in the mirror, he felt quite overcome with emotion. Carefully, he combed and adjusted his sleek damp hair, pulling it behind his ear on one side, so it looked exactly like Coco's jet-black, asymmetrical bob. Now with the bob, the jacket, the bag, the t-shirt, the trousers, he looked exactly as he had imagined he could – and that feeling was incredibly powerful. He felt as if he'd finally taken charge of himself, as if he could at last begin to create the life he wanted. No way was he staying in his room. He had to get out of the hotel and explore the town.

14

Lucie, teeth brushed and in her lightweight summer pyjamas, knew she was very tired, but still, when she lay down on the bed in the dark, she couldn't sleep. So now she was at the window of her room, looking out and catching glimpses of the fireworks in the night sky.

When she thought about the very long day she had just lived through, she couldn't help smiling. From the moment they'd all climbed into the car together, yes, it had been stressy and hassle-filled and right out of her comfort zone, but also... The ferry journey, the motorways, the visit to the glamorous heart of Paris, the blasting disco music, even all the Chanel anecdotes – everything had been completely new and interesting. This journey was giving her the break from the humdrum routine of post-divorce life that she hadn't even realised she'd needed.

To her surprise, her phone began to ring. When she went over to pick it up, she was even more surprised to see that the name Melissa, Deva's mother, was flashing up.

'Hello, Melissa?'

'Lucie? Lucie, is that you?'

'Yes, hello, how are you?'

'Are you with Deva?' Melissa asked, voice urgent, ignoring the question.

'Ummm... no, not at the moment. We're at the hotel for our stopover. Deva is in his room.'

'What's the name of the hotel?' Melissa asked.

Lucie gave her the hotel's name and address.

'He's not there...' Melissa said. 'I've been messaging and calling. No reply. I've been following him on his phone and he's not there.'

Lucie could hear the obvious anxiety in Melissa's voice.

'Maybe he's gone out for a walk,' Lucie suggested.

'On his own? In a strange place?' Melissa practically squeaked.

'Deva does live in London,' Lucie reminded her. 'I'm sure he can cope with a teeny French village.' But she remembered that she'd also found it hard to let go of all those maternal worries as Zoe had turned from teenager to grown up. She too had sat up late at night, frantically trying to track her daughter's moves on the phone.

'But it is hard not to worry about them,' Lucie sympathised. 'Where does the phone say Deva is?' she asked.

Melissa gave her the name of a square.

'OK,' Lucie said. 'This is a very small place, so I'll go down there and have a look for him. Then we'll report back. But don't worry. It's a lovely little village. He'll just be strolling around, enjoying the atmosphere.' No need to tell Melissa there was a major celebration in progress. 'I'll get him to call you as soon as I see him,' she added.

Having hastily pulled on jeans, trainers and a top, Lucie went out into the corridor, where she was surprised to see Zoe.

'Oh, hello, I thought you were going straight to sleep,' she said to her daughter.

'Yeah, you too,' came the reply.

'I've just had Deva's mum on the phone. Apparently, he's gone out.'

'Why is she worrying? He's a big boy in a tiny town...'

'Well, it can be hard to stop worrying about your children, no matter how old they are,' Lucie said, giving Zoe a smile. 'So I've said I'll go and have a look for him.'

'I'll come with you,' Zoe said.

'Are you sure?'

'Can't sleep anyway...'

'Everything OK with you?' Lucie asked. But Zoe just shrugged and Lucie took that as a signal not to ask any more.

Whatever Lucy and Zoe had been expecting as they arrived out onto the high street of the village and then into the wider central village square, it wasn't this. The place was completely mobbed. Loud, jostling, standing-room-only mobbed. The dark of the night lit up with bright bar windows, random jagged fireworks and crackers that erupted with bangs and sparks of showers, and a multi-coloured carousel blasting out dance music as it spun screaming teenagers round and round on its painted horses. Bars and restaurants had their doors wide open; tables and chairs were set out all over the pavements and the square, and there were people everywhere.

Lots of them were the worse for wear after a long afternoon and evening of partying and toasting la Révolution. An e-scooter whizzed past Lucie's elbow, hit a patch of wonky cobblestones further along the way and tipped its passenger straight out onto the square where he landed in a soft heap, but got up apparently unharmed, picked the scooter up again and got back on to continue weaving a wobbly path through the crowd.

'Oh boy,' Zoe said to her mother. 'Looks like we've arrived about half an hour before the ambulances will be needed.'

The atmosphere was definitely moving from cheerful and loud to rowdy, with the centre of the square acting as a magnet for the crowd. There was already a dense mass of people there, and more and more seemed to be thronging towards it. It looked like there was some kind of statue and fountain in the centre and something was happening there that was drawing the crowd.

'What's that all about?' Zoe asked, pointing towards the statue and the crowd forming around it.

As they got closer, they could hear a voice at full blast singing out the rallying cry: '*Aux armes, citoyens!*'

And, as one, the crowd now broke out into the stirring chorus of the French national anthem. Lucie and Zoe pressed on through the throng until they could see the fountain properly. It was an impressive mound, gushing with water that collected into a pool at the bottom. On top of the mound was the statue of a horse and on top of the statue of the horse was – to their complete astonishment – *Deva*! His eyes were fixed firmly ahead as he sang the French national anthem at full volume.

'Oh. My. God!' Lucie exclaimed. 'What's he doing? What on earth is he doing? And how the hell did he get up there?'

'And more importantly, how the hell do we get him down?' Zoe asked.

'He's wearing my Chanel jacket!' Lucie exclaimed.

'That's the least of our worries.'

'And carrying my cream 2.55 bag! Bloody hell. What on earth is going on? What is he doing? This is ridiculous!'

'He's picked quite the moment to try out his new look,' Zoe said. 'Maybe he was hoping for some audience feedback.'

'I don't know why you're joking—'

'Sorry, trying to see the bright side is a big part of my job.'

'He's on top of a statue with a crowd at his feet that might clap or might rough him up. What are we supposed to do? And what do I tell Melissa?'

'Let's leave Melissa out of it for now...'

The rowdy singing went on as the chorus was blasted out for a second, then a third time.

'Deva!' Lucie shouted out.

'Maybe don't distract him, Mum. That might make him fall,' was Zoe's advice.

'Do you think he's on drugs?' Lucie asked as she watched him lead this huge crowd in a patriotic singsong.

'No, but maybe he should be,' was Zoe's verdict. 'You stay here and keep an eye on him. I'm going to go and find out about ladders... the fire brigade, that kind of thing.'

'Keep an eye on him?' Lucie protested. 'He's about twenty feet up in the air. There's not much I can do. I can't catch him if he comes off that horse!'

The song was rising to a crescendo, with the crowd shouting out the words and throwing fists in the air. The atmosphere was a whisper away from being threatening. And Deva, he was completely carried away. He was twirling the handbag above his head like a flag or a lasso and suddenly, to a great cheer from the crowd, it spun out of his hands and soared into the air.

'That's a £3,000 bag!' Lucie gasped. 'A collector's item!'

Now the crowd seemed to surge in the direction of the

falling bag and when it landed, that's when the scuffling broke out.

A deafening five minutes began, full of shouts and cries, but it did at least move the crowd from the base of the statue. And now Lucie could hear her name being called out as Deva caught sight of her from his vantage point.

'Aunt Lucie! I'm up here!'

'Oh, hello, Deva! Hold tight! Hold very tight. Someone is coming with a ladder to help you down,' she added hopefully, as Zoe wasn't back yet, so she had no idea if help was going to arrive.

'But I don't want to come down!' Deva shouted. 'This is amazing! I've never had so much fun. I want to sing, all night long.'

And he launched into what sounded like Édith Piaf's 'Non, Je Ne Regrette Rien', but it was hard to tell over the din of the crowd.

'Please hold on!' Lucie shouted as Deva spread his arms wide, carried by the emotion of the song and the moment. Who was this person, she wondered. He was such a jumble of different moods and energies. Quiet, nervy, almost shy for long stretches and in some situations. But then he'd also run about fizzing with excitement on the ferry, she remembered. Been quite carried away in Paris... and now this – he'd transformed with a touch of Chanel into a crowd-rousing extrovert.

'Keep holding on,' she instructed once again, trying not to think of Melissa or having to explain any of this to her. 'Singing is good... and holding on is very good.'

* * *

It was almost an hour later before two burly bar owners with a very long ladder had managed to coax Deva back down to earth.

Once all the fuss was over, the ladder down, the rescuers on their way, the crowd moved along by harassed-looking gendarmes, then Deva sat on the edge of the fountain, with Lucie on one side and Zoe on the other, looking thrilled but also slightly shaken and dazed, giving off matador vibes in that pale, cropped jacket.

'You OK?' Zoe asked. 'Feet back on the ground?'

'Sort of,' he said quietly.

'That was quite a surprise,' Lucie told him. 'I think there's quite a different Deva inside than the one you show the world most of the time.'

'Maybe that's true of all of us,' Deva said, and something about the way he looked at her made Lucie feel a little unnerved. 'Maybe we should all be our real selves more often.'

'Maybe...' she agreed. 'But maybe not in a way that involves a ladder rescue.'

'Everyone needs to have at least one ladder rescue in their lives,' Deva said, giving her a little dig with his elbow. 'You should try it. I mean, I sang to the crowd,' he went on, 'I led the singing. And I only know the words to the chorus of the French national anthem... Must learn the verses.'

'I need to send your mum a message,' Lucy began. 'I'll tell her that we've found you... well... enjoying Bastille Day in the village and everything is OK.'

'There's something else you need to tell her,' Deva began.

'Yes?'

'Tell her, even though she hates the idea, no, make that, *loathes* the idea. I think I might be born to perform.'

15

'But we are so close...' Deva wheedled, hoping that if he persisted, maybe there was a chance he could change Aunt Lucie's mind.

'No, Deva, we're sticking to the main road and that is final!' Lucie said, and she knew it sounded a bit harsh, but really, she had already detoured through Paris and talked him down from a statue; hadn't she done enough? And not forgetting that he'd thrown her extremely expensive bag into the crowd! Although, by some miracle – maybe the spirit of Coco Chanel was looking out for Deva – on the walk back to the hotel, they had actually found it, somewhat squashed, grubby and trampled, hanging from a railing.

'But I don't know when I'm going to get this chance again,' Deva pleaded from the back seat.

'If it's so important to you, why don't you book a trip over before the end of the summer?' Lucie suggested, hands on the wheel as she looked forwards, eyes on the road. There was a straightforward plan for today and she didn't want to deviate from it. No impromptu trips to Paris, or evenings on top of statues.

Today was about getting though the hours of travel and then arriving safely at the wedding destination in good time. There, Zoe and Deva would join the rest of the family for the pre-wedding dinner, while Lucie would head south on her own to the little B&B on the coast where two days and nights of relaxation would be hers before she drove Zoe all the way home.

Deva was staying on in France with his family for a few days before flying back to London.

'But I can't afford to come all the way back out here on my own,' Deva said sadly. 'Or honestly, I would.'

After a few moments of silence, he picked up again with a description of the detour and how fascinating it would be for them all and how little extra time it would add. In fact, according to Deva and his phone map, there was a good chance of avoiding at least one major traffic jam if they took this route that went through the mountains and then down right through the two towns so closely associated with Coco Chanel's early years – Aubazine, where she grew up in a convent orphanage, and Brive la Gaillarde, where she had her first job as a seamstress.

'The turn is coming up in just a few minutes. What can I do to convince you both that this is a great idea? What can I say? What can I offer? What can I promise?' Deva wheedled on from the back seat. 'This could be so exciting, such an adventure. This is Coco Chanel we're talking about.'

Exasperated, Lucie glanced over at Zoe, who just gave a non-committal shrug. This was all on Lucie.

'Look, is there any kind of compromise that we can make here?' she ventured.

The look of hope that passed over Deva's face tugged too

hard on Lucie's heart strings. She kept thinking she was annoyed by him, fed up with him, totally exasperated, but then some look of his would remind her that he was still young, and a bit over-sheltered, over-enthusiastic, and somehow just a little too sensitive. And then, despite herself, she wanted to help... look after him, even.

'I don't think it's a good idea to do the full detour,' she said, suspecting almost immediately that Deva would only try to keep convincing her. 'But I'm prepared to drive into the mountains for twenty minutes or so, to let you take a look and take pictures and then we'll turn back, get onto this road again and carry on. Can you live with that for now?'

'Yessssss!' he exclaimed, while Zoe shook her head in disbelief.

So Lucie indicated and then turned the Jag off the long, black, beautifully tarred main road and into the smaller road that led towards the hills.

The pale and rocky hills quickly grew into mountains, while the road rapidly became steep and twisting, and Lucie, glancing at the satnav's clock, decided that fifteen minutes of this was really all she was going to allow before she turned around sharpish and drove back to the main motorway again.

Around the next bend, the road ahead rose very steeply. Plus, they were now in the shimmering midday heat of another sizzling summer's day. Halfway up the ascent, Lucie glanced at the dashboard to check that everything was OK, and that's when she saw that one of the temperature gauges – oil? Water? She wasn't sure, but this gauge was clearly in the red zone.

'Oh no, we'll have to stop when we get to the top,' she exclaimed. 'The car looks like it's overheating!'

She slowed right down and changed down into a lower gear, hoping that would take some strain off the engine, but this just seemed to make things worse. Now there came a grinding and hammering sound that she didn't like at all. Just as the car crested the brow of the hill, they all heard a strange snapping sound and then the horrible noise of metal grinding on metal. The engine began to lose power, so she steered towards the verge and turned it off immediately.

'Oh bloody, blinking, bloody hell!' she exclaimed. 'Now what?'

She felt a burst of panic. The car was broken... her dad's precious car, that she had promised to take care of, was broken. They had to get help, and get it fixed, and get back on the road to the wedding.

It was hard to believe, but hours and hours had passed and now the sun was dipping down in a reddening sky towards the tops of the hills. Soon it would be dark. And they were still by the roadside in what was clearly the most deserted road in the whole of France, with no phone signal, hoping that *someone else* would come past. Because that was the most frustrating thing – two young guys in a car had stopped, hours ago now, and they'd taken the registration number, Lucie's phone number, and promised to get help and send a garage tow truck to them.

The guys had even given them two bottles of water and a banana. So she, Zoe and Deva had all relaxed a little and had been expecting help to arrive soon. But now, all this time later, where was the help? It was going to get dark and they were absolutely marooned here.

'OK, I have officially given up,' Lucie told her passengers, trying to sound much calmer than she felt. 'I don't think those guys have done anything. Or maybe they did contact a garage, but it's done nothing. Either way, we are stuck. No one is coming and we're going to have to decide what to do.'

'Maybe Zoe should eat the banana,' was Deva's first suggestion. 'She's eating for two, isn't she?'

Zoe snorted. 'At this stage of coffee deprivation, I'm not sure I can be held responsible for my actions.'

'Do you think I should walk back towards the main road?' was Deva's next question. 'Try and get a signal on my phone. I could take all our phones,' he added. 'Maybe we've got different networks.'

But a quick check of the three phones revealed they had all been transferred to the same French service provider.

Lucie thought about Deva leaving the car for this walk into the growing darkness. Her mind raced ahead to not being able to contact him, not being able to find him and then having to explain to a frantic Melissa that she had managed to lose Deva somewhere in the mountainous French wilderness.

'No, Deva, good of you to offer, but we can't have you going off on your own down an unknown country road in the dark without a working phone. That would be madness,' Lucie said firmly.

And she meant it. She could curse herself for trusting those two guys in the car and letting them all sit here waiting for hours on end. Instead, they could have set off to the main road and flagged down help for themselves hours ago. Yes, it would have been a very long, hot walk. But by now, the car would probably have been fixed and they would have been back on their way to the bloody pre-wedding dinner.

'My mum is going to be very worried,' Deva pointed out.

'Dad too,' Zoe added.

'There's nothing anyone can do right now,' Lucie added. 'No phones... It's like the 1980s.'

At least this made Deva laugh for a moment.

'I need a full run down of supplies,' she said. 'If I know that we have enough water to at least get the two of you through the night, then I can cope with everything else.'

'This isn't the desert,' Deva informed them. 'They get their mineral water from here.'

'While that is good to know,' Zoe began, 'I'm not sure I should start drinking from mountain springs just at this point in my life.' She ran her hands over her stomach to remind him of the situation.

'I suppose that's true,' Deva replied.

For a moment, they all searched around the car, and together, in their three assorted bottles, they seemed to have about one litre of water left. It wasn't entirely reassuring but at least it wasn't an immediate crisis.

'So... what do you think we should do?' Zoe turned to her mother. 'All walk the five miles or so back to the main road, me waddling along beside you?'

'No, Zoe, it's pitch dark. We could get lost... have a fall... lose each other. We're going to have to wait here until first light and set off then.'

'Wait in the car all night?' Zoe protested. 'My back is already aching. I don't know if I can take another five or six hours of just sitting here.'

'I am so sorry. Dad assured me the Jag was serviced and absolutely good to go, otherwise I'd never have set off in it,' Lucie said. She was struggling to remain calm. Really, she would quite like to shout and rage about literally everything – she could start with bloody Miles and his bloody business fail and his bloody wedding and move on to her dad being terminally ill, him making her go on this trip in this car, and then end with bloody train strikes and those bloody boys who had said they would get help!

Yes, it was definitely tempting to just lose it and let fully rip at the current situation. But here she was with a daughter who dealt with terrible stressful calamities every working day and a nephew who was sensitive and easily upset. So, really, the grown-up thing to do was to just jolly well hold on and keep it together.

'Look, it could be much worse,' she said, trying to convince herself. 'We have water. We have a car to sleep in. The weather is much cooler now with a breeze. We'll be safe here until dawn and we know where the main road is. We'll be able to find it easily, so we'll walk there first thing. Yes, it might be about four or five miles, but we'll take it slowly and we'll get there eventually. Then we'll flag down help and we'll probably be on our way by... by early morning. So, just stay calm, everyone.'

'Well said, Mum,' was Zoe's response. 'And you're probably right. Probably best to stay put for now. Even if it's not going to be the most comfortable night ever.'

'I could give you a shoulder rub, if that would help,' Lucie offered.

At this point, Deva got out of the car.

'Where are you going?' Lucie asked anxiously.

'All the way to the boot,' was Deva's reply. 'Don't worry, I'm sure I'll make it there and back. But cover me.'

'Very funny,' Zoe said.

'Don't look now, I'm changing,' he added. 'And then I'm going to do some practice songs. I'm supposed to be the singer at a certain wedding tomorrow... hopefully.'

'Fingers crossed,' Lucie added, still not able to believe that they were honestly trapped here, just five miles or so from a major road.

'I should still get some practice in,' Deva said.

He seemed to spend some time changing. He opened the boot and then must have been rummaging through bags in search of whatever it was he was looking for.

Then finally, through the open car windows, they began to hear Deva running through practice scales, arpeggios, and warm-up exercises.

'He sounds good,' Zoe said.

'Yes, I remember him singing at a family event when he was much younger. He seemed to transform,' Lucie recalled, 'from this shy little person into someone who really was enjoying every moment of entertaining us all. Came completely alive for the song. Seemed to feel every note.'

And now they could hear that Deva had begun singing in earnest, unaccompanied, of course, so there was just the sound of his voice travelling out over the hillside, as the darkness began to close in around them.

'What song is that?' Lucie asked her daughter in a whisper. 'I recognise it. And he's very good. Don't you think?'

'"Eternal Flame" by The Bangles,' Zoe told her, adding, 'He has a gorgeous voice. Too good a voice for a future chief financial officer.'

'Hmmm...' As quietly as she could, Lucie opened her car door to better hear the singing. Zoe followed her lead.

Then Lucie stepped out of the car and turned, propping her elbows up onto the car roof so she could see Deva as well as hear him.

His back was turned and he was belting his tune out towards the barren hilltops ahead of them, glimmering in the very last of the pink light of the sunset.

His arms were spread wide and Lucie saw now that he was wearing her long, lace Chanel evening gown. After a first burst of recognition and surprise, she had to admit that the dress looked completely right on him and perfect for this performance. In fact, she couldn't help smiling. And she suspected that Deva still had a lot to find out about himself.

They were all turned towards the hilltops, still shining as the light grew inky, both Zoe and Lucie's eyes and ears on Deva. But still, there was something else, a step, a movement, some kind of sound behind her, that made Lucie turn around.

To her surprise, there was a skinny young man standing on the other side of the road. His hoodie was pulled right up over his head and his face was dark. He was standing, looking uncertain, and neither she nor this man seemed to know what to do next. Lucie felt a burst of protectiveness towards her pregnant daughter and the young man in her charge.

'I think we should get into the car,' she said urgently and loudly enough for Zoe and even Deva to hear.

Both of them turned around, and Deva's song came to an abrupt halt.

'Get in, get in,' Lucie said urgently.

Both she and Zoe got into the car and closed their doors. But it was obvious once they were inside that Deva wasn't going to do the same.

'What's Deva doing?' Lucie hissed. 'Is he going to talk to that guy? I don't think he should talk to him. He might be trying to rob us.'

'Or help us,' Zoe suggested.

'What is Deva doing?' Lucie asked again.

The young man began to cross the road towards the car, so Lucie wound down her window.

'Hello,' she began, trying to sound crisp and in charge and not nearly as worried as she felt.

And then Deva, still in his dress, of course, appeared at the side of the car. Sounding warm and friendly, he said, 'Hey, hello. How are you? Do you speak any English? Because *mon Français est mal.*'

'Yes. Hi...' the young guy began hesitantly. 'I see your car... long time. You... help?'

'The car has broken down... It's not working,' Deva explained.

Through a series of gestures, ragged phrases and words, the young man let Deva know that he had fixed cars before and could maybe have a look.

'Would that be OK, Aunt Lucie?' Deva asked. 'Let him look under the bonnet?'

Lucie could feel her heart hammering in her chest. She just couldn't let go of the fear that this was some kind of trick. It was dark, this was a very quiet road, no one's mobile had a signal and now this scruffy man had approached them. There might be others out of sight. All her instincts warned her to be careful and that this wasn't a safe situation.

'I'll open the bonnet, but Zoe and I will stay in the car,' she said anxiously.

'Mum,' Zoe began in a slightly disapproving tone, 'I'm sure everything's OK.'

The young man came closer to the car and smiled at them. It was a sweet smile, showing strong teeth against his dark skin. He was young, this guy, and thin. He didn't look much older than about nineteen or twenty, a similar age to Deva, probably.

Lucie lowered her window a little further.

'You like drink?' the young man asked, and he held up a small plastic bottle of water.

Zoe was the one who replied, 'Yes, that is very kind, thank you,' and reached out to take the bottle from his hand.

At that, Lucie felt the knot of tension in her chest loosen just a little.

'Could you pop open the bonnet, Aunt Lucie?' Deva asked. 'This guy would like to take a look and see if he can work out what's wrong. You never know, it might be something simple. Maybe he'll be able to fix it.'

Lucie reached down under the dashboard for the button and pressed, wondering what her dad would have to say about this young dude poking about under the lid of his precious car. And now she was realising, for the first time since they'd turned off the main road, that she was completely out of contact with him. If he'd taken any sort of turn for the worse, no one would be able to reach her.

Just as the knot of tension began to tighten again, she reminded herself that her dad had been the one to persuade her to come on this trip and he had promised, *promised,* that nothing was going to happen to him while she was away. She would just have to believe him.

Once the bonnet was up, the young guy and Deva went to the front of the car to peer inside.

'Use the light on your phone,' Lucie called out to Deva.

'Yup, thanks, thought of that,' he replied.

She turned to Zoe. 'Do you think he will have any idea what the problem is?'

'Who knows,' Zoe replied, 'but my guess is he's a refugee from Africa, heading north, maybe even headed to Calais to try to get onto a lorry or a boat.'

'Really?'

'Yeah, he's not French. He doesn't have a French accent, didn't offer to speak French to you or me. And he's had to be surprisingly resourceful to get this far, so maybe he'll turn out to know something about delicate older car engines. More than us, anyway.'

Still on Lucie's mind was the thought that this was not a risk-free situation. What if the guy had a knife... wanted to stow-away in their car... was going to force them to drive him to England... was going to kidnap Deva and his passport. Her imagination was completely running away with her and she had to tell herself to stop it.

Hadn't he offered help and smiles and a bottle of water? Maybe everything was as it seemed and she should feel relieved that help of some kind had finally turned up.

Sitting in the front seats of the car, Zoe and Lucie could both hear and feel as parts under the bonnet were tapped, turned and explored. A little time passed before Deva appeared at her window with a bright expression on his face.

'He thinks he knows what it is!' he exclaimed. 'And he can maybe get the car to drive for a short distance, hopefully enough to get us to a garage for a proper repair.'

Lucie, feeling the beginnings of relief at this news, opened the car door and stepped out, so she could discuss it with them both.

As she approached the bonnet, the young guy looked up, pointed to himself and said, 'Petros... Pete.'

'You're called Pete?' she asked, and he nodded in reply. 'Hello, Pete,' she said, but held back from giving her own name.

Deva, however, jumped in; pointing at himself, he said, 'Deva, and this is my Aunt Lucie. Zoe is in the car.'

Pete pointed under the bonnet and with some simple words tried to convey the problem.

Lucie's grasp of car mechanics was not exactly extensive, and from the sliver of light from Deva's phone and explanations only along the lines of 'bad here', 'make fix good', 'only short, short', she was not learning anything more.

'We can drive for a short time?' Deva clarified.

Pete nodded vigorously.

'Where is a town? Where is help?' Deva asked him.

Pete pointed back down the steep hill they'd climbed up in the car all those hours ago now and then pointed right.

Right was away from the main road, Lucie realised. Right was deeper into this unknown region and away from their route.

'Maybe we should go back to the main road,' she suggested to Deva. 'We have no idea where this town is, how long it will take to get there, or if the car could even make it. We could end up sitting at the side of another deserted road.'

'Town?' Deva pointed right. 'Or big road?' He pointed left, hoping Pete would understand him. 'Which one is close? Is near? Is soon? Quick?' He tried a variety of words, hoping Pete would understand.

'Car... town,' Pete said emphatically, pointing right again.

'Can you make the car work?' Lucie asked.

'Yes,' was all the reply she got as Pete turned his attention back to under the bonnet.

Pete began to turn the cap off one container and moved a wire or two around, talking to himself in a language that sounded completely unfamiliar and unrecognisable to Lucie. She wondered where this young guy was from and how he had ended up here, in the middle of the barren French hillside. She didn't think it was going to be a happy story.

After a few minutes of this, he smiled at them and with the words 'make drive', indicated that he had done what he needed to do and they could hopefully get to the nearby town.

'Thank you very much,' Lucie said, eager now for them to be

in the car and driving away from a situation that still made her feel uneasy.

But Pete, putting the bonnet carefully back down on the engine, then turned to them and, looking first at Lucie, then Deva, asked: 'Help me? Brother, sick.'

Now her sense of mistrust was dialling up again.

'Where is he?' Lucie asked.

The boy pointed off the road into the hillside. Could he be trusted? Could she really be sure it was safe to follow this guy off the road and towards who knew where?

'I'll go and ask Zoe what she thinks,' Lucie said to Deva.

Opening the car door, Lucie leaned in and told her daughter: 'He thinks he's fixed the car enough for us to drive to a nearby town...'

'Well, that's pretty amazing. Good for him,' Zoe replied.

'Yes, but now, he's asking if we can come and see his brother, who is ill. And apparently, this brother is off the road, into the countryside. I don't know how far... hopefully not too far. I just don't know if we should trust him, Zoe. Maybe it's a trick. Do you think I should go and take a look? I can come back and tell you what I think.'

But Zoe was already opening the car door and hoisting herself out of the passenger's seat.

'Zoe, you are going to stay here,' Lucie insisted. 'I'll go and look, find out how far away the brother is.'

'Mum!' Zoe protested. 'I'm the nurse, and I'm pregnant, not unable to walk.'

'But... but... what if the brother doesn't exist? And, anyway, you must be so tired,' Lucie countered.

'I work in ICU. Believe me, this is a picnic,' came Zoe's reply.

'OK... OK,' Lucie relented. 'But I'm going with you and Deva can stay with the car.'

'Fine. Let me get my kit out of my bag.'

'What kit?'

'I always carry a medical first aid kit, ever since...' She broke off because she didn't need to remind her mother.

'Oh,' was Lucie's quiet response. There was no danger she would ever forget that very close call. Her daughter had been one of four nursing students out for dinner when her friend had accidentally eaten peanut sauce and a last-minute change of handbag meant she wasn't carrying her epi pen. The restaurant had no first aid kit and the ambulance had almost not made it in time. Lucie remembered now that Zoe could hardly even tell her about it the next day because she was so upset and almost completely hoarse from running up and down the street, into other restaurants and bars, screaming for an epi pen, to no avail.

'Nothing worse than knowing what you need to do, but not having the kit,' Zoe said briskly, as she opened the boot of the car and unzipped her travel bag.

When the robust, neatly packaged kit was in her hands, Lucie told Pete that she and Zoe would walk with him to where his brother was. The smile and obvious relief in his face when he realised what she was saying gave Lucie a little more faith that this was all as it seemed and everything was going to be OK.

But still, in a low voice, she told Deva, 'You'll stay here with the car. I've locked the boot and I'm taking the key, so if anyone else turns up, they can't ' – she wanted it to sound light, almost jokey – 'drive off with you, or anything.'

'Yeah, of course... no worries, it'll be fine,' Deva said. 'He's a good guy, I can tell. He's a 'fugee. Like my dad was once. Dad always said everyone suspects you're a villain when you're just a human who wants to be alive, in a safe place.'

Lucie took a last look at Deva and hoped he was right, hoped his trust had been put in the right place. She smiled at him, liking the cheerful and alert look on his face. It was only when she was walking away, following Pete with Zoe by her side, that Lucie realised Deva was still wearing her black lace dress... Yes, she glanced over her shoulder to check. He was.

It suited him so completely, fitted him so well, and clearly he was so at home and comfortable in it that she hadn't even noticed. And no one else seemed to be noticing it – or mentioning it either. She shrugged. Time to concentrate now on Zoe and this young man just ahead of them leading the way over the stony, dusty ground towards, hopefully, not any kind of trap or trick, but another young man who needed their help.

16

They followed a rocky, even at times gravelly and slippery, path away from the road and down the side of the steep hill they'd climbed in the car. All of them used the lights from their phones to guide their footsteps.

'Take care,' Lucie warned Zoe as she heard the scrape of a shoe sliding in the gravel over the dusty earth.

'I'm fine,' Zoe insisted.

In the dim darkness, Lucie could already see the outline of things on the ground; from this distance, it looked like bags, sleeping bags and other items. And yes, as they approached, it was obvious that there was someone in one of the bags.

Pete began to speak in his native language as they approached the person in the sleeping bag.

'This him,' he turned to tell Lucie and Zoe. 'This my brother.'

'What's his name?' Zoe asked. 'His real name, if that's OK.'

'Fikru,' Pete replied.

Carefully, Zoe lowered herself down until she was kneeling,

so she could take a close look at the young man lying in the scruffy bag on the ground.

'Can you shine the light for me, Mum? But at a distance and not in his eyes,' she asked.

'No problem,' Lucie told her, and she redirected the beam from her phone.

'Hello, Fikru,' Zoe began, 'I'm Zoe. I'm a nurse and I'm going to check you over and make sure you're OK.'

As Zoe unzipped the first aid kit and brought out a thermometer and a stethoscope, it was already obvious to Lucie that Fikru, who looked even younger than his brother, was not OK.

He was only dimly aware of them. He could open his eyes a little but he didn't lift his head.

Zoe had the thermometer in his mouth and was now opening the sleeping bag so she could listen to his heartbeat.

'Tell me when he started to be ill, Pete?' she asked the concerned young man, who was now kneeling on the other side of his brother.

Pete looked at her, worried and not fully understanding the question.

'Two days sick?' Zoe asked, holding up two fingers. 'Three days sick?'

'Yes.' Pete began to nod. 'Three days sick.'

Lucie took a moment to look around at this place where these young brothers had been living, possibly for a few days. There were only the barest essentials here: some empty water bottles, several plastic carrier bags with maybe food, maybe a handful of belongings inside. There was a big box – something battery-operated, she guessed – attached to an extension cord with a row of plugs, and in those plugs, two phone chargers. But out here, no one could get a signal.

Lucie imagined the boys at night, hunkered down beside

this row of plugs, trying to send messages to their family back home, trying to keep track of other friends on the move across other countries. All of them trying to find somewhere else to lead their lives. Imagine if her child was on a perilous journey into the unknown like this.

She had no idea what the answer was to enormous international problems like immigration. But she did know that her lack of trust and her suspicion were quickly being replaced by sympathy and what she most of all wanted was to be helpful and kind.

'A cut?' was Zoe's next question. 'Is he injured?'

When Pete didn't follow what was meant, she asked, 'Blood? Bleeding? Pain?' in the hope that any of these words would trigger his understanding.

Then she gestured sawing at the skin on her forearm and pinching it.

Finally, Pete seemed to understand. He unzipped the sleeping bag fully and pulled up the leg of his brother's track-suit trousers. Lucie shone the light onto the leg and they could all see a large swelling with an oozing opening in the centre.

Pete made a buzzing sound and moved his finger to indicate an insect.

'An insect bite?' Lucie asked. 'That's got infected?'

'I think so, and it's serious,' Zoe said. 'I'm worried about sepsis and we've got to get him to hospital.'

Looking up at Pete, Zoe said slowly and clearly, 'I have medicine,' and she held up the small box of antibiotic tablets that she carried in her first aid kit.

Pete looked almost tearfully relieved.

'Take medicine... be OK?' he asked hopefully.

But Zoe shook her head. 'No, we must take him to the car. We go to hospital.'

These words seemed to alarm Pete.

He shook his head and repeated, 'Take medicine, be OK.'

'No, Pete. He could die.' Zoe did her best imitation of a dead person here. 'Hospital,' she repeated. 'Hospital now.'

The cause of the distress quickly became obvious as Pete began to urgently tell them: 'No moneys, no papers. No moneys, no papers.'

Zoe gave the universal calming hands gesture. 'Is OK, is OK,' she soothed. 'Need doctor first.'

'You doctor?' Pete pointed at her and sounded almost as if he was accusing her of not doing what she should do.

'Nurse,' she said, pointing at herself, 'not doctor. Need hospital. Need big, big medicine.'

'How on earth are we going to get him to the car?' Lucie asked, beginning to feel properly worried by how quickly this situation was unravelling.

'I don't know, but we have to try,' Zoe said. 'He could die out here. Honestly, if we don't have him in hospital within a few hours, he might not make it. Even in hospital he might not make it.'

The words were frightening, but Zoe's tone was completely calm and controlled, which helped Lucie to breathe and to calm down too.

'Is it that bad?' she asked her daughter.

'Yes, it's bad, but luckily we're here now.'

As they helped Fikru swallow the pills with some sips of water, Lucie couldn't help feeling that it was amazing to watch a human being that you'd once carried on your arm, read bedtime stories to, blown the nose of, helped with her Maths homework – all those other tiny hours, days, years of parenting – it was amazing to see her as a fully separate, professional, human being, doing her difficult and responsible job. There she was, the all grown-up Zoe, doing what she was trained to do and doing it so well. She could tell that the boys were now trusting her to take charge just as much as Lucie was.

'Pete, we must take Fikru to the car,' Lucie said, thinking that two voices telling him this was what had to happen were better than one.

'I get things,' Pete said, and in just a few rushed moments, he'd packed up the power source, plugs, chargers and carrier bags into one much bigger plastic bag.

Then it took all three of them to get Fikru to his feet, where he wobbled and swayed against Lucie and Zoe as Pete hastily draped the two sleeping bags over his shoulder and scoured the ground to make sure he hadn't left any of their few belongings behind.

'No point asking him to leave the sleeping bags and heavier things for now?' Lucie asked her daughter.

Zoe shook her head. 'Looks like everything is very precious. He would just worry even more.'

'How are we going to do this?' Lucie asked.

'You and me with Fikru between us... Pete carrying everything else? We'll have to try. I'll shine the phone light ahead of us. Just one step at a time,' she encouraged her mother.

It was steep, and gravelly. It was very hard work. All Fikru could do was keep his feet on the ground and bear some of his weight for part of the walk. At other times, Lucie and Zoe were almost dragging him along, bearing his full weight. Not that it was much, because, just like his brother, he was slim and slight, making Lucie wonder when he and Pete had last eaten a full meal.

Just as they reached the brow of the hill, Deva spotted them and hurried out of the car to help.

Then together, they all made progress towards the Jag.

'Come on,' Zoe said, urging them onwards, 'we need to get on our way. We need to get to this town and hope there's some help for him there.'

'I too in car?' Pete asked.

'Yes, of course,' Lucie replied, 'big car.'

And so, instructed by Zoe, Pete put his sleeping bags and possessions into the boot alongside their bags. Then he got into the back of the car, while they all managed to help guide weak and barely conscious Fikru into the middle, so he could rest his head on Pete's chest, then Deva got in beside them. Zoe took up her place in the passenger's seat and Lucie got behind the wheel.

For a moment, she looked in turn at all of her passengers, not quite able to believe how this day had developed, but it was certainly different from the usual and she was proud that hopefully she, Zoe and Deva were going to be able to help and do something useful today.

She put her key into the ignition and turned. There was a grinding, followed by almost a mechanical sort of cough, then the engine started and turned over... and kept turning without any strange sound.

'Oh, that's amazing, he's actually managed to do it,' she exclaimed.

'Slow, slow,' Pete instructed from the back seat.

Lucie made a very awkward five-point turn at the top of the hill, sure that she'd heard the crunch of the bumper meeting a fence post, but never mind that now. Then, with the car going at no more than ten miles per hour, she drove down the hill, listening nervously to the engine for any sign or sound that something may have gone wrong again. She listened also to the sound of Fikru's small groans and Pete's soothing words to his brother.

'Do you think he's going to be OK?' she asked her daughter.

'I don't know, Mum,' Zoe replied. 'Depends how soon we can get him treated. I mean, will this town have a hospital? With an A&E department? With the right kind of medicine and equipment? He doesn't need a GP; he needs a hospital. He needs IV antibiotics as soon as possible. But I know you have to drive slowly. Better to drive slowly and get there than break down again and leave us all stranded... That would be a disaster right now.'

'Yes,' Lucie said, her fingers tight around the steering wheel as she willed the repair to hold and the car to keep going.

'He really needs help,' Zoe said.

'You've given him some medicine though, haven't you?'

'Yes, as much as I can for now...'

'Well, let's just keep driving and hoping,' Lucie said, trying to stay calm and focused, both on the road ahead and on the patient propped on the seat behind them, who she glanced in the mirror to look at every few minutes.

'He sort of reminds me of Rafi,' Zoe said after a little while. 'Fikru,' she added, to clarify. 'I know that sounds strange because we've not been able to exchange even any words, but he's got the same kind of bone structure and he's very sensitive to touch... So a few parallels there.'

'Sensitive to touch... and bright light?' Deva asked from the back seat.

It was almost a little startling to hear Deva speak, as he'd been quiet ever since the car had set off.

'Rafi? Yes, he is,' Zoe confirmed, 'and totally not a hugger.'

When Lucie turned to look at her daughter with her eyebrows raised, Zoe added, 'Well, so long as he's prepared, ready for me...' She smiled. 'But he jumps if you make unexpected moves.'

'OK, here we are at the junction, turn right for Brive La Gaillarde... five kilometres. Fingers, toes, everything very, very crossed that we're going to get there.'

'Brive La Gaillarde?' Deva repeated.

'Yes, have I heard you mention that place?' Lucie asked.

'Brive La Gaillarde... This is the dream...' Deva said, but quickly added, 'Although obviously it's a nightmare for our poor friend back here.'

'So I'm guessing it's a Chanel destination?' Lucie asked.

'Oh yeah...' and Deva's full-on enthusiasm was right back, but in consideration for the patient beside him, he kept his voice low. 'Brive was where Chanel...' he began, but then stopped himself and added, 'You know, for now, never mind. I'm not sure if everyone wants to hear all the ins and outs of Coco's early years right now, do they?'

'Maybe not,' Lucie agreed, 'but I will ask you all about it when the time is right.'

'Deal... but if it's OK, there was something I was going to say to Zoe...' Deva went on in a quiet voice.

'Go for it, Deva, I'm all ears,' Zoe replied from the front seat.

'Well... don't take this as anything other than one friend, well, in fact, cousin, just thinking out loud to another friend... cousin.'

'Of course, it's fine, go ahead, think out loud to me,' Zoe assured him.

'Well, you've heard of the "gaydar", I'm sure?'

Zoe laughed a little uncertainly. 'I don't like to think of gaydars. I find it's best just to not make any assumptions about anyone's sexuality. We should all just mind our own business on that.'

'No, I mean, yes, I totally agree... and what I was going to say is I have no clue about the gaydar; I mean, I don't even know if

I'm gay,' he blurted. 'I really have no clue. But I do have the "A-dar".'

'The A-dar?' Zoe repeated. 'What on earth is that?'

'Just a sense when someone is on the spectrum like me, but they don't know it yet. I know what to look for, and I've developed this feeling about when people might be... The word I like is "spectrumy".'

'I am a nurse, Deva. I have heard of autism,' Zoe replied.

'Yeah, and sometimes it's obvious. But sometimes people miss the subtle things. I was just going to suggest, from what you've said... I could meet Rafi and see if my A-dar picks anything up.'

'Rafi? Look, just because he lives alone and likes computers doesn't mean... And anyway, I don't know if that would help.'

Zoe sounded a little frosty now.

At this, Deva threw his head back and let out a long sigh. 'Everyone says that. Everyone thinks they don't want a label and how would it help? But, I promise, it is always better to know. If you're diabetic, it's better to know. If you're manic depressive, it's better to know. So, if you're on the spectrum, it's better to know.'

Then he went on, 'And it's a spectrum. No two people are the same. But it's very easy to mis-read us, misunderstand us. And as for the myth that people on the spectrum are insensitive. Sometimes, it's the opposite; sometimes we are so sensitive, we can hardly even... *live*,' he declared.

'It's better to know you're diabetic because there are treatments for diabetes, but...' Zoe began, then she petered out and seemed to think better of it.

'There are treatments for all the things that come with autism,' Deva countered. 'There are treatments for the anxiety, the OCD or the insomnia... and then there's all the psyche stuff – the understanding, self-care, self-management. That's the really important bit. Plus, if you know you're on the spectrum, you join the club of all the awesome auti people... like Chanel, is my guess. In fact, I want to go back through history and "out" all the autistic people.'

'Why Chanel?' Lucie asked him.

'She had an incredible sense of smell... It was usually her first comment about people and places, how they smelled. She had a phobia of dirt, could never be a morning person, was obsessive about work, but it's not fair to judge people you don't know. You can have autistic traits from growing up in a family where maybe one parent is on the spectrum without being the full bhoona.'

'Full bhoona?' Lucie asked.

'I think it's a Glasgow thing. The whole hog?'

'Right.'

'I don't think you should judge people you haven't met,' was Zoe's verdict.

'No! Of course not,' Deva was quick to add. 'But all I'm saying is that it is honestly better to know. Helps you to understand yourself... and helps other people to understand you. That's all.'

Lucie glanced over at Zoe, but Zoe's arms were folded over defensively. Whatever Deva might be getting at, Zoe didn't appear to be interested.

Lucie drove on, carefully, steadily, listening all the time to the engine, and when she didn't hear anything suspicious, she picked the pace up slightly to the 20 mph mark. And the miles passed. Her passengers didn't talk much. They were tired and of course deeply concerned about the young man in a semi-conscious state on the back seat. She did hear Deva asking Pete where he was from and Pete replying 'Eritrea' before asking where Deva was from. 'Scotland,' Deva said, but he followed this up with, 'My dad was a refugee from Sri Lanka.'

And even though Lucie had known this, she'd never really thought about it. She'd never thought about what it might really mean to have to leave your homeland and possibly all of your family because of war, or famine, or a political regime that suddenly meant you were on the wrong side and had to get out. Imagine leaving Sri Lanka and landing in Glasgow. That must have been a culture shock.

Now, she could see that there were a few houses appearing at the side of the road, the first signs that they were out of the deep countryside and approaching the town.

Then came a series of beeps and buzzing sounds and Zoe dived for the handbag at her feet, saying, 'It's my phone! We must have signal again.'

'Thank God! Try the map,' Lucie instructed. 'See if you can get it to direct us to a hospital.'

After a few moments, Zoe exclaimed, 'It's working! *L'hôpital* in two kilometres.'

'Oh, thank goodness,' Lucie exclaimed as Zoe turned to Pete in the back seat and told him as simply as she could, 'Hospital, doctors, very soon. In ten minutes.' She held up her ten fingers to demonstrate.

'Does anyone speak a decent level of French?' Zoe asked next. 'We need to explain what I think could be wrong.'

'Google translate,' Deva said. 'Let's look up everything you need to say.'

* * *

Arriving at the hospital, everyone was nervy. Lucie wasn't sure where to put the car, while anxious Pete kept repeating 'No *paperis*, no *papières*...'

Zoe made her mother drive right up to the A&E entrance, while she practised the sentence in French that Deva had found for her on Google translate: 'Emergency – I have a patient in the car with suspected sepsis. I am a nurse.'

Turning to them all, as the car approached the A&E area, she said, 'Don't panic. This is my territory, I've got this. I'm going to get help.'

Then she smoothed down her hair, took a tiny moment to apply full-blooded wine-red lipstick, then, pulling herself out of the car, despite being rumpled and exhausted from a full day in a broken-down car on the hillside at almost eight months pregnant, she looked tall and powerful and magnificent.

This was Zoe, Lucie couldn't help thinking, her own person, making her own choices, living her own life. Lucie was still her mother, of course, but the active childhood part of parenting and influencing was over now. This was Zoe, fully in charge of her own life. And Lucie realised she could let go and be fully proud of who her daughter was becoming.

'There's my wonderful girl,' Lucie said out loud with tears welling up in her eyes. 'She's a nurse. And what a nurse!'

17

Just as Zoe had promised, help arrived quickly. Staff were not rushing but acting with speed and focus as they brought a trolley stretcher, then helped Pete and Deva to move Fikru out of the car and get him lifted onto it.

Lucie saw him trying to keep a hold of Pete's hand, but he didn't have the strength, and Pete wanted him to go, was smiling at him and talking in a reassuring voice.

Then there was nothing for the rest of them to do but re-park the car in the appropriate area, then come back to the starkly lit A&E waiting room and wait.

It was already 1 a.m. in the morning, Lucie saw when she was finally able to sit down, take out her handbag and check her phone. There was a text from her dad, sent hours ago, which she opened, as always, with a little burst of anxiety.

It read:

> Hope you're having fun, my girl, and kicking up those heels. All good here, Dad xx

Fun? Fun! She couldn't help giving a little smile. Well, there had been fun, but this wasn't it. Still, she was glad of the trip, even glad of the breakdown. What would have happened to Fikru without Pete repairing the car so they could scoop his brother up and bring him here?

She looked up at their little party, gathered in a huddle on the plastic waiting-room chairs. Zoe looked understandably exhausted, but still poised and quite together, as if she was determined to keep her energy going. Pete was slumped in his chair, gazing with a worried expression on his face. Every movement in the waiting room seemed to make him jump, and Lucie knew he was worried about his brother, of course, but also about police, the authorities, and the stress of not having the right papers. Deva, by contrast, seemed totally alert and alive. He was smiling at his phone, typing out messages, no doubt studying the map and working out how close he was to the Chanel sites he was longing to visit.

'Just giving my mum and my sisters the update,' he explained, 'telling them that we've been broken down without phone signal, but we are in a town now. Not been abducted by bandits, aliens from outer space, or whatever she's spent most of the day imagining. She really will have had her tights in a tangle.'

Lucie took a second, longer look at Deva. He was still in her prized lace evening dress. She tried to remember the price tag on that dress... £3,000... £4,000... maybe more. She'd only worn it twice and now here it was on her nephew in a hospital waiting room. But she couldn't help smiling. He really suited it. It fitted beautifully around the high neck, the armholes; it clung gracefully to his narrow waist and swished at his ankles. It looked surprisingly good with chunky white trainers. And they'd all stopped noticing that he was a boy in a dress. Maybe quite soon a boy in a dress would be just as unremarkable as a girl in trousers. Hadn't he told them Coco Chanel in trousers one hundred years ago was a scandal?

'Do you think someone will come and tell us something about Fikru soon?' Lucie asked her daughter.

Zoe shrugged her shoulders and said, 'Depends how long it takes to stabilise him, establish treatment, assess how it's working. They'll come and talk to us when they're sure about what to tell us. As sure as they can be at this stage...'

'He's still got a long way to go, hasn't he?' Lucie asked her quietly.

'It's still fingers crossed time, definitely.'

* * *

It was almost an hour later when someone finally appeared and told them in a combination of English, French and Google translate that Fikru was on IV antibiotics and seemed to be responding as well as could be expected. It was harder to convey this to Pete, who mainly wanted to know when Fikru could leave.

'We should try and get some sleep,' Lucie said, because her eyeballs felt scratchy and it honestly seemed like days and days since she'd had a proper sleep. 'Why don't I see if there's a hotel or B&B nearby?' She took her phone out of her bag again.

'Sleep?' Deva asked, sounding astonished. 'How can anyone be thinking about sleep? We need to wait for more news about Fikru. And we're in Brive! There's so much to see and do!'

'Deva, it's now... 2 a.m. in the morning,' Lucie told him after a quick check. 'Not usually the ideal time for sightseeing. When we take the car to the garage in the morning, maybe you could have a look around the town then.'

'Great idea! But only if everything is OK with our new friends.' He nodded at Pete.

Zoe gave a huge and heartfelt yawn. 'I'm shattered,' she admitted. 'Mum, maybe you and I should try to find a place for at least a few hours' sleep. But Pete won't want to leave, so Deva, do you want to stay with him?'

Deva nodded enthusiastically.

'Are you sure?' Lucie asked. Yes, she would just about kill for a bed, but was leaving Deva and Pete here the right thing to do?

'Look, we'll keep our phones right beside us, volume up high,' Zoe added. 'And if there's any news or any kind of... I don't know... any sign of the authorities, trouble about papers, the things Pete's worried about, you'll phone us straightaway, won't you?'

'Of course,' Deva replied.

'Fikru is in good hands, Deva and Pete will be fine here – I think we should sleep,' Zoe told her mother.

'Is that nurse's orders?' Lucie asked with a smile.

'Yes!' Zoe smiled back.

'Oh, well then...'

* * *

First came sleep.

Lucie and her daughter slept for six hours straight in twin beds in a faded but comfortable room in a small hotel. Then in the morning came much-needed cups of coffee and a consultation with the hotel owner in basic French and Google translate about garages and paying for another two nights in advance so that Pete could have somewhere to retreat to if needed.

A similar kind of basic French/Google translate conversation with a mechanic followed. Once he'd looked under the hood and heard about the wedding in Perpignan at 4 p.m. later that day, he'd assured them that it wouldn't be difficult and if they waited for about an hour, he would replace the part and have the car back on the road.

In the daylight, Lucie was upset to see the prang she'd made on the front left of the car with the fencepost. It had spoiled the Jag's classy good looks and would no doubt be pricey to fix. But she could worry about that when she was back in England.

She worked out how to buy a card with some credit for Pete's phone and when she and Zoe went back to the hospital, they listened to the encouraging update on Fikru, then Lucie insisted on giving Pete some money as well as the phone card and the details of the pre-paid hotel room.

He tried to refuse everything but finally relented when Deva got down on his knees and pretended to beg.

'I will come back to Brive on Monday,' Lucie told Pete, making sure that he understood. 'I will see you in two days and check that you and Fikru are OK.'

Pete looked so young and exhausted that it still felt bad to leave him alone at the hospital.

'Go to the hotel room and have some sleep,' Zoe encouraged him. 'And you will call us, if there is any problem?' she asked him several times, and although he nodded and seemed to have understood, none of them could be sure that he would.

Finally, it was approaching 11 a.m. by the time they were back in the repaired Jag and at last setting off for the wedding.

'It's supposed to be a four-hour-and-fifteen-minute drive,' Lucie informed her passengers, looking at the satnav with some concern. 'If there's any traffic, it's going to be tight – the ceremony starts at 4 p.m.'

In the back seat, Deva had an expression of utter gloom on his face.

'What's the matter?' Lucie asked.

'I haven't seen anything in Brive,' he complained. 'Not one single thing apart from the hospital.'

'You can come back with me and Zoe on Monday,' Lucie told him.

'But I'm supposed to be flying back with Mum and the sisters,' he told her moodily.

'Well, maybe you need to tell your mum that you're coming with us because it's really important to you. We can see how much singing and the spirit of Chanel matters to you. You seem like a different person when you're singing or talking about your friend, Coco. It's inspiring, Deva! This is who you would be if you weren't afraid of what your mum or anyone else thinks. So, you need to tell her.'

For a moment, Deva seemed to smile quietly to himself as he let his auntie's words sink in, then, face brightening further at the prospect, he asked: 'Will you take me to the convent in Aubazine?'

'Is that where Chanel—' Lucie began.

'Grew up, basically. She was there from age eight to eighteen, I think. It was a major formative influence.'

'And it's not too far from here?'

'No, just a short drive.'

'Then yes, we'll do that on Monday too,' she told him.

And with those words, Deva leaned back into his seat and pulled his headphones on, a totally thoughtful and absorbed look on his face.

* * *

Listening to some of his favourite music as the Jag moved back onto the main road towards Perpignan, Deva slowly and carefully revisited his cherished daydream. The one where he was walking up the steps of the convent, in a trail-blazing outfit that paid perfect homage to his muse.

He couldn't possibly describe to anyone how important this was to him... or why. Why did Coco Chanel matter so much in his life? Why did he admire what she had done, what she had thought, so much? Why had a female fashion designer with a black bob in cream trousers, who died over fifty years ago, cast such a spell on him?

He smoothed over the lace fabric of the Chanel dress that he had put on last night and was still wearing. She mattered so much to him that it was almost as if he knew her.

No matter how crazy it sounded, Coco Chanel was like an auntie to him, or a fairy godmother. And he was determined to somehow live up to her influence.

18

'I think you might have to entertain us with the latest news from Jacasta's Instagram?' Lucie told Zoe once they were back on the motorway and the smooth miles were rolling them towards Perpignan.

Zoe scrolled for a few moments before revealing: 'Well, let's see... Luckily the wedding stress hasn't got to her and she's still feeling "#blessed". So, we have a photo of her and her "wedding girls" in yoga clothes in the garden, where they have been eating "nourishing granola" and "spending beautiful time together in meditative gratitude".'

No, it wasn't very nice, but Lucie couldn't hold back her honk of laughter at this.

'What else? Scroll back, we must have missed a few instalments with all our drama.'

'Hmmm... so, we have some pictures of the "#enchanted" venue. Some photos from last night's dinner captioned "thankful for the wonderful people around me", although it does seem to be mainly pictures of her. Oh, and here she is in front of the food table "nourishing my friends with good food and good thoughts". Wow,' Zoe added, 'that is a lot of salad... Many, many different shades of salad.'

'Do you think this is going to be a salad-based wedding?' Lucie asked.

'Most definitely. Look forward to some harissa-flavoured grains and a handful of rose petals.' After a pause, Zoe added, 'I hope that doesn't make too many people too angry, or should that be "hangry"?'

'Oh, it will, no doubt about that,' Lucie said, feeling just a little bit delighted at the thought, even though she had promised Zoe to be very nice about this wedding. 'People will not want to have travelled all the way to the South of France from the UK, from New Zealand even, to be served a wedding-themed salad. Even Miles will not be happy with a wedding-themed salad. I don't know how he stands it...' she added, but quietly, not wanting to rile Zoe into leaping to his defence.

'Some kind of two-seater bridal swing is being installed,' was the next detail Zoe unearthed from the Instagram treasure trove.

'In the bridal bedroom?' Lucie didn't want to ask but still did.

'No! Mum! Please, I don't want to think about that and neither should you! No, in the garden... Probably she and Dad are going to pose for photos on it.'

Lucie could not help herself from giving another burst of laughter. It was so ridiculous. How on earth had Miles been talked into all this? But then, she had thought over the years that Miles had become increasingly vain and full of himself. So maybe he was quite enjoying the social media attention from Jacasta's army of followers. He'd certainly made himself much more insta-worthy. Every time she'd seen him lately, something else had been done or tweaked to his hair, face, even body. She suspected he'd had liposuction on his waistline. Either that or he was eating one heck of a lot of wedding salad.

'How are you doing, Deva?' Lucie called over to her nephew in the back seat. He pulled down his headphones and looked at her with slow and tired eyes. He'd had even less sleep than her, she remembered, and did finally seem to be feeling it.

'Planning on a little disco nap,' he said, then moved the headphones back in place. He was still in the exquisite dress. She wondered if he'd ever take it off. Maybe he would wear it to the wedding... So did that mean it would be forever melded into the shape of a slim twenty-year-old Glaswegian, who was still figuring himself out?

Maybe she should just give it to him. And just having that thought was weirdly liberating. Yes, she could just unpack those old boxes and give some things to Deva, some to Zoe, if she wanted them... and sell the rest. There was nothing about past burdens that she needed to hang on to.

'You know, Mum,' Zoe began, 'we are being pretty mean about Jacasta, but that's strictly between us, OK, just for laughs on this trip. Because you should know that I think she's actually alright.'

Lucie tried not to mind how she felt about this revelation. Of course Zoe should think Jacasta was alright; that was the generous and right thing for her to think. And maybe one day, Lucie could think that about Jacasta too. But for now, she had to focus on not feeling too hurt or betrayed by Zoe's admission.

'It's not the way you think it is...' Zoe went on.

'And what's the way I think it is?' Lucie asked, because she needed to hear from Zoe exactly what she thought was in Lucie's head, before she began to argue or defend herself.

Zoe looked over at her mother. 'Well,' she began slowly, 'I think... and look, I don't blame you. I think you see her as someone who's not completely serious, or not completely committed to Dad. Someone who might think there's an advantage to marrying a pretty sussed businessman... even if he did almost go bankrupt. But they met when he was down, really flat on his back. He was crashing at a friend's house... He hardly knew what to do with himself all day and he was broke.'

'I don't think so, Zoe. There was something he held on to, registered abroad that he didn't want me to know about,' Lucie said, deciding she would put it out there, all the cards on the table.

'Yeah... Dad did tell me about that and he also said that's how you would see it.'

Lucie shot Zoe a look. Really? Miles had told her about this. Had he told Zoe the truth, or had he told her the version he hoped Zoe would pass on to her?

'He kept one office block off the books when you got divorced. That's a fact,' Zoe began.

'An office block?' Lucie repeated, astonished. 'A whole *block*?'

'Pretty small block, I think. But, at the time, he thought it was criminally undervalued and he had a massive mortgage on it, so selling it would have caused an even bigger hole in the finances.'

'Nice of him to share all this with you... and not me.'

'I know, Mum. And I haven't known about it for long. In fact, I kind of dragged it out of him because I was trying to understand why you were still so angry with him.'

'You know, we ended up losing everything, including our home and my business too. Do you not think I'm entitled to hold on to a bit of anger about that?' Lucie said, gripping the steering wheel tightly.

'He did his best,' Zoe countered. 'He didn't mean for it all to play out like that.'

'He could have told me much sooner what was happening.'

'Maybe he was trying to protect you, or not worry you, or maybe you wouldn't have been very understanding, maybe you'd drifted too far apart by then... I don't know.'

'OK...' Lucie could see that there was a chance for both of them to get very upset and she didn't want that, so instead she hoped she could calm them both by saying, 'Look, time has passed, we're all getting over it. So why don't you just explain about the office block and I promise to keep calm and listen. OK?'

Zoe's shoulders seemed to lower with relief at these words, so she went on. 'He hung on to this thing, scraping together to pay the mortgage on it, asking everyone he could think of for help. But no one wanted to help. And he decided to just keep on asking, literally everyone he could think of, then two people did turn up for him – one was some old friend and the other, all he said was "an unlikely source". Maybe someone on Jacasta's side – I don't know. And this office block, and keeping hold of it, this is what's really turned things around. It's making him decent money now, it's worth much more, so he can refinance. But my point is, Jacasta met him when he was broke. She took him in, bought the groceries, even bought him a suit to wear for his meetings, according to him. She's definitely not a gold digger and she's not at all as fluffy as she comes across on Instagram. They do seem very happy together.'

'I see...' Lucie said finally, trying to take it all in. The successful office block, the younger woman who'd helped him get back on his feet – and now she was a jangling mix of emotion. She recognised jealousy in there, a lot of jealousy. She wanted to be much more back on her feet too. Why wasn't she starting a new business? Or looking out for a new companion for herself? Or just in general getting on with her life, instead of watching from the sidelines while Miles got on with his? Well, there was her dad, of course. But even very committed daughters could still find the time to get on with their lives... couldn't they? And she knew that was exactly what her dad would want to see.

'I think he knows that he owes you something from that building...' Zoe added.

'Well, half, I think you'll find.'

'Probably not, Mum, because when you two divorced, it was worth minus money. So it would have taken away from what you were left with. He sort of protected you from that.'

'OK, I'm not sure I want to talk about this any more, Zoe,' she said finally. 'Thank you for trying to explain it. Hopefully, at some point in the future, Miles and I will be able to talk it through – with or without our lawyers – and come to some kind of agreement over it. Right... how much longer do we have to go?'

'One hour and twenty-two minutes with some orange and red bits ahead,' Zoe told her. 'It's going to be really tight to get there on time. Dad will be chill... but Jacasta probably not so much.'

As if on cue, Deva pulled down his headphones and looked at his phone, which had just buzzed.

After reading the message, he told them: 'Uh oh... Message from Jacasta asking if we're going to make it, or if she has to make another arrangement for the wedding song.'

Lucie looked at the dashboard clock... 2.28 p.m. and the wedding was due to begin at 4 p.m. If they made it in the one hour and twenty-two minutes promised by the satnav, that gave Zoe and Deva only ten minutes to change and get to the ceremony. It wasn't exactly the ideal amount of time you'd want to give yourself to prep for being a wedding guest, let alone the singer, but it was doable… in a crisis.

'Can you change in ten minutes?' she asked Deva and her daughter. 'Or could you change in the car?'

'I'll start putting on my makeup,' Zoe decided, reaching down into the footwell for her handbag.

Deva pulled a face. 'Change in the car? I mean, I'll try but I'm not a gymnast. So long as you two don't mind being enveloped in a cloud of No 5… Actually, as this is a formal event, with my mother present, better make it Pour Monsieur.'

19

'I thought you said left!'

Lucie felt as if all her energy, all her patience, was completely used up and she was going to crack.

'No, second left... after this one,' Zoe insisted.

Lucie manoeuvred the great big car into a three-point turn in the narrow lane, then came out onto the main road again.

'So next left?'

'Yes...'

It was just twenty minutes before the wedding was due to start. Everyone in the car had been through every emotion – from hope and elation, when the traffic freed and they could pick up speed, that they were going to make it on time, to despair and frustration when they hit yet another stretch of congestion.

Now, there was just tension mixed with a wearied acceptance that maybe this event, which they'd been thinking about and planning and travelling towards for days, maybe they weren't going to go to it after all. Or in Lucie's case, maybe she wasn't going to manage to get them to it. According to the map, there were still four kilometres to go and the minutes were ticking down with alarming speed.

'So down this road,' Lucie said as they turned into another narrow road, 'and the venue is off this one. This should be the final stretch?'

'Yeah,' Zoe confirmed.

'Foot down!' Deva urged.

But it wasn't that kind of road. These were tight corners where you could meet someone hurtling the other way, or a tractor tootling along at 10 mph, or even worse, a deer... a rabbit.

Lucie did the best she could, even taking one corner at a speed that made them all lurch to the right in their seats.

'Mum! I did not know you could drive like this!' Zoe blurted.

'Well, maybe you don't know every single thing about me, Zoe. Now, shush, I'm concentrating on getting us to bloody Miles's bloody wedding.'

Green verges, hedges and tall poplars passed by. The miles between them and Jacasta's 'magical French ceremony of love amidst the peonies' began to close. Meanwhile, Deva, having instructed them not to turn around, eased the Chanel lace from up over his head and arms, folded it tenderly into a little bundle and then began to put on the sober white shirt, black jacket, trousers and even gold-coloured tie that his mother had picked for him for the event.

'My shoes are still in the boot,' he said. 'But otherwise, I'm good to go.'

'Fantastic,' Zoe told him. 'At least one of us can head straight for the ceremony. But I am not going to be able to slither out of this dress and into the fuchsia pink marquee I have rented for the occasion. My slithering days are over, for the time being.'

'Fuchsia pink?' Lucie asked, because she didn't know

anything about Zoe's wedding guest dress. 'That sounds gorgeous. That will light up your beautiful face.'

'I am so tired that nothing short of floodlights is going to light up my face, and there's absolutely no disguising the bus-sized bump at this point. So might as well go big. Wait till you see this dress.' There was a momentary hit of energy and excitement in her voice. 'It has a huge flower at the front, all in fuchsia fabric – Carrie Bradshaw, eat your heart out. I love it. It would have been lovely to have had slightly more than a handful of minutes to get dressed though. I thought I'd be putting my hair up, curling the front strands... I mean, these are family wedding pictures. They'll hang around.'

'I'm so sorry,' Lucie said.

'Oh... not your fault. None of us expected to run into two refugees with one in need of urgent medical help. Has anyone heard from Pete?'

When the answer turned out to be no, both Zoe and Deva sent him messages.

'There!' Deva shouted, as he spotted the sign ahead. 'Maison Violette on the right!'

Lucie gave a glance at the dashboard again... Eleven minutes to go. She turned right and drove, as fast as she dared, up the driveway towards the beautiful French mansion house ahead. As they approached it, Lucie wondered where she should put the car. Was there a car park? And where should Zoe rush to change? Where was Deva supposed to go to head straight for the ceremony? And how could she turn around and get out of here just as fast as humanly possible? As all these thoughts were flying through her mind, a man in a white suit ran past, then stopped in his tracks, turned, looked at the car and began to run towards them.

Just as he broke into a broad smile of welcome, Lucie realised it was Miles.

Miles in a white suit, Miles with lashings of black hair, Miles with a too-deep-to-be-true tan, Miles, minus at least half a stone of weight on the last time she'd seen him.

Bloody Miles and his bloody, *bloody* wedding.

He was speeding towards their car, mercifully heading for Zoe's side.

'Hello, hello!' he was shouting out. 'You made it! Oh my goodness, you made it. How fantastic! How absolutely amazing! Jacasta is having kittens about Deva not being here to sing. And I didn't want to get married without you there, Zoe, sweetheart.'

As Lucie pulled to a stop, Zoe flung open her door and he was there, her ex-husband, leaning in to kiss his daughter and greet them all.

'Hello, Deva, good to see you, and hello, Lucie...'

His smile tensed just a little as his eyes met hers.

'What a journey you've had by all accounts,' he went on. She gave a polite smile in reply.

There he was, Miles, looking like a low-rent imitation of Piers Brosnan, she decided on the spot. Really, it was quite easy to channel all her anger, annoyance and disappointment at him when he was making such an obvious twerp of himself.

'Well, they're here now, thank goodness,' she said stiffly. She knew she was over an hour's drive from the hotel she'd booked for herself on the coast, and she was wondering where she could find a stiff gin and tonic and whether she could somehow sleep it off before driving to the sea.

'You look exhausted, Lucie. Why don't you come along?'

'Come along where?'

'Come to the wedding? Have a few drinks, meet Jacasta, have dinner... and the Wilsons, remember them? They cancelled at the last minute, so there's even a room for you, if you want it.'

Before Lucie could even begin with why she definitely was not coming to the 'Ceremony of Love Amidst the Peonies', Zoe and Deva both turned to her and began a chorus of... 'Please', 'Yes, definitely', 'Muuuuuum', 'Auntieeeee', 'You've got to come', 'You've got to see me sing', 'And the fuchsia dress!' 'And you've come so far, might as well stay for the best bit'.

'But I don't have anything to wear to a wedding,' Lucie said, deciding that this might be the simplest way to get out of it.

'Well... you do, actually,' Deva admitted, a little shamefaced. 'I've borrowed... well, quite a few of your Chanel things, which are in the duffel bag in the boot. Including shoes...'

'Well, there you are then,' Miles said. 'Dress up in the finery and come along. You'll love it, Lucie. So many old friends, old faces for you to catch up with.'

Bloody Miles...

'C'mon, Mum, we've got about five minutes to get gussied up.'

'Deva,' Miles urged his nephew, 'we'll get ourselves over to the marquee, get everything delayed for just a few minutes and give these ladies a chance to freshen up.'

'But where do we go?' Lucie asked, already vaguely furious with Miles as soon as she had accepted the invitation. How dare he commandeer her, tell her where to dress, what to wear, and, worst of all, refer to her and Zoe as 'ladies'. Ugh, for some reason that just tipped her over the edge. She could still leave. She could still get in the car and go. Head for the sea... be sipping a cocktail on her own by the beachfront, talking to her dad by sunset.

But... Zoe, Deva, so many others – God, even Miles – were her family. Not going would be like missing a major family milestone. And maybe she could enjoy a family event even more if she wasn't Mrs Miles. Whatever annoying, irritating, downright embarrassing things Miles did, they didn't have anything to do with her. She would be free of having to worry about him. That was now Jacasta's problem.

And didn't she want to see some of this ceremony after she'd heard so much about it? #Loveinthepeonies or whatever it was. Plus, she was just a guest... She could drink a few cocktails at Miles and Jacasta's expense, maybe even consider letting her hair down. Not that she was entirely sure what that would involve.

'Ask Marcel,' Miles replied, gesturing to the vast house. 'He's knocking about downstairs.'

So Zoe and Lucie, with a small bag each, plus the bag Deva had given Lucie, headed as quickly as they could to the enormous wooden door of this three-storey mansion, so high and so wide, it cast a shadow from quite a distance away. There was the most incredible purple and white wisteria growing up the front, but as they got closer, they could see it was all artificial silk blooms.

'Someone's been watching *Bridgerton*...' Zoe commented.

'That may explain this entire wedding,' Lucie said.

And to her relief, Zoe started to giggle at this.

'Are you at all annoyed, Mum, that he's having such a lush party when you guys had something much more modest?'

'No, that is not annoying. If I were going to get remarried, which is hard to imagine—'

'Not at all,' Zoe insisted.

'Nice of you. I'd go all small and bespoke and bijou. How about you? And that's not in any way a loaded question,' she added quickly as they hurried through the front door and into the reception area.

'I'm picturing a garden, trees, greenery, calm, lovely, and yeah, on the small side.'

'I absolutely love you, Zoe,' Lucie blurted. 'Thank you for forcing me to drive down here. I think we both needed to talk about things...'

'Yeah, thanks, Mum. I'm sorry you've been so sad and so upset. I hope you'll be able to think about what you want on your little holiday by the sea.'

'I will... definitely.'

There was no one in sight downstairs in the impressive reception hall of the Maison Violette, which was all wood panelling, flowers and more flowers and the scent of lavender, but there was a door open onto a small sitting room abloom with chintz curtains and chintz-covered sofas, so they decided to hurry in there, shut the door, then strip off, rummage about in their bags for clothes, and do the quick change needed to get to the wedding before curtain up.

'At least you know what you're wearing, that is a major advantage. I'm just playing lucky dip in here,' Lucie said as she opened the bag Deva had handed her.

'Oh my God...' Zoe held up her silky, fuchsia concoction. It was horribly crushed from two days in the bag in a hot car, and the big flouncy flower sewn on to the front looked wilted and dejected.

'That is such a beautiful dress,' Lucie soothed. 'Look, pop it on for now, with your lipstick and earrings, then after the service, come back to the house, find Marcel, find your room and ask him for an iron. And when you come back down to join us, you and the dress will be all perked up and refreshed. Is that a good plan?'

'Yeah, that will have to do.'

'It's a gorgeous dress,' Lucie told her, 'I can't wait to see you in it.'

'Thanks, Mum. And what about you? What's in the bag Deva packed?'

One by one, Lucie pulled out the clothes. On top was the lace dress Deva had been wearing until he'd changed in the back of the car.

'Black floor-length lace?' Zoe asked.

'No, that looked amazing on Deva... I can't live up to him in that.'

They both smiled.

Next came the creamy tweed jacket with the oh-so-distinctive black edging around the collar, cuffs and jacket edges that Deva had worn to climb to the top of the statue on Bastille Day. Followed by the matching creamy tweed skirt.

'These are beautiful and appropriate, but I will boil alive out there,' was Lucie's verdict.

'Agreed. Come on, Mum, we've got about thirty seconds left,' Zoe reminded her as she pulled her own pink dress over her head, smoothed it down and began to fix her hair into the hurried version of the up-do she had planned.

Another tweed jacket, a silky pussy-bowed blouse, the creamy handbag, a little battered from its rough-and-tumble in the village square, then she was nearing the bottom of the pile. There were some strappy black heels down there, and her black version of the classic Chanel 2.55 quilted handbag.

'I just don't want to wear my Chanel things,' she complained, 'They're unhappy memories now.'

'Crack on Mum, no time...' Zoe insisted.

And there, down at the bottom of the bag, as soon as she touched the fabric, she knew.

That vintage silver and black cocktail dress! No fancy label, from a secondhand shop. Oh yes, the one that was sleeveless, with thick shoulder straps and a square neckline, cinched in at a high waist, then falling in three, flapper-style tiers to below the knee. That was the one. She'd bought it more than ten years ago for a Christmas party.

'Silver, gold and black? Not exactly wedding-style,' she said a little doubtfully, holding up the light, silky, slithery creation.

'Oh my gosh, that is fabulous!' was Zoe's verdict. 'Perfectly appropriate for you to wear black.' She winked. 'It's a funeral of sorts, your ex's wedding.'

'Do you think I can get into it?' was Lucie's next concern.

'Only one way to find out...' Zoe said.

Lucie fumbled to undo all the many, many buttons down the back. Then with Zoe's help she got it over her head and down.

She looked down at herself. Definitely not the willowy late thirties she'd been when she bought this. Boobs were bigger, bulge around the middle curvier, arms heavier too. But this was a clever dress. The tight waist was high, close to empire line, and those shifting, shimmering ruffles skimmed the body beautifully. Despite herself, she smiled. There was no mirror in sight, but she suspected this looked pretty OK.

'You are bringing it, Mum!' Zoe exclaimed. 'Can't believe you've kept this locked up in a box for so long! And I am definitely borrowing it when I'm back down to my fighting self again.'

Zoe busied herself doing up the buttons at the back. A few around the bust would have to stay undone, but Zoe provided a drapey scarf to slip over her mother's arms and hide the situation until there was time for Lucie to change into a camouflaging black bra later.

'Shoes, bag, lipstick, let's go!' Zoe commanded.

So final touches were added and they got out of the room as quickly as they could.

Out in the reception again, Marcel had materialised, a little man, wizened and brown, who sensed the urgency and directed them through the house, out of the majestic wood-and-glass doors at the back and towards the gorgeous silky awning set up in the garden, full of flowers and brightly coloured wedding guests.

Over to the far left, Lucie was aware of Jacasta and her party of wedding girls waiting. So, she sped up towards the tent.

'You go to the front, to your dad,' she urged Zoe. 'I'm going to slip in on a back row.'

For a moment, Zoe looked at her and she thought her daughter might protest.

'That's the right place for me,' she hissed. 'This is Jacasta's day. I'm going to be right in the background.'

'OK, see you after. No crying,' Zoe said, but this came with a cheeky smile and a wink.

* * *

As Zoe hurried down the aisle in full bloom fuchsia, turning all the heads, Lucie located the back row of seats on Miles's side. Mercifully, there was a spare single seat just a few chairs in, so she only had to ask a few people to stand up and let her through. At a glance, she wasn't even quite sure who they were, maybe business colleagues she'd met once or twice but didn't clearly remember. Once she was sitting down, the music continued and she had a few moments to settle and gather her thoughts. She could see Miles, of course, standing expectantly at the front. Beside him was his pompous older brother, Jason.

In terms of Miles's character development, Jason probably

had a lot to answer for. Maybe if Jason hadn't been such a proud, selfish, bullying alpha-boy, Miles might not have turned out quite the way he had – always thrusting, pushing, trying, never satisfied with his lot.

Oh! And there was Deva, on a seat to the side of centre stage, beside the keyboard player and the violinist, who were busy making soft, relaxing, waiting-room style mood music. Deva in a black suit, white shirt and tie, looked buttoned up and tense. Even from the back row, she could see that he looked strained and his face was a little shiny with nervous sweat. Now and then he tugged at the tie, ran his fingers round the collar and shrugged his shoulders in his suit, as if he couldn't wait to throw off this constricting contraption.

Then the music stopped and that expectant hush followed as people stopped talking, heads turned and everyone waited for the bride to enter to her bridal theme tune.

The opening chords of something soft and familiar were struck... Oh, Debussy's 'Clair de Lune'. That was a classy choice, Lucie had to admit.

Then Jacasta entered, looking beautiful in an ivory satin column number, and began her walk down the aisle. Her dark hair was swept elegantly up with a cascade of glossy ringlets at the front, giving Empress Josephine vibes. There were flowers in her hair, and in her hands a trailing bouquet of pink peonies, white roses and sprigs of lavender. The wedding girls behind her were two in pink and two in lilac satin versions of her column dress. All so pretty.

The celebrant was a cheerful looking woman waiting for them at end of the aisle. Miles stepped forward and the smile that he gave his bride-to-be, well... Despite all the angry confusion of emotion rushing around in her head, that smile, to her surprise, it was causing a little lump in the back of her throat. It was a long time ago now, but he had once smiled at her like that. And now she realised that maybe it could be OK to let go of feeling angry with him. She could be happy for him that he had found someone who would hopefully love and cherish him in the years ahead – he'd moved on. Let Jacasta deal with Miles now; she looked more than up to the job. Lucie was free now to spend way less time thinking about them… and much more time thinking about herself and how she was going to move on too.

Turning her attention away from Miles, she began to do some guest-spotting, looking at the heads, shoulders and hats in the audience in front of her. The front row was easy to identify – her ex-mother-in-law, Betty, followed by Deva's mother, Melissa, then Zoe, then Jason's wife, Tina. The cousins – Deva's three sisters in multi-coloured saris and Jason's two children – were all in the row behind.

In the row beyond this, she picked out various aunties, uncles, and several of Miles's cousins. It was a surprisingly big family turnout for a wedding which was thousands of miles from home for most of them.

Now she looked in the rows beyond for friends, curious to see who had shown up for Miles. She wondered if this meant they had chosen him and not her after their divorce, or if she would still be able to count these people as her friends after today.

She recognised haircuts and profiles and found it intriguing to see which friends and business associates were here. She'd not been good at keeping up with most of these people since the divorce. Too busy, too traumatised, plus she'd moved much further away from 'leafy' Bromley once their house was sold. She'd chosen her father's town as her first post-divorce base, but not forever, she had told herself when she'd put down the deposit for the rental.

Would these people be pleased to see her, she wondered. Most likely they would be surprised to see her here.

She smoothed down the ruffled tiers of the dress.

Deva would be very pleased to see her in this dress. He would appreciate it to the full. She found herself looking over in his direction, where he still looked strained and nervous. She looked and looked at him, willing him to glance up and catch her eye. When he eventually did, she gave him her warmest, most encouraging smile. *You've got this, superstar!* was what she wanted to tell him. She was sorry that he'd rushed off with Miles, before she'd had time to say those words to him.

He gave a small, tense smile back.

'...man and wife,' the celebrant was announcing now.

Really? Already? How had she managed to miss the home-made vows that Jacasta was sure to have penned for them both? Never mind, she could look it up on Insta later, when she was somewhere where she could have a quiet giggle to herself. She wondered if Jacasta fully realised what she was letting herself in for – but then again, different people brought out the best and sometimes the worst in each other. Maybe Miles with Jacasta was a different kind of Miles to the one he'd been with her, especially in those stressed-out, angry, resentful later years.

As the couple stepped over to the side table to sign the documents, that was when Deva stood up and both the keyboard and the violin began to play the opening chords of... She waited for a moment. It was familiar... It was old-fashioned, not what she'd expected for this song. But maybe it had a special resonance for the happy couple: Frank Sinatra's 'Come Fly With Me'.

Frank Sinatra? Really? Maybe it had been playing in the

elevator when they'd first set eyes on one another, she told herself with a repressed giggle.

Deva broke into the opening lines and his voice sounded nice... steady, even quite good. But it didn't feel like full-throttle Deva. It didn't feel as captivating and glorious as Deva doing The Bangles, arms held out, dripping Chanel lace and belting the words over the barren hillside and into the sunset. No, it didn't feel like that at all. And Lucie thought it was sad that this audience was getting such a restrained version of the original.

She scanned over the heads in front of her, looking again at the few she'd not been able to place. There was a tall man, two rows ahead, four chairs along to the right. Broad shoulders under a light grey suit, hair a dark steely grey. On either side of him was a blonde woman, one with long, loose curls, the other with her hair done up into a chignon. Even just glimpsed from behind, all three looked totally wedding elegant.

The man happened to glance to the left, so Lucie got a clear view of the side of his face. He was clean shaven and tanned and she felt a strong beat of recognition. Her heart began to pick up the pace. As she took a sharp in-breath, she felt the silk dress tighten around her. She looked – no, she stared. It may have been over twenty-five years since she'd last seen this face, but there wasn't any mistaking him. She was sure it was Clark, her former colleague, that constantly unavailable, funny, lovely man she'd once thought she was so connected to, so... in love with all that time ago. But what on earth was Clark doing here? At Miles's wedding. What reason could there possibly be for Miles to reconnect after such a long time? And they weren't even friends, just slight acquaintances back then. Why was he here? Clark? Clark! Maybe Jacasta knew Clark? Lucie's heart was drumming rapidly now and she could feel an uneasy blush creeping up from her neck and over her cheeks.

Nothing had ever happened or been said between them, nothing that she needed to feel embarrassed or awkward about. But still, somehow, she was sure back then that he knew how she felt about him. And she'd had the strongest sense that he'd had those feelings for her too. Something a little tense, exciting and physical had always been present between them. One of them taking glances at the other when they thought they were unobserved. Both of them finding reasons to talk, go on site visits together, and always finding it so easy and a little thrilling to talk to one another about anything and everything. And the pain of not being able to say anything, or do anything, because one of them had always been in an on-off relationship at exactly the wrong time. That photo, she remembered, of the two of them talking, laughing, hardly able to take their eyes off one another. That's how it had felt between them. All the time. Until she couldn't stand it any more and she had taken a friend's advice to get out there and find someone new.

Clark had taken off to the US for a work project and she had met Miles. And once she was pregnant and then married, she hadn't looked back. She'd never looked him up again and hadn't even allowed herself to think about him. Until Deva had unearthed the photos and it all came flooding back. All that unexpressed want and the deep regret that she might have spent over two decades with the wrong man.

She found herself staring at the two blonde heads on either side of him. Both were facing forward, so she couldn't tell anything. One was going to be his wife or significant other, surely? And the other maybe his daughter? Or maybe one of those women was here with someone else. Or maybe both were here with someone else... For a moment, she allowed herself the thought that he was here alone, but she immediately squashed it down as completely unlikely. What was he doing here? The complete surprise was making her head spin.

More music was playing as Jacasta and Miles began their walk back up the aisle, smiling delightedly and stopping to hug, kiss and say hello to family and friends. The glamorous wedding girls with armfuls of bouquets followed on behind.

The happy couple were soon out from under the canopied ceremony area and into the beautiful garden, and gradually the guests began to file on out behind them. Lucie realised that in a few minutes, she would be standing outside too. She needed to gather her thoughts. Within moments, she would be greeting her ex-mother-in-law, her ex-brother-in-law, her ex-sister-in-law and all their families, not to mention old friends... and that would all be difficult enough, but she was also about to meet Clark after all this time. And all those emotions from the past year that she'd laid to rest and moved on from – was there any chance that they would all come bubbling up again?

It was a lot, she had to admit, feeling another sharp in-breath; a lot, a lot. She felt a wave of something that took a moment to register. Tension, nerves, almost nausea.

Hello, Lucie, got to get a grip, she told herself. She ran her damp palms over the silky sides of the dress and strangely found herself trying to remember some of Deva's favourite Chanel facts... It all started with hats, and she gave No 5 away to American GIs after the war.

And breathe slowly in... and breathe slowly out.

You've got this, she told herself. Even though she was pretty sure she didn't.

20

Coming out from under the wedding awning, Lucie found herself a little awkwardly on her own in the beautiful garden that was now rapidly filling up with some people she knew vaguely and didn't really want to get to know better, other people she knew well but didn't much want to see, and then there was this reunion with someone who'd last known her when she was twenty-four and a different person altogether. It was all making her quake with nerves.

A waiter passed and offered her a glass of champagne. She took two, mumbling something about 'Best get one for my friend' and drank the first one down in three swallows. OK, that helped with the nerves a little. She parked the empty glass and began to walk around with the intention of saying a breezy hello to her in-laws and their children. Just 'hello' and move on, she thought. Meet and greet, short and sweet.

'Hi... hello, how are you?' She smiled, nodded and aimed to just keep on walking past the Marshal family – brother-in-law, Jason, and his wife, Deva's mother, Melissa and Miles's prickly mother, Betty.

But Miles's mother looked up sharply at the sound of Lucie's voice and then gave Lucie a penetrating once over. Lucie found her eyes meeting Betty's and there was no mistaking the harsh glare she directed at Lucie before turning her back and carrying on talking to her oldest son.

Not very friendly, Lucie thought to herself. That woman had never liked her. And now, she no doubt didn't like Jacasta either and somehow wanted to blame everything that had happened with Miles's business and Miles's marriage on Lucie. And *why am I here?* And *why am I wearing this old dress*? No doubt she was absolutely dying to ask Lucie these things, but instead she had decided to snub her – the ultimate insult.

And now Deva's mother, Melissa, in full feathered hat and peachy dress with sparkles, was approaching to greet her. After they'd said their hellos, she wanted to know all the details about the journey, the breakdown, and convey to Lucie just how worried she'd been.

'How did Deva cope with everything? Was he really OK?' she asked. 'He can struggle so much when his schedule changes. He can go into complete meltdown mode, or just totally shut down. I'm sure he's been absolutely wrung out by all this.'

Lucie took a breath, sipped from her glass and wondered how much Deva would tell his mum about the detour to the Place Vendôme, the visit to the Chanel shop, singing to the sunset in a lace dress and perhaps, *perhaps*, opening his heart to a new version of himself.

And if he did tell her about it, would Melissa encourage him to be that version? Or would she squish it down, like she'd tried to extinguish his talent for singing, and make him conform to his parents' version of himself? With that thought, Lucie suddenly realised how important aunties and uncles could be to give young people another trusted perspective, a different view of themselves, and the support to challenge their parents even when there was a clash.

Up till now, she had to admit, she hadn't been a very good auntie. Too focused on her own family, her work and not giving enough of her time to the young people who might still enjoy some of her time and her input. Really Must Do Better, she thought to herself.

She realised Melissa was still waiting for her to reply.

'You know, I understand. I did worry about how Deva was going to take it all too,' Lucie sympathised, 'but you know, we all got along really well. And if anything, I think he quite enjoyed the chaotic bits. They seemed to give him... well, I think "inspiration" might be the word.'

Melissa raised her eyebrows and gave a 'huh' kind of sound. And then Lucie was re-introduced to Deva's older sisters, who were all smiley, beautifully dressed and much older and more sophisticated than she remembered, twinkling with gold earrings, necklaces, rings, nose studs, and glossy with the application of eyeshadow, powders, creams and shiny lipsticks.

'Oh, you're all looking so fabulous,' Lucie told them. 'Your dresses and the colours are gorgeous. I only decided at the very last minute to come to the wedding, so this silver-and-black number was the only thing I had to hand. I know it's not really wedding-y,' she explained, wanting at least one member of Miles's family to hopefully report this back to his mother, as well as Jason and Jason's snooty wife – she in the lemon-yellow perfect wedding guest dress and matching Princess Catherine-worthy hat.

And now here was Zoe at her side.

'Such a lovely ceremony, wasn't it?' Zoe said, a big smile on her face. 'I thought you might want some moral support when you go and congratulate the happy couple?'

Lucie gave her daughter a grateful look.

'That's very good of you to think of me,' she said, knowing that having Zoe by her side would make it better. 'You're an absolute morale boost, when you're not snarking at me, obvs.'

'Ha,' Zoe replied, but with a smile.

'And you look amazing,' Lucie added. 'You should only wear pink from now on. Do you have pink scrubs?'

Zoe laughed and, taking her mum's arm in hers, she led her through the throng towards the queue for Miles and Jacasta.

And as they walked, Lucie couldn't help herself from looking about, just wondering where... Oh, big jump of the heart, there he was, Clark. And his two blonde women. Just as she passed, just as she was about to look away, he happened to look up, spot her, catch her eye and... She couldn't exactly tell, but was that a look of astonishment? She smiled at him, of course, but couldn't stop to wonder, because now the queue for Miles and Jacasta had moved on and within a few moments, she was giving the man she'd lived with for twenty-five years a hug and congratulating him on his marriage.

'Thank you, Lucie,' he said simply, before turning his attention to Zoe, who got a bear hug over the top of her bump. And now Lucie was face-to-face with Jacasta, meeting her for the very first time on her wedding day... to Lucie's former husband. For a moment, both appeared to be at a loss for words.

'Hi, Jacasta, I'm Lucie. Congratulations,' Lucie said with as much warmth and generosity as she could, and she extended her arms so they could have a little hug. 'It's lovely to meet you. What a gorgeous ceremony in a beautiful venue. I hope you'll both be very happy.'

It seemed to take Jacasta a few moments to react. It wasn't until she had looked at Lucie properly and then spotted Zoe beside her that she seemed to realise just who she was.

'Oh my gosh! Hello, Lucie,' Jacasta began with a big smile. 'Lovely to meet you. Come here!' And she held out her arms and brought Lucie in for a second, longer hug.

'You're part of the family,' Jacasta added. 'I hope we can get along great, and I love your dress.'

That was very generous of her and a nice sentiment. Easier for her to say though; she was coming to them all fresh – not dealing with twenty-five years of past history. Nevertheless, it was right to be positive today – on the wedding day.

'Oh, your dress is definitely nicer,' Lucie replied. 'I love it, and agreed, let's try to be good friends.'

'Thank you for coming.' Jacasta smiled again, then turned to Zoe with an excited 'Look at you! Not long to go!' and Lucie found herself moving down the line, shaking hands now with the wedding girls and then with a couple nearer her own age who turned out to be Jacasta's mother and father. 'Hello, I'm Lucie, Zoe's mum,' she said, deciding that was a bit more subtle than 'Miles's first wife'.

But both couldn't seem to stop their eyebrows shooting up their foreheads at those words. And she couldn't help feeling a little buzz at that. *Yes*, she thought, *I remember when I used to make people's eyebrows raise a lot more. And I liked it.*

Then she was at the end of the line, with her greetings all over. She took a sip of champagne and stepped out onto the lawn with a vague idea of going to a quiet corner of the garden to calm her thoughts for a few moments and find some shade from the fierce afternoon sun.

Eyes a little dazzled, she didn't see until she was only a few feet away that she was walking straight into the path of two blonde women... and the man who still, after all this time, seemed to be able to make her heart leap.

His head was turned in her direction. A smile was splitting his lean and handsome face. He didn't even look so very different. No, he looked pretty like himself, just a time-has-passed version. His hair was grey, not brown, and the lines on his face had deepened. But he was still tall and slim. He had been into a sport, she remembered – football? No, possibly tennis... He looked as if he was still playing regularly.

She was smiling back, her heart in her mouth.

'Lucie?' He was stepping towards her. 'It's you, of course it's you! It's me, Clark. Remember me? I had no idea you were going to be here.'

'Clark!' she exclaimed, a smile across her face.

'It was a last-minute decision to come, believe me,' she added. 'I drove my daughter down, because of the train strikes. And agreed, it is a surprise to be here and even more of a surprise to see you.'

He was holding out his arms to her, a huge smile across his face. Did he want to hug? Were they going to hug?

Yes... they were.

He briefly put his arms around her and, for a moment, she felt the strong, safe warmth of that hug, got a hint of lime, grapefruit, mossy greenness, and then she was released.

'It's amazing to see you,' he said, continuing to look right into her face. 'You look fabulous – as you should on your ex's wedding day.' His smile broadened. 'Can it really have been twenty-plus years since I've last seen you?'

'Must be twenty-eight,' she said, not quite sure which of her emotions was going to take charge – the rush of nervy excitement, the burst of sharp sadness that she hadn't seen him for so long, or the shy awkwardness enveloping her that almost made her want to run and hide in the powder room, or really anywhere.

'So this' – he turned to the blondes to introduce her – 'this is Lucie, who used to work with me, a long time ago now when we were both fabulous young people in our twenties.'

'Hello,' Lucie said to them both in turn. Both were very pretty, slim and glamorously dressed. One in her late twenties/early thirties; his daughter, perhaps? The other woman was older, glamorous, hard to put an age to her. Must be his second wife/significant other, was Lucie's guess.

'This is Sienna, my daughter and this...' – he turned to gesture to the other woman – '...wife, Dita.'

'Hello, lovely to meet you both.' Lucie shook their hands and tried to somehow deal with the sense of disappointment washing over her. For a few minutes there, she had allowed herself to wonder, just wonder, about what it might be like if he were free. Could they possibly have re-connected? Started to get to know one another again? Have rekindled something from the swirl of feelings that had surrounded them when they were young?

But here was Dita, who looked just so together and totally the kind of woman she could imagine him with.

And she hadn't seen him since she was in her twenties and hadn't even allowed herself to think about him, so what on earth was going on in her head? She was being completely ridiculous.

'Aunt Lucie!' Here was Deva at her side. 'I've been looking for you!' he exclaimed.

Yes, it was lovely to see Deva, and she had to tell him about his performance and give him her thoughts about how to throw it all out there with the next big number coming up after dinner. But did he have to appear at this exact second? Because politely, Clark and the blondes drew back and began to talk to someone else to give her and her nephew some space. When she would so loved to have talked to Clark and found out how he was and everything that was going on with him.

'Oh my word.' Deva stepped back to admire her outfit. 'Now, I know this isn't Chanel, but it's beautiful and it feels like a bit of a homage to the Chanel 1997 collection, which featured a throw-back "flapper" dress. It looks amazing on you,' he added, gently reaching out to touch the fabric. 'Silk, heat treated to give it that ribbing. It's gorgeous.'

'Well, you would know. You're the one who spirited it out of my boxes and into your suitcase,' she reminded him.

'Yeah... you're not too angry about that, I hope. It wasn't stealing, it was borrowing.'

'It's fine, and I know. My things are in the safe hands of a true connoisseur. And you're back in your suit now...' she added gently.

Deva gave a nod but didn't say anything else about that.

'The Sinatra song sounded really good,' she began.

Deva looked at her, really met her eye, and seemed to be asking for her absolutely honest opinion. 'But?' he asked. 'Because I know there is a but...'

'Well, only because I know you want me to be honest, and you probably know what I'm going to say anyway,' she prompted.

'I didn't really bring out my best for that one, did I?' He looked crestfallen.

'Hey, don't be hard on yourself,' she soothed. 'The Deva that sang into the sunset, fully lost, heart and soul pouring into every note – that's the one we want to hear. But I know that must be so hard to do when you're tense and everyone's looking at you and there's all this weight of expectation.'

'Yeah,' he agreed, 'but I've no idea how to recreate those perfect conditions in my head so that I can blast it out the way I should.'

'Plus' – her voice dropped – 'I never liked that Sinatra song much. Bit twee, bit trite. Doesn't punch at the gut.'

'Agreed.' He smiled.

'You'll be amazing doing The Bangles later, I know you will. You love that music, so just go for it. Release the real Deva. Be yourself, Deevs,' she added, realising it was the first time she'd ever shortened his name.

'Really?' he asked, eyebrows raised.

'Yeah – go for it. You do you. Give it full throttle.'

'*Gie it laldie*,' he said.

'What?'

'Glaswegian for what you said. Thanks, Aunt Lucie.' And he reached over to give her a small, slightly awkward hug.

'Sorry… I'm not good at this. Not a hugger,' he added.

'Ah, hugs are not so bad, when you mean them. So, shoot the lights out. Go full Deva,' she added.

A grin split across his face and his shoulders seemed to drop as some of the afternoon's pent-up tension began to leave him.

'I will,' he said. 'Thank you.' And with that, he turned away and she suddenly wondered if she'd said the right thing. She'd meant the singing, right? Give the singing full throttle.

But Deva seemed so happy, so lit up, that now she was wondering if maybe he had something else in mind and she had inadvertently given him encouragement, permission even, to do something extraordinary.

This was a guy, after all, who had sat on top of a horse statue on Bastille Day and urged the drunken hoards '*Aux armes, citoyens!*'

Permission to do something extraordinary... Maybe that was something she needed to give herself. She was just about ready to do her own equivalent of standing on the hilltop and blasting out The Bangles in a lace dress.

21

It turned out that dinner was not going to be inside that beautiful oak-floored cool dining room. No, they were led, by the violinist and a woman with a flute, to another part of the garden where a vast pink marquee had been set up. Oh, the flowers! So many flowers... An entrance archway of flowers, and inside, extravagant bouquets on the tables, bouquets hanging at strategic points on the bunched fabric ceiling and all around the small stage. Lucie found herself wondering what all these flowers, not to mention the rest of the wedding, had cost. Or if Jacasta, as an influencer, had in fact managed to call in lots of favours and freebies. All very different from her wedding, where the flowers had been her bouquet and two table arrangements for the dinner at the hotel.

And now, as she followed the guests into the marquee, she saw the cake – an astonishing three-tiered wonder on its own small table slightly to the side of the stage. It was a cream, gold and pink pinnacle of a cake rising from the rose and peony-strewn table. She felt she had to go and have a closer look at the gold marbled icing and the miniature bride and groom on top. The fondant Jacasta and fondant Miles were tiny works of art, with faces carefully created to look as like the happy couple as possible.

As Lucie studied those little figurines, she felt a surge of anger. Look at these people in this tent all so delighted that her ex-husband had moved on, had found a nubile young woman to share his life with. And some of these people had been at her own wedding, eating a much humbler cake, by the way.

Smug Miles, starting his business and his married life all over again. Moving on without her, while she seemed to be stuck, hunkered down in the little post-divorce bomb shelter she'd built for herself. She looked at his slim fondant figure in its slick fondant tuxedo with his smooth black fondant hair on his fifty-six-year-old head. That man! She had been trying hard to be magnanimous, giving the happy couple her congratulations. But, as she thought about the fact that she was still paying for his new hair, there was no use denying that maybe it was a little too soon for her and Miles and his wonderful new life was, now and then, going to get right on her nerves.

It was the work of a moment to first glance about to make sure no one was looking, then take a knife from the place setting at the nearest table, and with a single, deft swipe, she scalped the Miles figurine. Yes, with one little chop, she gave him back the bald patch he would have had if he hadn't spent *her* money on hair treatments and hair plugs. Yes, that was definitely better, she thought, looking at the nice white patch that now shone from the top of the figurine's head. That definitely helped her anger to settle back down again.

People were starting to take their seats and, in some confusion, Lucie went over to the board and wondered where she was supposed to sit. She doubted there had been time to replace the name of the guests who'd cancelled with her name... And who did Miles say had cancelled? She couldn't remember who it was.

She looked around the marquee and suddenly it felt overwhelming. In just that one quick scan of the room, she'd seen Miles and Jacasta kiss and laugh, Miles's mother turn to Jason's wife with that sour look that meant some stream of criticism was about to emerge, and Clark sharing a joke with the beautiful blonde wife.

No – this was too much. Way too much. No vegan, salad-based dinner was worth this amount of personal discomfort. And imagine having to listen to the speeches. Good grief! What was she thinking? She had to get out of here as quickly as she possibly could.

With that, she skirted the side of the marquee and headed, as unobtrusively as she possibly could against the flow of traffic, towards the house. She got in through the glass doors, mercifully unlocked, and was walking through the beautiful sitting room and into the reception area, wondering where her bag could possibly be.

That was when she ran into the maison's keeper, or maybe fixer, Marcel, who immediately offered to show her to the room where he had taken 'Madam's bag'.

Thanking him, she followed him up the sweeping, polished wooden staircase that she'd already had a chance to study thanks to Jacasta's Instagram.

Up they went on a second set of stairs to the higher floor, and Marcel opened a substantial wooden door and gestured her into the room. Now this was a lovely room, old-fashioned and traditionally furnished, but by someone who had an eye for detail and harmony. For a moment, she couldn't decide which of the elements was the loveliest – the tall windows, framed with beautiful salmon-pink silk curtains, which no doubt looked over the beautiful lawns, shrubbery and driveway at the front of the house, the double bed with its polished mahogany bedstead and velvet bedspread in pinks and golds, the gilt-framed mirror on the wall, the antique lamps, or the luxuriously thick cream carpet and pink rugs underfoot.

It was all very prettily done, and now that she was admiring the bed with its thick mattress and freshly ironed white sheets, she realised how little sleep she'd had since leaving England. Nervous energy and many, many cups of coffee had kept her going for all this time, but now she was absolutely running on empty. She thanked Marcel and once he'd left the room, she wondered if slipping into that bed and allowing herself an hour or two of nap time while the wedding went on without her would be a good idea.

She sat on the bed, enjoying the deep, soft springiness, and realised with a wave of guilt that she had hardly thought about her dad since she'd arrived here, and with that, she was desperate to speak to him and check everything was OK.

She called his number immediately.

'Hello, Lucie, my girl,' he answered within a couple of rings. 'How are you? How is France?'

'How are you, Dad? That's much more important!'

She found herself listening carefully to his voice, his tone, trying as hard as she could to read the energy levels and whether he was comfortable, happy and if it was going to be OK for her to stay away for another night or even two.

'I'm as well as can be expected,' he insisted. 'Nothing dramatic to report. Now how about you all? Has my gorgeous Jag got you all there safely?'

'Well... she did have a bit of an issue in the heart of the Auvergne.'

'Oh dear... tell me all about it.'

So Lucie did, leaving out for now the bit about the dented front panel. She would get that quietly and unobtrusively repaired so he didn't need to know that the Jag had been pranged and her good looks were currently spoiled.

'So some refugee lads did a temporary patch up and helped you on your way?' he asked, having listened to her recount the story.

'Yes... and we took one of them to hospital.'

'What?'

She told that part of the story too, thinking she must phone Pete and see what the update was on his brother.

'Well, you've certainly had an adventure then, just like I told you. Has it done you some good?'

'Yes,' she said with a smile, thinking of Deva and The Bangles on the hillside... and permission to do something extraordinary. 'I think so. But right now, I'm a little tired. There's not been much sleeping.'

'Ah well... hopefully, you'll have a chance to catch up with that and the sun and the sea. So, where are you now?' was his next question.

'Well, you may not believe this, but I've just retreated to my room at the wedding venue. I watched the ceremony and it was... nice,' she decided. 'But I'm too tired to sit and have dinner and make polite small talk with people who are all probably wondering what the heck I'm doing here, let alone listen to the bloody speeches, so I've retreated to my room. And a very nice room it is too.' Then, before she sounded like she was appreciating Miles too much, she added, 'Wonder if he'll send me the bloody bill.'

This made her dad laugh.

'Good for you,' he said. 'Good for you for going along. I hope you're looking fabulous. Make sure he knows what he's missing.'

'I looked just like a fifty-two-year-old woman who has spent too long in a car, but at least I was wearing a nice dress. Turns out Deva "borrowed" some items from the box under the bed, including the prized Chanel pieces.'

'Well, this all sounds very intriguing! A proper adventure, like the old days,' he added. 'Remember them? We'd get a phone call on a Sunday evening and have no idea where you were going to be calling from.'

'Ha... happy but slightly crazy days.'

'Right, I'm going to push off now,' her dad told her. 'Why don't you sleep now, then go back to the party later and let your hair down? You're not too old, my darling. And I would argue that one is never too old.'

'Love you, Dad. See you soon.'

'Look after yourself... and the Jag!'

And with that, he was gone. She was left smiling at the phone, reassured that he sounded cheerful and as well as could be hoped.

She tried Pete's number next, but there was no reply. A little worried for the brothers, she sent a text.

> Hi Pete, how is Fikru? Hope the news is good. We are thinking of you both. Love from Lucie.

Once that one was sent, she messaged Zoe too.

> Have gone to my room. Exhausted. Can't face the dinner, speeches etc. Need a nap. Call me if I'm about to miss anything big. Marcel will tell you where I am. Have fun, loads of love Mxx

Then she lay back on the bed, closed her eyes and let all the events of the past two days swirl around her head. Images of Paris, of the hospital, of the statue in the town square, of Fikru and Pete, Jacasta and Miles, flowers, flowers, all came rushing into her mind.

Processing... she thought to herself. *I'm processing...*

It did feel as if more had happened in the last two days than had happened in the last two months... two years, even.

And now she found herself thinking about Clark and the blonde daughter and the blonde wife. It was almost thirty years since she'd seen him last. Thirty years! Could that even be right when she was so surprised, almost overwhelmed, at the strength of her feelings? She found herself remembering fragments of their conversations all those years ago, the good advice he'd given her, and a work trip they'd gone on in the car together – her all jumpy, nervy, determined to do her best work, but aware of how strong her feelings were about him.

She remembered too how exciting it was to go to work every day, just to see him and talk to him, then how depressed she would be afterwards, because she was convinced he could be perfect for her, but it didn't look as if anything was ever going to happen between them.

And this situation had gone on for months, until a good friend had given her a stern talking to, telling her this was ridiculous and she had to stop pining for the impossible; there were literally millions of other people in the world and she had to get over this guy and get on with her life.

Her eyes closed, her head still reeling, she dropped into a light sleep with the last conscious thoughts being a troubling *Was all this time spent with Miles a mistake? Am I ever going to recover from a mistake on that scale? Am I ever going to be able to emerge from the divorce bunker?* Mixed with the reassuring *Zoe is my compensation for marriage to Miles.* But then Zoe was growing up, growing away, would soon have her own baby to care for. Lucie's dad wouldn't be there for her much longer either. Yes, she would have to put on her helmet and her flak jacket if necessary, but one way or another, she would have to get out of her bunker.

22

Zoe sat in the quiet of the bathroom and stared at her phone. Over the course of this afternoon and evening, she had sent Rafi six WhatsApps, four texts, even an email and a message on Instagram. She'd tried to call him twice and left one voicemail… but there was still no sign of a reply.

She had no idea what was going on. This was so unlike him. So out of character that she wasn't sure whether to be worried that something had happened, or just furious that he wasn't responding.

What was really going on?

'What is he thinking, baby girl?' she asked her bump in a low voice. 'Does he want to be with us? Does he want to be on his own? I just don't know.'

The pregnancy had been unplanned.

There, she had to admit that. Even if she was never going to tell anyone else in the world, including her daughter, she had to admit it to herself.

So the pregnancy months so far had been about catching up with herself. Getting to grips with the fact that this was going to happen, and sooner than she might have wanted. And, although she had realised that Rafi was behind her in terms of getting to grips with it, she had thought he would get there eventually. And she really had believed that they would at least move in together.

But ever since he'd said no to buying this latest flat and no to attending her dad's wedding, well, she had felt serious doubt begin to creep in. Nothing had changed between them, nothing at all. But... but... but... she was having a baby. This monumental change was coming to her life and she needed him to accept the changes too and start planning for the future of their little family.

Maybe, despite all her protestations, maybe her mum was right; maybe she did need a commitment of some kind from Rafi.

And if not...

'Well,' she told her bump, 'you and me will just have to come through for each other. Somehow, we will just have to do this, together.'

She had loving parents, she had great friends, she loved her work colleagues too. Somehow, if she had to do this all without Rafi, well, she would.

She would... she would... but... She gave a big sigh at the thought and could feel a small, sad tear slip from the corner of her eye. It was terrible to be at a perfect wedding like this, watching Jacasta and her dad radiate so much love and happiness towards each other, and feel so alone and so questioning about how much the love of her life loved her back.

That was all she had been able to think about as she watched her dad and Jacasta make their vows.

Does Rafi love me?

Does he love me like this?

Would he do this for me?

Or was he going to let her and their baby down?

* * *

Meanwhile, in the small room that had been assigned to him on the second floor of Maison Violette, Deva was pacing anxiously around.

First of all, he began to hum gently, then he began the proper vocal exercises that he had been taught back at the out-of-school drama classes he had absolutely lived for during his school days in Glasgow.

He could hear teacher Jeanette's instructions in his head: 'Empty your mind, breathe into every note, then work slowly, slowly up and down the octave, bring your concentration to every single note.'

That was the aim with this next song. *Don't think about the audience, don't think about the occasion, just think about making each and every single note the best I can possibly make it.*

Deva looked at himself in the mirror in the dark suit and the constricting shirt and tie. Then he thought about singing yesterday, singing with his heart and soul right out across the hilltops and into the sunset. That was the kind of singing he knew he was capable of. That was the voice and the heart that he wanted to bring to the world.

He glanced over at the ornate wooden wardrobe in the corner of the room. On a hanger on the front of the wardrobe was the other dress he had liberated from Aunt Lucie's boxes at the last minute and stuffed into his backpack.

It was another long, black lace Chanel. Vintage, he thought... She must have bought some vintage pieces too. This was maybe from a 1980s pre-Lagerfeld collection. But nonetheless beautiful for that.

Without even thinking about it too much, he took off the tie, the suit and the shirt and decided he would just try on the dress, just to see.

And once it was on, well, the decision was made for him.

He had never felt more powerful, more in touch with his talent than when he'd sung to the hilltops. Even as he'd been singing then, he'd wondered if this was the pinnacle, if this was the best he was ever going to be able to sing, his perfect moment.

But now, now that he was encased in Chanel lace once again, like every true artist, he was wondering if that performance yesterday could just be the beginning.

Could he get even better than that? Could he push himself? Practise much harder? Find his inner diva and become a truly star performer?

He smoothed down the dress. Then he began to style his hair, emptying his mind and getting into the zone. Yes, he would aim to tune out the audience, tune out what his mum might think, or his sisters, or anyone else. Instead, he would focus on the song, the notes, the emotion and how to give the next, even better, performance of his life.

23

There was a tapping on the door. Lucie opened her eyes and found her room in darkness. She sat up abruptly, glanced at her phone and saw that it was almost 7.30 p.m. She'd lost almost two hours.

'Mum?' She heard her daughter's voice on the other side of the door.

'Hi, Zoe... door's open.'

Zoe stepped in as Lucie sat up and smoothed out her hair.

'Dinner over?' Lucie asked.

'Yup... and the speeches too. Very gushy. I'm glad you didn't have to hear all that.' Zoe smiled. 'So now the happy couple are about to get their photos taken on the wedding swing and then Deva is going to sing for their first dance. I didn't think you'd want to miss all that.'

'Oh, no, definitely not!'

Lucie stood up. 'Hang on a few minutes, let me do a little refresh in the mirror,' she said, scouting about for her hair-brush, lipstick and mascara.

'How are you doing?' she asked Zoe as she applied her fresh coating of makeup. 'Having fun? Or pretty tired?'

'Both,' Zoe decided. 'But Dad and Jacasta look very happy and it's nice to catch up with so many people. So I'm pushing on through. There was coffee at the end of the meal, so that helped.'

'And how about Rafi? Have you been in touch with him?' Lucie asked, but gently, suspecting it was sensitive ground.

A look seemed to pass over Zoe's face.

'Is everything OK?' Lucie asked.

'I *hope* everything's OK,' Zoe began. 'I've just not had any reply from him all day, which is not like him,' she added. Then she quickly followed this with, 'I'm sure everything's fine.'

'Don't worry yourself,' Lucie reassured her while feeling her own familiar burst of worry that Zoe was worried, and who was this guy anyway? And how dare he make her daughter feel anxious about anything at all at this late stage in her pregnancy.

'Right,' she said, setting a cheerful smile in place, 'let's go support Deva and find out all about wedding swings.'

* * *

In the garden, they found flowers, more flowers, and now lanterns, subtle outdoor lighting, scented candles and guests milling about in the glow of the marquee.

Knots of people had gathered around this elaborate double swing, its ropes all festooned with flowers and greenery.

Miles and Jacasta were sitting side by side on the swing, one arm around each other, one arm holding a rope as the photographer bounced about beside them snapping away.

'And look into her eyes... and Jacasta, slightly to the left...

and chin up just a little... Perfect, hold it there... Now looking over to me...'

Both were smiling, apparently enjoying this whole ludicrous performance. *A swing*? Lucie couldn't help thinking, *weren't they a little old to get excited about swings.*

But as most people seemed to be enjoying the performance, she took the chance to snag another glass of fizz from a passing waiter, then stole glances around the audience. There was no point in kidding herself; she was definitely looking for Clark. *So he's married. That doesn't mean I can't catch up with him, be friends with him again... does it?* Having an old friend like Clark back in her life would be a start, wouldn't it?

She scanned the faces and just as she thought she couldn't locate him, there he was. His back to her, his arm around one of the women he was with; she couldn't tell from here which one. And now, the sharp feeling of being all alone, and on the edge of it all, swept over her.

She took a deep swig from her glass, turned her attention back to Miles, Jacasta and the swing, and quite honestly wanted to laugh out loud at this pantomime. Instead, she brought out her phone, set it to record video and held it up at the scene. Maybe in ten years' time, when Miles and Jacasta had split acrimoniously, she could play this back to him and remind him what an absolute tit he'd made of himself at this over-the-top wedding.

She wondered whether Miles and Jacasta would have children. She tried to picture her fifty-six-year-old ex changing a dirty nappy. He'd never been the keenest on baby tasks the first time around. Was Zoe's baby soon going to have a playmate who would technically be her aunt or uncle? Lucie really didn't know whether to sigh or giggle at that thought.

She looked back at the couple on the swing and for a

moment thought one of the ropes looked a little longer than the other. She had barely registered this thought when the right-hand rope came fully loose and slapped hard onto the ground, very quickly followed by Jacasta and then Miles on top.

For a moment, the entire audience gasped and stood frozen with shock, taking in the heavy grunts, cries and waving arms and legs from the tangled heap of bride and groom in front of them, then there was a surge of the people at the front rushing to help.

As first Miles was helped to his feet, and then Jacasta was pulled up from where she'd been crushed underneath him, it was clear that there may be some pain, scrapes and bruises, but both were thankfully unharmed.

Lucie quickly clicked off her phone recording but couldn't quite tear her eyes from the scene as Miles went from feeling shocked to finding the whole thing pretty funny. He began smiling and, once he was sure Jacasta was alright, he began to properly laugh. Meanwhile, Jacasta was examining her bouquet, which had taken a serious crushing, and her dress, which now had an obvious green grass mark on the side, and she was looking as if she was suffering a serious sense of humour failure.

As Miles tried to take her arm, she pulled it away from him. Then she dumped the crushed and mangled bouquet onto the grass and stomped off across the lawn, the wedding girls clustering around her in sympathy.

Once the girls had made off in the direction of the house, Miles went up to a group of his closest friends, knocked back a glass of wine and began to roar with laughter. Much of the wedding audience took their cue from him and all the pent-up humour in the situation was released. Almost everywhere you looked now people were creased up with laughter and... oh dear, comparing their videos of the moment and laughing all over again.

Across the crowd, Lucie caught sight of Zoe, who met her eye too. Zoe wasn't laughing; in fact, Zoe rolled her eyes, scowled and then hurried towards her dad. After a few moments of conversation – which looked a little like Zoe ticking her dad off – Miles headed off across the lawn, hopefully to find Jacasta and help her recover from this ordeal.

Only when Miles had left the scene and Lucie could see Zoe heading towards her, only then did Lucie allow herself a smile at it all.

'Well done,' Lucie told her daughter once she was within earshot. 'You're quite right to send Miles off after her. I mean, poor her, coming off the swing in front of everyone, crushing her flowers, staining her dress, not to mention having Miles land on top of her...'

Zoe seemed to be struggling with her face... She was clearly trying to keep a calm and sympathetic expression in place, but now there was an unmistakable twitching at the corners of her mouth and crinkling round her eyes.

'It was bloody funny though,' Zoe said finally, allowing herself a broad smile but no actual laughter. 'Please tell me you've got it on video.'

Lucie just tapped her phone and gave Zoe a knowing look.

'I would replay it to check,' Lucie said, 'but there's too much risk that Jacasta will hear me laughing in her bridal suite on the other side of the maison.'

Zoe tried not to giggle, but had to give in.

'Oh... don't think I'm being mean, please. I wish them the best, I really do,' Lucie tried to explain. 'I'm getting over being furious with your dad and one day in the future I'm sure we'll all be friends. But for now, I'm allowed to laugh because he is still a bit of a tit and I can't help feeling that she is going to keep him on his toes and give as good as she gets.'

'That's fair enough,' Zoe decided, before adding, 'And what about Deva? Have you seen him? I thought his song was coming up next.'

'No, but we could go and look around for him. And what about you, have you heard from Rafi yet?'

Zoe paused for a moment, as if she wasn't quite sure what to tell her mother. Then she decided on: 'Only a quick message saying stand by, he will be in touch very soon, which is a bit mysterious. Sounds as if he might have some news.'

Please let it be good, Lucie thought to herself.

The tables in the marquee had been pushed to the side and the lighting dimmed. The keyboard player and violinist were back, along with a DJ with full equipment. The bar was set up at the back and of course everything looked stunning. Flowers – check, low and careful lighting – check, actual wafting scent – check, projection of lovely photographs and arty images – check. Thank God for the swing moment, Lucie couldn't help thinking; this perfect bloody wedding had to have some hiccups.

She decided to refresh her drink and as she made for the bar, she stopped to say some brief hellos to familiar faces. As she was talking to one former business friend, over the woman's shoulder, she caught sight of Clark. Then he saw her and their eyes made contact. It momentarily stopped her in her tracks. She lost the thread of what she'd been saying to the acquaintance and stumbled over her next sentence.

Now Clark was completely filling her thoughts. In that one

look, she remembered so many things about him. How funny he could be but also how serious when required. And how calm and unflappable, whatever was going on around them. Five years older than her, when she was in her early twenties, he'd seemed like the best possible grown up. The kind of man you wanted to marry, have children with, hope your son grew up into.

Was he still all of those things? What had happened to him over the years? How had life changed him? Was he still the same kind of man with the same kind of values? She realised she was quite desperate to know. Still, the woman she was with kept on talking and she could see that Clark had moved on to another conversation. But when she looked over in his direction once more, she saw his eyes move towards her again and he gave a slight nod, which she took to mean that he'd seen her and they must talk some more. Even the thought of that made her heart jump and some sort of blush or flush travel from her collarbone up across her cheeks.

* * *

'My lovely guests!' Miles was heading towards the raised dais. 'I hope you're all enjoying yourselves.'

There were cheers of approval in reply to this.

'Bet you can't wait to start dancing and letting what's left of your hair down.'

Another cheer, along with a heckle of 'Especially the over sixties!'

'So, before we let rip with the DJ, my wife, Jacasta...'

Amidst the cheers that followed this, Lucie couldn't help thinking how odd it was to hear Miles say 'my wife' and then follow it up with another woman's name. In fact, she thought she'd heard his momentary pause as he checked himself to make absolutely sure he didn't automatically say the wrong name. Old habits die hard, after all.

'Jacasta and I are going to open the dancing to our song. So step forward, Jacasta!' Miles announced.

Jacasta emerged from the side of the stage in a different dress. This one was lacier and a better cut for dancing than the column dress. Her hair and makeup had been retouched and there was a corsage of wedding flowers on her shoulder and on one of her wrists. She was young, beautiful, full of energy and ambition. Miles had landed so much more than he deserved, Lucie thought.

Maybe people had thought the same of her when she'd married him. And she felt jolted by that. She couldn't bring back her youth or the beauty she'd had in her twenties and thirties, but she'd allowed her energy, ambition and focus to slide over recent years. She'd felt beaten down by what had happened and she'd retreated. Whereas Miles had been through the worst, picked himself up and set his sights on a whole new chapter. And that's what she needed to do too.

As the music for the opening dance began to play, Zoe appeared at Lucie's side.

'And let's welcome my nephew, Deva, up here,' Miles went on. 'He's going to sing this absolutely perfect song, which was playing the night I met Jacasta.' Then he gathered Jacasta into his arms and they stepped onto the dancefloor together, all broad smiles, eye contact and, Lucie suspected, carefully rehearsed steps.

Her eyes moved from the Happy Couple to Deva, who stepped up onto the dais, took hold of the microphone, and positively shimmered under the dimmed, twinkly lights, in another head-to-toe black lace Chanel dress even lovelier than the one he'd worn to sing to the mountaintops. His shining hair slicked into a smoothed approximation of a very short Chanel bob.

And the voice, the voice that emerged now, that brought all the emotion to every note, that wrung everything out of each word of 'Eternal Flame', this was the voice that had rung out over the hillside and echoed into the sunset.

Zoe and Lucie looked at one another, and Lucie felt a little shivery tingle pass down her spine.

He was just so good. She took a quick glance around the audience to see if everyone was as bowled over, as spellbound, as she thought they should be. And yes, it did look as if everyone in the room had come to a surprised standstill. Yes, he was definitely bringing everyone to their knees with this song.

Soon, other couples were making their way onto the dance-floor. And Deva was hitting the higher notes, ramping up the emotion and knocking it right out of the park. Oh yes... prompted by the words of the song, we could all *feel his heart beating*, we did all *understand*.

Lucie could feel the tightness of emotion in her throat and it was certainly not caused by the sight of Miles and Jacasta making puppy eyes at one another. This was a glorious song, and not appropriate for Miles. How could he dance to 'Eternal Flame' after twenty-five years of marriage to someone else, the silly arse. She put Miles out of her mind and turned her attention back to Deva, who was spreading his arms wide for the finale, giving it all to them: all the sound, all the song, all the heart came right down into the microphone and flowed out over the audience.

Did they understand? Did they feel the same? Or was he only dreaming...

The words of this song seemed so perfect and so personal to

Deva, as he stood there in front of them in the dress by his beloved Chanel. He just wanted to be heard and understood.

She could feel tears of emotion pricking at the back of her eyes.

When he'd sung his final note, there was a pause as it reverberated around the tent and then long, loud appreciative claps and cheers from the audience as he took his bow.

But what Lucie noticed as she watched Deva come off-stage, glowing and grinning with the effort and the appreciation, was that he went up to his mother, Melissa, but her face looked angry. She appeared to say sharp words to him, then she turned on her heel and walked away, right out of the tent.

24

Without hesitation, both Lucie and Zoe made their way through the crowd to get to Deva's side.

'That was amazing!' Lucie told him, putting a hand on his shoulder and making sure he met her eyes and understood just how sincere she was. 'I really mean it. You were absolutely brilliant.'

'Totally,' Zoe added. 'We are so proud of you. All that clapping and cheering was for real. I don't think you have a career in accounts ahead of you, Deevs... I think you're going to be A Star!'

They could see the mixed emotion on his face... He was part smiling, part frowning, as if he might break down and cry but with happiness or sadness, or maybe both.

'My mum...' he began, voice breaking. 'She's furious... about the dress. Blames you, by the way' – he directed this at Lucie – 'said she always thought you were a bit wild under the surface.'

'Oh, for goodness' sake,' Lucie blurted. 'If I've encouraged you to dress as you want to and sing your absolute best, then I'm proud of that,' she added. And she followed this up with a robust, 'So your mum didn't approve, so what? I don't think my dad approved of anything I did until I was about forty-five. So don't worry about it. She'll come round. In fact, at your age, if your parents fully approve of you, you're probably doing something wrong. OK? Coco would definitely approve.' She smiled at Deva, then gave him an encouraging hug. 'Coco and her dress have given you permission to do something extraordinary, and you might have inspired us and maybe half the people in this room to do the same.'

And now Zoe, wide smile on her face, broke in with, 'Yes... I think you two have totally inspired me – Deva with the song and Mum with that very good advice to never mind what your parents will think!'

Her smile turned into a grin and she looked as if she was about to take a castle by storm.

'Wait... what?' Lucie couldn't help asking.

'I've made my decision... now I'm going for it. Now or never... yes or no... do or die...'

'What are you talking about?' Lucie wanted to know.

But Zoe already had her phone out and she was calling up a number...

'I'm changing to speakerphone,' she said, 'so you two can be my witnesses... Let's just step out into the garden so we can hear him.'

Lucie and Deva looked at one another. What was she talking about?

'Zoe? What?' Lucie urged, but they followed her hurried strides out to the stillness on the other side of the tent.

The ringing tone came through the speaker for several moments, then a male voice answered.

'Zoe!' The voice sounded excited, almost flustered.

'Rafi! Yeah, it's me. I'm phoning to ask you something. It's important. Very important.' Then, before he could say anything in reply, she came out with: 'I want to marry you, Rafi. Please can we get married? I don't care if you don't want to live with me, but I do want to be your wife. I want our baby girl to have our surnames and I want you to be legally tied to us...' Then, taking another breath, she went on. 'And if that doesn't sound romantic enough – I want to marry you because you are one of the very best men I've ever known and I am so, so lucky to have you.'

At this, Zoe looked up at her mum... and Lucie found herself swallowing hard. Because that was enough, wasn't it. You wanted your girl and her girl to be with one of the very best guys. And if Zoe thought he was, then he really must be.

There was a pause and Zoe, Lucie and Deva all exchanged nervous glances. Zoe began to look slightly panicked.

Deva made a calming motion with his hands and whispered, 'It's OK, he's processing... Let him just take a moment.'

'Zoe...' Rafi began, and his voice sounded husky and a little choked. 'I've just arrived at the airport in Perpignan. I've come to ask you the same question.'

At this, all of them screamed with excitement and grabbed hold of one another's arms.

'What's going on?' Rafi asked into the cacophony. 'Who else is there?'

'Never mind, never mind!' Zoe exclaimed. 'I'm here. I'm waiting for you... This is amazing!' Then she repeated the address several times to make sure he knew it and told him to hurry.

When she hung up, they all had to hold one another's arms and have another little scream.

'He's coming here!' Zoe exclaimed. 'He wants to ask me! I

need to get upstairs, do my hair and makeup again, get prepped. This is big! This is huge! Almost as huge as me!'

Then she took hold of her mother's hands and asked her, 'Is this a good idea? Am I doing the right thing?'

'Zoe.' Lucie smiled and tried to stem the tear that was threatening to squeeze from the corner of her eye. 'You're amazing. Totally awesome. I am so proud of you. And if you think Rafi is the right man to be your husband – then so do I. Go for it, darling, but...'

'But?' Zoe asked anxiously.

'No wedding swing, OK, sweetheart?' Lucie said with a smile.

They all had to laugh at this.

'OK, gotta go prep,' Zoe said, and giving them both a kiss and hug after a quick 'Is a hug OK?' to Deva, she hurried off towards the house.

'Well...' Lucie began, turning to Deva with a smile.

But Deva was looking beyond her shoulder.

'Uh oh...' he began. 'Angry mother incoming.'

'Lucie!'

And here was Melissa, approaching rapidly with a very unhappy expression on her face.

'Is Deva wearing your dress?' she began.

There was no use in denying this, so Lucie simply said: 'Yes.'

'Why?' Melissa asked beseechingly.

Lucie looked at Deva, who looked at her, as if he was hoping she could somehow say something to make this a bit better and smooth it over.

'Because he wants to...' Lucie began.

'That's not a reason!' Melissa snapped. 'He's making a complete fool of himself. Is that what you wanted? This is your ex-husband's wedding. I mean, why are you even here? To make a fool of yourself?'

'Ooft!' Deva exclaimed, 'That was a bit harsh, Mum.'

'We've had a very long journey and Miles offered me dinner and a bed for the night,' Lucie said simply. 'I'm also enjoying catching up with old friends... and family.'

'But Deva... in a dress?' Melissa blurted. And somewhere mixed in with that anger was upset and an inability to understand what was going on.

'Deva is a wonderfully talented singer and performer.' Lucie smiled at her nephew. 'When he's wearing Chanel, he performs even better. I don't think it's anything more complicated than that...'

'But...' Melissa began. 'I don't want a son who wears dresses, who thinks he's a girl!'

'When you're twenty, you've got to try a lot of things out to work out who you are and what you want. I know I did that. Luckily, my mum and dad just let me get on with it. They cheered from the sidelines... because that's what we're supposed to do.'

Whatever Melissa might have wanted to say next was interrupted by the appearance of Miles by their sides.

'Great song, Deva,' he said. 'What a talent. Lucie, can I have a quick word?'

At this, Melissa took hold of Deva's shoulder and turned him away. Lucie didn't like the look of that move very much. It was quite controlling, as if Melissa was taking charge of her son. She fully expected that the next time she saw Deva he would be back in his suit, and whatever feelings were bubbling up in his mind as he tried out dresses and singing and figuring out who he was and what he wanted to be would be pushed firmly back down again.

'Miles?' Lucie turned with a pleasant smile to her ex.

'Lucie, did you scalp the cake groom?' Miles asked, sounding angry.

Oh boy... this was not what she'd expected.

'Ah... well...'

'You did, didn't you? What on earth did you do that for? Jacasta is very upset. She's upset about that. She's upset about the swing. She's upset about her bouquet getting squashed and the stain on her dress. She thinks this whole thing is a disaster.'

Lucie took a breath. 'This is a gorgeous, beautiful, memorable wedding. Please tell her that. People will take wonderful memories away from tonight.'

'But why did you scalp me?' he demanded.

'Well, maybe, Miles, it was because you deserve to be scalped!' Lucie said, determined to remain calm but to stand firm. 'You used *my* credit card to pay for your shiny new teeth and your stupid new hair and I'm still paying the bill!'

Then, while she had his ear, she thought she might share a few other home truths with him. 'Do you not think I might have a few other reasons to be pissed off with you? I'm living in a rented one-bed in Tonbridge while you have a flaming chateau wedding in France! What's that all about?

'Half of my pension fund has been signed over to you!' she went on. 'And on top of that, you seem to have some secret office block that you've never told me about. So yes, I scalped the bloody fondant groom. Quite honestly, that was restrained. I should be scalping you!'

25

After delivering these words and feeling the relief that came with having got them off her chest, Lucie was all set to turn on her heel and walk away from Miles, but something about his expression caused her to stay.

His face seemed to soften, his shoulders sag, and he looked her in the eye with an almost pleading expression.

'What's up?' she heard herself ask with much more sympathy than she had expected to use.

Miles didn't exactly run his hand through the recently applied hair, but he sort of felt and patted it in an exasperated way.

'Look... I'm sorry,' he began. 'There was a lot going on in the final months of... well, the business, the divorce... and I may have lost track of some of the details. I honestly didn't realise you were still paying that card... I thought, God... Well, I don't know what I thought. There are still a lot of payments and bills going out. Things are far from sorted out. But obviously you shouldn't be paying that bill.' He looked appropriately embarrassed. 'So give me the details when you're back home and I'll take it over.'

'Thank you...' She paused, totally surprised by how quickly he'd climbed down over this and wondering if there was anything else he wanted to add.

'And what about the office block?' she prompted.

'It's registered overseas,' he admitted, 'under a different holding company. The reason I kept quiet about it was because it was financially under water when we split and would have added another £300,000 or so to our debts if they'd come for that too.'

'Right... So are you wanting me to thank you for your amazing financial acumen?' was her heavy-on-the-sarcasm reply to this.

'No... no, of course not,' Miles said. 'Not after everything I've put you through. But that office block has come good. It's back in credit and we should sit down and work out what share you should get of the rent going forward.'

'Probably half,' Lucie said, determined to stand up to him.

'Yes... probably half.' Miles seemed to agree without any big debate. 'You know, the funny thing is that I asked everyone I could think of to lend me money so I could keep paying the loan when it was in the hole... I literally went through all my contacts, even my old address books. Two people came through for me and one was Clark Patterson, remember him? Your old work colleague... I only met him once or twice back then...'

A jolt of nervous tension shot through Lucie at the mention of Clark's name.

'He's done well,' Miles went on. 'Runs a big architectural and building development company now. He hadn't heard from me since before we got married, but he heard me out, saw the opportunity and put up the cash. He's here, by the way, you should say hello.'

'Oh... yes... right...' she said vaguely, hoping she'd covered any sign of her feelings.

'So, yes, Lucie, I'm sorry about everything that happened and I will square up with you, I promise,' Miles said.

'Thank you. I'm sorry too,' she added. 'And, honestly, I am glad you've found someone to be happy with.'

There, she'd said it and she meant it. Surely that was enough talking with Miles. Surely she'd done her bit and they could both head back to the party.

Miles paused. He seemed to be thinking and choosing his words carefully, considering what he should or shouldn't tell her, then he said, 'I do love Jacasta...'

'I'm happy for you,' she said, but a little coolly. Really, she wasn't the one who could gush over this.

'But she's so young,' he added, looking somewhat unhappy at the thought.

'Yes... she is.'

'She wants a baby.' He shrugged. 'I'm really not sure about all that... and I hate her taste in music. No offence to Deva, but that song...'

Lucie couldn't help a small snort of a laugh.

'And oh my God, the influencer life,' Miles complained. 'This whole wedding. It's pretty much a business expense, all done for the clicks and the affiliate links to buy stuff.'

'Oh...'

'She makes me feel very old sometimes,' he admitted. 'I've got to look good, tanned, with the hair and the teeth. I've got to go jogging. I'm even wearing' – he looked properly embarrassed now – 'man Spanx under this suit.'

Now Lucie laughed.

'Man Spanx? I didn't even know they existed, but I'm all for equality,' she joked. 'And they're working. You're looking pretty trim.'

Miles pinched at his side, pulled the fabric away and it made an audible twang as it snapped back into place.

'She's got you under the thumb, Miles. I am delighted for her. I'm sure it's doing you a lot of good,' Lucie said, feeling a burst of amusement.

'I'm only allowed to drink at the weekend,' he added with a shake of his head. 'Anyway, how are you doing?' he asked. 'Really? Not the airbrushed answer.'

She took a steadying sip at her glass. 'Getting it together,' she began. 'I won't stay in the flat forever, but it's good to be close to Dad.'

'And how about him? How's it going?' Miles asked with such a sympathetic tone that she felt her eyes tearing up.

'He's not got long...' she managed. 'Which is incredibly sad. Because I'll really miss him.' She swallowed and blinked hard because she didn't want to break down in front of Miles, because then he'd have to put his arm around her and that would probably make everything worse and she just didn't want that scene here in front of potential passing guests.

'I'm really sorry,' Miles said gently. 'I always liked your dad.'

'He doesn't like you,' she said, mainly to take herself from the verge of tears.

Miles put his hands up. 'Deserved,' he said. And he followed this up with, 'And what about Zoe? She's doing OK, isn't she? Seems to have picked a nice guy.'

'Have you met him?'

'No... but she keeps telling me it's going to happen.'

'He's coming here, tonight. Last-minute change of plan. Wants to be with her and... meet the family...' Lucie didn't want to spoil her daughter's news. 'I think they're making good plans together,' she said.

'Well… I know you might not want this straight away, but can we try our best to be friends? For Zoe's sake and for our sake too.'

'Yes, Miles. You sort out the credit card bill and my share of the office block payments and we can definitely work on being friends.'

He held out his hand for her to shake.

As she took it, he said, 'Nice to talk to you, Lucie. And thank you for all the good years.'

That gave her an unexpected lump in the back of her throat.

'Yes, well… Congratulations, Miles, I hope you and Jacasta will be very happy. Just be honest, be open. That's all that matters in the end.'

He gave her a long look. She wasn't quite sure what to read into it – regret, sadness, relief, annoyance, nostalgia – maybe all of those things, because she felt them all too.

'Enjoy the evening,' he said.

'Yes… you too.'

Her phone in her hand buzzed with a message, and when she looked down it was Zoe:

He's here! Come to the front of the house!

And now, with a jolt of excitement, nerves, expectation, she made her way to finally meet the man that Zoe had chosen.

* * *

As Lucie passed through the garden, she saw Deva and tapped him lightly on the arm.

'Want to come and meet Rafi with me?'

Because it seemed perfectly right that after their adventures together Deva should be there too.

'Of course,' he said, so together they walked out of the garden, through the beautiful building and out to the wide, lit-up driveway at the front.

There, a taxi was pulling away and a tall, slim, young man, dark-haired, Middle Eastern looking, undeniably handsome, all suited and booted with a backpack and a small suitcase was walking towards Zoe. She was hurrying, as best she could in her pink kitten heels and heavily pregnant state, towards him, arms out, calling his name.

As they reached each other, they didn't hug and kiss; instead, they held out their hands and took hold of them and looked into one another's eyes. Then, to Lucie's surprise, Zoe began to kneel.

'Oh my God! She's going to propose,' Lucie whispered to Deva.

Rafi was laughing and trying to pull Zoe up, but when it was clear she was determined and not going to budge, he went down too, so they were both kneeling right there in the dust and gravel of the driveway.

Words were exchanged and smiles and laughter and, judging by Zoe's eye wiping, also tears.

And then they kissed and hugged over the top of her bump.

'Well... what do we think of that? Looks like they've both said yes,' Lucie murmured, feeling quite weak-kneed at the emotion of it all. She might be a fifty-two-year-old divorced woman, but she certainly hadn't forgotten how it felt to be young, optimistic, full of love and full of hope that everything would turn out wonderfully.

'That is very nice...' Deva said. 'He does look like a super nice guy, but my A-dar is picking up the vibes...'

'Your what?'

'My A-dar, my autistic radar... The way he holds himself, the hints of overwhelm, touches of awkwardness... I can't quite describe it to you. I just get the vibes, even from here. And from what she's said about him, of course. It's a spectrum,' Deva added when he saw the anxious look on his aunt's face. 'Best to know you're on it and learn how to manage yourself rather than thinking you're just "weird" and don't get people and can't seem to do anything right.'

'You think Rafi is autistic?' Lucie spluttered.

'We prefer "neurodiverse" these days, and honestly, it is everywhere. Where do you think the expression "black sheep of the family" comes from? Almost every family has a bit of neurodiversity going on. As I say' – Deva gave a shrug – 'best to know. Best to figure yourself out and learn the tools of the neurodiverse trade. And on that note, I really need to retreat to my room, get my headphones on, the tunes on, process the last hour or two and chill. Say congrats to them from me...'

'Yes, of course...'

Just before he turned to go, Deva had one more question. 'Auntie L?'

'Yes?'

'Will you take me back to Brive? To the convent?'

'Yes, of course. I am going to spend one day and night at my beach hotel, so we'll go on Monday. And we'll visit Fikru and Pete too.'

'Perfect. Turns out my mum, if she's still talking to me, has booked us to stay on here for three nights before we fly home. So Monday is perfect. Thank you. And I can take the train back from Brive, so you can carry on driving. In fact, I want to take the train back from Brive.'

And with a swish of Chanel lace over the gravel, Deva strode towards the front door.

Lucie stood where she was. She thought Rafi and Zoe might want some moments together before she approached them. In fact, she decided to take out her phone and snap a few pics of them from a distance. Here they were, beautifully dressed, beaming with happiness at one another in this gorgeous, floodlit driveway. She held her phone steady and snapped a few frames.

Then, hand in hand, Zoe and Rafi turned and began to walk towards the house, catching sight of her as they approached.

'Mum! Hello, meet Rafi, my lovely fiancé!'

Everyone dissolved into smiles and laughter at those words.

'Hello, Rafi, and huge congratulations to you both!' Lucie said.

Rafi held out his hand for her to shake as Lucie cast her eyes over him and tried to work out everything she could from just looking at this man who was about to join her family. Tall, handsome, quiet, gentlemanly, he didn't look entirely at home in that dark suit and white shirt, but he didn't look entirely uncomfortable either. He'd picked a nice tie, she saw, navy blue with a subtle white dot pattern. It was a bit mumsy, but she couldn't help noticing that his shoes were well made and spotless. All this spoke to her of a man who cared about the details, someone who knew how to look after himself and would help to look after both Zoe and their baby.

He had a nice smile. And he felt like a quiet presence, but not as shy or uncomfortable as she'd maybe suspected. He seemed like a grown up, his own man, when she'd expected a troubled computer geek, someone Zoe would have to care for and cajole and rescue. This was all promising, very promising.

And Zoe, tucked in under his arm, radiated sheer happiness.

'This is lovely, lovely news,' Lucie told them. 'I am so happy for you both. Are you going to announce it here? Let everyone know?' she asked, knowing that for now, all those other questions – *When? Where? Before the baby is born? After?* Could wait until the couple had spent some time thinking them through.

Rafi and Zoe exchanged a look before Zoe said: 'No! Absolutely not! We'll tell Dad tomorrow, no stealing any limelight from his big day. I think we should just go in, say hello and maybe have a dance, Raf... Are you up for that?'

Rafi smiled, shrugged and looked at Zoe as if he couldn't possibly refuse anything tonight.

'OK, lovebirds,' Lucie said, 'you lead the way.'

So there was Lucie, holding a fresh glass of something. The waiter had pressed it into her hands. It tasted strong, a vermouth-based cocktail, she guessed. Woosh, it seemed to travel straight to her head. Maybe for some people the night was still young, but she was beginning to feel about one thousand years old and as if she doubted she could last another ten minutes here in this marquee. She pulled up a chair at a deserted table and for a few moments sat alone, sipping at the drink. The lights were dim and people were mainly dancing close, like Zoe and Rafi over there, or talking in little huddles away from the speakers.

Her eyes were drawn back to the dancefloor – Miles with Jacasta, Rafi with Zoe, other couples she had known during her married life, who'd managed to stay close, stay together. *Oh no,* she couldn't help thinking to herself, *I'm going to be that faded middle-aged lady who sits alone on the sidelines at parties, feeling a bit sorry for herself... feeling that the glory days are all behind her.*

She decided she shouldn't do that.

She should get out of there, with the remains of her cocktail, into the garden and either find someone interesting, or at least amusing, to talk to, or go and admire some artful arrangements of lighting and flowers. Maybe she should take an upbeat selfie and post it on her Instagram account. Maybe she should take that upbeat selfie and post it on Tinder... or whatever the singletons were using these days.

Another swig of cocktail, then she set a smile on her face, tried to shrug off the lonely faded-lady thoughts and stepped out of the tent and round to the quieter part of the garden along the side, where she'd seen some tables and chairs set out earlier.

Out here, it was full of flowers and pretty, dimly lit with fairy lights and small lanterns on the tables. Quite beautiful really. At first, she thought no one else was there. Then she saw there was one lone man, sitting at a table, a single glass on the tabletop beside him. He turned his head at her approach, almost as if he was waiting for her.

And it was Clark.

26

'Oh Lucie, hello!' He jumped up.

'Clark... Hi...'

He pulled out a chair for her.

'I'd love you to come and sit with me,' he said. Then with something of a small laugh he added, 'I was sitting out here hoping you would somehow come along. Because I remember that you used to only like partying for so long and then you want the quiet again.'

Wow. She felt a little bowled over that he could remember that.

She liked his accent, English but with an unmistakable Californian twang. He must have been over there for a while. He still looked Californian. The way he casually wore that white tux jacket with the shirt undone by a few buttons, a little rumpled too. He was tanned, his hair was well cut and he had nice teeth, straight, strong, not too glaringly white. Plus, he was relaxed, a little slouchy in the chair. And his eyes didn't seem to leave her face. That was... no denying it: sexy.

Lucie took her time, placing her drink down on the table,

settling down onto the chair, pulling it to the right angle to face him. She took her time because this was making her so nervy and excited that she had to try and calm down. And he had been so insightful about her that she needed a little time to think about how to make sure that her reply was as perfect as his words had been.

Finally, she went for, 'It's just too good to see you again. Why have we not been in touch for decades?' with as much eye contact and sincerity as she dared.

'It's so good to see you too...' he replied with that half smile and something of a light laugh. She remembered it exactly and could feel the hairs on the back of her neck stand up.

'I didn't expect you to be here...' he began. 'In fact, what the hell are you doing here? This is your ex-husband's wedding night – you should be on the other side of the world in a hot tub full of eligible young men.'

She slightly splurted a little bit of cocktail at that.

'I had no intention of being here,' she insisted. 'But I had to drive Zoe and my nephew down and... long story. And probably a total mistake. Until I bumped into you, obviously.' She gave him her best smile and they held the look.

'I have missed you,' he said.

'Really? Clark... twenty-eight freaking years have passed. You never wrote, you never called.'

'Please don't remind me how old I am. Don't do it.'

'And what in the bloody hell are you doing here, by the way?'

'Stalking you, obvs,' he joked immediately.

'Ha!'

'No, I'm here because I did a business thing with Miles...'

'Oh yeah, I heard. I will be informing my lawyer and claiming my share...' she replied. She remembered how easy he was to talk to, how open, honest and how funny he was. How he used to make her funny too.

'Very good. So I told him we were holidaying nearby and he insisted we drop in on his wedding.'

Ah, there was the 'we'. The chill of the 'we'. Whatever warmth, lingering eye contact and interested vibes she'd thought she wanted to put across, she reined them right in now because, once again, he was oh-so-interesting, but unavailable.

'So here we are... in a glorious French garden...' he went on. 'And how are you? How has it been?'

'What? The divorce?' she asked, startled by the question.

'No, being married to Miles for all this time? I mean, that is one pompous little prick. I always thought that and nothing about my recent dealings with him has proved me wrong.'

She felt another snort of cocktail coming on.

'You are well shot of him. Hot tub full of eligible young men. That is the way to go. Oh, there's a waiter. Hello! Yup, over here,' he called, then with a winning smile, he asked for, 'Two more of those gorgeous drinks, please, for me and one of my oldest friends.'

Two fresh cocktails were set out on the table in front of them.

'Oh boy,' Lucie said, unsure if she could manage another mouthful.

'We've got a lot of catching up to do. Cheers.'

They clinked glasses together, eyes meeting, Lucie flooding with the memory of being twenty-four and being just desperate for this man to feel the way about her that she felt about him.

'So you're shot of Miles, you're shot of the suburban home in Bromley, shot of the millstone businesses. I'm guessing you're coping admirably, living the life, planning your next big move,' he told her. 'And... can I just say, looking not at all so different from when I knew you. How do you manage that? Is there a lot of excellent quality "tweakments" involved? C'mon, you can tell me. We're old, old friends. But not so old,' he corrected himself quickly.

What was this look he was giving her? So warm, so connecting, so understanding. It was almost too easy to talk to him, too easy for him to understand her thoughts. That was what she remembered from before. The natural barrier that existed between people, it just seemed to blur and melt between them. That was exactly how it was before. Too easy. Too straightforward to talk and be understood by him.

And how could he still be so handsome? He must be past the mid-fifty mark... Could she ever have imagined she would be attracted to someone who was that age? But look at those shoulders, the waistline, the lean, rangy physique, hair that was steel grey, but still thick and well cut.

He looked at ease with himself, no hair dye, no need for plugs. She doubted very much that there were man Spanx under his suit. And she suddenly longed to tell him about Miles and the man Spanx... Another sip or two of this cocktail and she probably would.

'So, what about Clark?' she asked. 'Tell me all about you. How long did you stay in the US? When did you meet your wife? Are there any other children to go with the lovely daughter?'

She thought these sobering questions would be the best way to back off from all the complicated feelings passing between them. Questions like this would give them both a brisk reminder that they couldn't just pick up from where they'd been in their twenties.

Clark seemed to jerk back in his chair slightly.

'My wife? I managed to stay in America long enough to acquire two ex-wives.'

'Oooh dear. That sounds expensive.'

'Correct. I could be living in a mansion in Kensington now without those vultures – and I mean the lawyers. The ex-wives are fine. All perfectly civil. Four children, Lucie, four...'

He held up four fingers and added, 'All in the States, but almost all grown up, so the co-parenting gets easier. They want a lot less parent time.'

He took a swig of his drink. 'Good luck to Miles,' he added. 'Because Jacasta has the look of a woman who will be clamouring for babies very soon. I foresee twins, who will need university and a car and a flat and he is going to be working forever. No, no, strictly no more wives or children for me.'

Lucie couldn't help her smile at this and she could also feel just this little surge of hope. Hadn't he just said 'no more wives or children'? Did this mean Dita was his girlfriend? Or could this possibly mean that he was somehow... free?

Just to make absolutely certain she'd understood what was going on, she had to ask him, 'But didn't you introduce Dita as your wife?'

Clark's eyebrows rose.

And there was a pause.

Lucie could feel herself holding her breath.

This answer mattered. It really mattered. It was make or break, do or die...

'No!' Clark exclaimed. 'Or... I think you've misunderstood me. Dita is my daughter's wife. Does that clear up the mystery?'

'Oh!' Lucie let her breath out in a rush and felt a smile spread across her face. 'Oh, of course! I must have misheard... or, I'm sorry, assumed...'

Absolute rush of inner relief.

Inner laughter.

Inner dancing around on the lawn barefoot under the sprinkler.

But... but... whoa... hold your horses, she warned herself. How does one get from here – two old work colleagues meeting at a wedding after two and a bit decades... to where her crazed, quite wildly overheated imagination seemed to want to lead her?

Overthinking, overthinking...

Maybe – take a steadying sip of cocktail, she told herself – *maybe just sit out here and talk a bit more and let's slow it right down and take this one baby step at a time.* She had been in a marriage for most of her adult life. Even thinking about moving on to a new person was huge.

But moving on to someone who'd been so important to you in your early twenties... that was even huger. Yes, she needed to slow this right down and just focus on the talking part. Talking to Clark.

'So you're single?' she asked.

'Oh yes,' he replied. 'Just like you.'

'Hot tub full of models?'

'Not so much these days,' he said and then laughed. 'To be honest, I've been more or less single for four years. No good people left out there... I hate to tell you.'

'Single? You? You could charm anyone into bed when I knew you.'

'And look how that worked out for me – two ex-wives, four children, that I know about.'

Single? This man? This gorgeous, emotionally connected, successful, good-looking man. That was a red flag right there. How in the heck was he still unattached? Even if he had become a little commitment phobic.

She was all caught up in his eyes, in his smiles. *He's been waiting...* she found herself thinking. *Waiting for the right time... the right person... Maybe I could be that right person at the right time?* And just thinking that felt as if she'd poured some sort of exhilarating glass of chilled water over her head.

'So... Lucie Chilvers,' Clark began. 'Still sneaking pop stars out of bars? Still crashing the very best parties? Wearing the very best outfits?' he asked, tipping his head a little in the direction of her dress. 'That dress... it looks very 1990s... looks like something I remember you wearing one very good night.'

'Oh...' She smiled at him. 'Yeah, that was a good night. I remember it. I remember that dress...' she said. It felt exciting that he still remembered *those* stories about her.

'I was in danger of getting extremely boring – until I set off in the car to France. And it's been non-stop adventure since then. Non-stop, and still an adventure right now.' She looked at him.

'I suspect there's still a vein... still a rebellious streak that you like to tap into... that you can't deny,' he said.

Maybe the cocktail had gone to her head, but this, the tone of voice as he said it, the eye contact, the smile... she felt, for the first time in a long time, oh yes, she felt sexy. And daring... and that it was, just like all those years ago, quite a real physical effort to keep her hands off this man. She wanted to move right up to him, put her arm and her shoulder against his, move her leg next to his and feel his warmth, feel what she suspected would crackle between them, just as it had before.

And it had been such a long time since she'd felt like this.

'Maybe,' was all she could manage as they held a long look.

'So what are you up to? Post-Miles, post Ultimate Interiors.'

'Oh... you knew about my company?'

'Yes, I used to look at your website now and then – you did very nice work. I was thinking of commissioning you...'

'You looked me up? You cyber-stalked me? And you never thought to say hello?'

Quite a heady, dizzy feeling was coming over her.

'But...'

The word seemed to hang in the air between them, as if he didn't want to say what stopped him. And she suddenly guessed, because he had worried their feelings would break out all over them again – and she had been married all that time.

'You're probably regrouping after everything that's happened. And I'm excited to see what you'll do next. Maybe we could do some work together in the future?' he suggested to her surprise.

'Regrouping,' she liked his suggestion that she was 'regrouping'.

That was a good word. Why hadn't she thought of it like that before? She'd gone through a brutal divorce, the loss of her company, now her husband's re-marriage and her dad's illness. Understandably, she might sometimes feel as if everything was over and hopeless and she wasn't sure what she was going to do next – but how much better to think of it as regrouping. There could be all kinds of exciting times and opportunities ahead, especially if this man could somehow be involved.

'Lucie,' he began, 'I don't know if you ever had the feeling that...' He paused and she could feel her heart revving up again. The way he was looking at her, she just knew he was going to say something serious, important... maybe even about *them.* 'We could have had something, together... back then?'

'Yes...' she heard herself reply, 'I definitely had that feeling... sitting here next to you, I'm remembering just how strong that feeling was.'

She leaned in a little closer towards him.

Could she really? she wondered. Could she come out of her carefully created and barricaded divorced mum self and start something with this intriguing man who was possibly going to make her have all those deep and difficult feelings all over again? Could she bear to have her hopes lifted? Risk her feelings? Risk having them dashed? She wasn't sure, but she was thinking that she could be willing to try.

Permission to do something extraordinary...

'I should tell you that my dad is very ill,' she began. 'He's going to die in a month or two. I'm going to be very involved with him. And I'm going to be very, very sad about it...'

She swallowed to clear the lump from her throat.

'I am so sorry.'

Clark reached over to put his arm around her, and it was comforting to be held tightly, wrapped up, in the way that she was used to comforting and wrapping other people up, but she hadn't had this for herself for a long time. So that made the lump in her throat even harder.

'I've waited all this time to connect with you again. I can wait a bit longer,' he said, and that felt like the best thing he could have said.

'You come to me when you're ready,' he added. 'Come on, get out your phone and let me give you all my details. Just promise me you will be in touch.'

Once the contact details were stored, they didn't say anything for a few moments, but became conscious of the music coming from the tent. Deva was singing again and Clark, a smile on his face, asked, 'Would you like to dance, wild girl of the nineties?'

She hadn't danced for an age... wasn't even sure if she could remember a single move. But still found herself getting to her feet and telling him, 'Yes, let's go dance.'

* * *

As soon as they had stepped into the tent and found a place on the dancefloor, Deva spotted her, stopped the song he was singing in its tracks and made an announcement to the crowd, over the backing music still playing.

'Wait a minute, wait a minute, everyone, someone very special has just stepped onto the dancefloor. Hello, Auntie Lucie, I'm going to sing something just for you.'

'Uh oh!' Lucie looked up at Clark. 'Rumbled...'

Deva conferred briefly with the DJ and musicians and after a few moments Lucie heard chords... Not the nineties anthem that she had perhaps expected, but still a familiar song. She remembered Zoe loving this, playing it in her room, listening to it in the car, both of them singing along.

And there was Deva, still rocking the dress, gripping the microphone right up to his mouth, as he cut straight to the chorus of the Kelly Clarkson anthem and told his auntie in song that what didn't kill her would make her stronger *and stand a little taller*.

Joining in with the words, Lucie started to dance. She felt uncertain, stiff and more than a little jerky and out of practice at first, but she carried on, inspired by Deva's voice, until she was warmed up and confident. And then she really was dancing the way she remembered from way back, and laughing, and looking deep into the eyes of this man from such a long time ago.

In the middle of that dance, with Clark holding her hands and dancing right alongside her, she remembered her father's words:

'Drink champagne, kick off your heels, dance on the grass, and remember that life is to be lived.'

Oh yes, life was to be lived again. How many times had she put off living today in the hope that her real life, all the good things, would come another day?

He was here, right in front of her. Maybe she shouldn't put anything about this off for another moment. They had wasted enough time already.

So she moved towards him, put her arms around his waist and moved in to kiss him. Right on the mouth. And that was electrifying. So much more exciting and interesting and quite frankly *hot* than she'd expected. That was some California kissing action, she suspected as he pulled her against him, there on the cosy darkness of the dancefloor, other bodies brushing and bumping against them.

Surprising herself even further, she said against Clark's ear, 'I have a gorgeous room in the Maison. What do you think about taking the kissing there?'

'We could definitely take the kissing there,' Clark agreed. 'This is your ex's wedding night... and if you don't have a hot tub full of guys to take your mind off it, I'll have to try and help.'

She leaned in to kiss him on the neck and found herself looking over Clark's shoulder directly into Zoe's eyes.

Zoe's eyebrows may have been up almost to her hairline, but she still grinned and gave her mum a distinct thumbs up.

27

Heading up the stairs hand in hand felt absolutely thrilling. Lucie couldn't help thinking that as she had gone through all the downside of a divorce, it was about time that she enjoyed the upside. And every step on that staircase made her feel as if she was de-aging by a year. So by the time she was opening the door with her key, she felt giddy, light-hearted and as free as in her early twenties.

But once they were in the room, the lights on, her crumpled travel outfit thrown over a chair, her makeup scattered across the bedside table, it somehow felt a little too real. Yes, there was a real, living, breathing man standing right next to her, his arms around her waist, his face against her hair. And a wave of uncertainty washed over her now.

'It's been a while... I'm not sure if this is...' she began and trailed off.

Clark kept his arms in place, but immediately moved his head back so he could look her in the eye. He smiled and asked, 'OK, so how nervous are you on a scale of one to ten, where ten is pre-colonoscopy or maybe root canal without pain relief? Because I'm at about a six or seven.'

'Me too.' She smiled back.

'I mean, I haven't waxed anything,' he added. 'No part of me has been waxed since I left the States eight months ago. You probably thought I was wearing a t-shirt, but no, it's white fur.'

She burst out laughing at this and put her arms back around him.

'Oh my God, waxing... I haven't salon waxed since the financial crisis in 2008,' she admitted. 'Bromley's best beautician went bust and that was the end of it.'

'Well,' he began, kissing her lightly on the lips, 'I blame that crash for a lot of things, but I hadn't thought of all the furry suburban mummies it caused.'

'I'm furry...' she blurted. 'And nervous. It's really been quite a long time...'

'So, we are going to kiss and only do what's completely enjoyable. Does that sound OK? And FYI, I like the seventies vibe. Low lights, fur, I'm going to put classic Grace Jones on speakerphone and we can roll around on that big bed over there and have come completely grown-up fun. How does that sound?'

She wanted to tell him that it sounded perfect. It sounded like the exact solution to every single moment of angst that this wedding had caused her. And she was so happy that he was here and so interested. But instead, she heard herself muttering something about putting on something else... although she couldn't even think what that would be. It wasn't as if she'd packed the silky negligee and matching dressing gown that she would quite like to be wearing right now.

'No, no...' Clark was telling her ear in a way that was making her neck tingle and shiver. 'Leave your dress on, I love the dress, but take your underwear off. Does that work for you?'

'Yes... I think that could work for me.'

As she slid her bra out from under the dress straps and let her knickers fall to the floor, he turned off one of the side lights, tossed his jacket and shoes onto the carpet and, to the promised Grace Jones soundtrack, they fell onto the bed.

In between exploratory kisses, he told her, 'Just forget about the outside world. Totally forget it. We are here, we're alive, we're very happy to see each other again. We should have done this in our twenties, but let's make up for some lost time.'

She pulled open his shirt and ran her hand over the fur. 'Waxing is over-rated.' She giggled.

'Oh, tell me about it,' he groaned. 'All the ingrown hairs. This is perfect, "La Vie En Rose" has started and it is still the sexiest song in the universe.'

And it was... and he was unbelievably sexy too... and finally, when she managed to leave the outside world behind on the other side of that door, so was she.

* * *

When Lucie opened her eyes the next morning, she saw a cream-coloured ceiling and an ornate gold and crystal chandelier. For a few moments, she blinked and stared, absolutely no idea where she was. Then she lifted her fuzzy head and remembered that this was the pink bedroom in the chateau.

Oh... the pink bedroom! The wedding, the wine, the cocktails, the dancing and... Clark!

She turned her head sideways...

Oh. My. God. Clark.

There he was, asleep, beside her. Her mix of excitement, confusion and panic was real. Now what?

Now what?

Now what!

As if he could hear her thinking, he suddenly opened his eyes, looked right at her, smiled and said: 'Now what, Lucie Chilvers?'

'I think I need some water,' she replied. 'And a shower.'

'Yeah,' he agreed. 'Water. Shower. Coffee. Then a plan of action.'

And it turned out that after the water, shower, coffee and more kissing, the plan of action was simple. Clark suggested it and Lucie agreed.

'We leave in your Jag. We pick up a few of my things at the holiday cottage and then we go to your hotel by the sea.'

'For twenty-four hours of getting to know one another again,' she said. 'Then real life intervenes again because I have to pick up the loved-up Zoe, drive Deva to Brive, check on the Eritrean boys and head home.'

'Deva to Brive... check on the Eritrean boys?' Clark asked with surprise.

'C'mon, I'll tell you all about that in the car. I just need to let Zoe know I'll be back for her tomorrow.'

'Let's go down, she's probably having breakfast by now.'

'Go down there? Together?'

Lucie wasn't so sure.

'Oh, yeah definitely, blatantly,' Clark said with a smile. 'I'm wearing my outfit from yesterday. I'm doing the walk of shame. You, you're the lioness who dragged her prey back to her lair.'

He gave her a look which made her stomach give the kind of flip she hadn't felt for years.

She took a little time to choose the best summer dress from

her suitcase, style her hair and apply makeup and perfume. There was no need to run into Jacasta, the wedding girls, or anyone else roaming about Masion Violette this morning, looking like a faded version of herself.

'I'm regrouping,' she told her reflection in the mirror, and she patted on her favourite lipstick. Because regrouping sounded interesting and full of new possibilities.

Then they did, blatantly, stroll into the breakfast room, where – after walking past Miles, who understood immediately, *ha*! – they found Zoe, Rafi and Deva sitting together in a companionable huddle.

'Oh, hello, Mum,' Zoe said, eyebrows shooting up her forehead. 'You need to know that my fiancé, Rafi—' – she broke off to beam at him – 'is flying me home tomorrow. So you'll be driving back on your own. Will that be OK?'

'A lot less pee stops,' Lucie joked.

'But we're still doing Brive tomorrow?' Deva wanted to check.

'Yes, I'll be here at breakfast tomorrow to pick you up.'

'Perfect – so are you going to your seaside hotel? And is your new boyfriend going with you?' were his next questions.

There wasn't going to be any sneaking things past Deva, that was for sure.

'Ermm… yes… this is Clark,' she told them as Clark took a step forward, smiled and said, 'Great to meet you all.'

'We're old friends… from the nineties,' Lucie said and couldn't help the smile at these words.

'Oooh, you knew her when she was wild then?' Zoe asked. 'Not the suburban juggler of work and school run schedules that I grew up with?' But this came with both a wink and a smile at her mother.

'And yes, we're going to the coast… together.' Lucie tried to say it seriously, but she was so happy that it burst out alongside a little laugh.

'Hugs,' Zoe said, holding out her arms. 'Have a lovely break and see you when you're back. Love you.'

And holding Zoe close for that moment, Lucie told her with all truthfulness, 'So happy for you, darling, so excited.'

* * *

They didn't even go out to eat that night because it was too good to be together and they didn't want anything, or anyone, to spoil it or intrude. Instead, they sat on the balcony of the hotel room in their bubble of happiness and watched the red sun dip into the sea as they ate a picnic involving cheese, baguette and peaches – each thing more perfectly delicious than the last.

'What in the hell are you doing with me?' Lucie had to ask him as he sat at the little table opposite her and seemed to be unable to keep his eyes away from her face. 'You look bloody fantastic! You obviously jog and lift weights and do intermittent fasting or something very Californian.'

He laughed. 'Don't undersell yourself,' he said, putting his hand over hers. 'I think you have a very sexy Monica Bellucci thing going on and you don't even know it. Plus you have a brain. You get my jokes and you make your own jokes back. This is ground-breaking, life changing. My daughter is going to be very excited for me.'

'You sound very Californian... and I like it,' she admitted. 'Big change from the man who never told me what was going on. Do we have to go back to reality tomorrow?'

Clark leaned back in his chair and took a long look at her, before saying, 'You're going to drive me back to my girl and my little holiday cottage. Then you're going to take your nephew on his visit and check on your Eritreans. After that, you'll drive back to England and be with your dad for as long as you need to be. And whenever you're ready to have the Clark love back in your life, you will call me up and I will be right there waiting for you.'

'Do you promise?' she asked, because everything between them seemed too good to be true. 'You're not going to turn out to be the Tinder Swindler, are you? A breaker of divorced-lady hearts. Those people are out there. They are real, they exist.'

Clark just looked at her with kindness, sympathy and understanding. Then he said, 'No, none of those things, Lucie Chilvers. None of those. I am looking forward to enjoying complex, grown-up fun with you.'

'I'm going to wax,' she decided, 'so much.'

'God, so the freak am I,' he exclaimed. 'We'll be gliding against each other like a pair of damp chicken fillets the next time we meet.'

'That's an image,' Lucie laughed, 'but quite erotic. I'm getting quite turned on at that thought.'

'Me too... we need to get back inside.'

What had her father said?

'Maybe you'll meet someone interesting there. Have a fling! And wouldn't that be a wonderful revenge?'

Oh yes... and this was so much more than a fling, she already knew. This could turn out to be... everything. And she'd be able to say, forever, 'Yes, we met again at my ex-husband's wedding.'

28

MONDAY

'So, here we are...' Lucie announced as she rolled the car to a halt in the dusty, gravelly car park.

She had left the coast very early this morning, picking Deva up at Maison Violette not long after 7 a.m. so they could get onto the road to the convent well ahead of the holiday traffic, and they'd made good time. On the journey, Deva had told her so much about the Abbey, she didn't think any tour guide was going to be able to tell them more.

Now, here they were parked up in front of the mighty Aubazine Abbey, where Coco Chanel and her sister, Antoinette, were just little girls when they were dropped off by their father after the death of their mother. They would stay here, looked after by nuns, until they each reached the age of eighteen.

Lucie looked over at her nephew in the passenger's seat. It would be fair to say that Deva had made quite the effort for this trip. And already, he was looking in awe and almost overwhelmed by the moment.

He was wearing his black suit trousers and his smart black shoes, then on top, one of Lucie's silky blouses and the vintage cream Chanel tweed jacket that he had liberated from one of the boxes under the bed at her father's house. He had also added a large sparkling brooch, several pearl necklaces, and smoothed his hair down into the short Chanel-homage bob. He carried the black Chanel handbag, while Lucie toted the cream one, which Deva had lovingly cleaned up and polished after its Bastille Day adventures. He had also insisted on blasting them both with his bottle of No 5.

'I think we're ready,' Lucie announced.

'I can't decide if I want to tune in to the tour guide or take my headphones and listen to my Coco playlist as I go round,' Deva told her, an anxious look on his face.

Once again, he was as twitchy and nervy as he had been at the Place Vendôme in Paris, when she and Zoe had worried that he wouldn't get out of the car.

'Take your headphones,' she told him encouragingly. 'The tour might be in French, so no one will mind if you decide to tune out and listen to the music instead. You do you, remember. Where would the world be if Coco hadn't done Coco?'

At those words, he turned and gave her a smile that assured her she'd said the right thing.

She opened the car door on her side, got out and was relieved to see that he did the same. Then they went to the entrance, paid for the tickets, and climbed the steps into the imposing building.

As soon as they set foot inside, it was so obvious to see all the rustic, but classically beautiful, influences that had followed Chanel her whole life. The walls, floors and staircases were all built of solid, creamy limestone, while the beams, benches and tables were pale scrubbed wood.

'She had an exact replica of this staircase built in her house in the south of France,' Deva whispered.

When they stood together in the high, vaulted chapel, Deva pointed out the simple black and white stained-glass windows with designs that could not have looked more like the famous interlocking Cs.

'Look at that,' he whispered to her. 'I think of her as a little girl gazing up at that window every day, seeing her initials and dreaming about how she's going to be not just an orphan girl, but someone important. Somehow, she knows that the world will recognise her initials and she has no idea how this is going to happen, but her ambition is huge.'

The guide walked them past cupboards of folded white linen, and everywhere was the smell of incense and the scent of lavender from bags of the dried herb and from the fields beyond the Abbey.

It was all magnificent and abundant in scale, but also pure, scrubbed clean and humble.

The silence of the stone corridors, the cleanliness, the purity and simplicity were awe-inspiring. The abbey was hundreds of years old, but Lucie could see that it was also as timeless and contemporary as a Scandi-inspired Pinterest page. Walking around, taking it all in, she was beginning to feel all kinds of inspiration of her own bubbling up.

When she was ready, she would go back to interior design, she decided as she took her phone out to capture the creamy flagstones in this corridor. But she wouldn't do things that were flashy or gimmicky like before, no. She would focus on solid, lasting, timeless, classic design. The very best materials, the most pared-back looks. Black, earthy tones, cream, white, wood, stone – all the wonderful neutrals. The name 'Classically Yours' came to mind. And for the first time in months, maybe even years, Lucie felt properly excited about going back to the work she was meant to be doing.

* * *

It was a wonderful visit and totally inspiring for them both. Afterwards, they had to sit in the car and talk it over. Lucie telling Deva how profoundly beautiful she'd found it and Deva sitting with a look of almost tearful rapture on his face.

'And how about your mum?' Lucie asked him when they'd shared all their thoughts about the Abbey. 'Have you two been able to make it up at all? Is she getting over her shock at The Dress?'

'I was really worried that we would fall out forever,' he admitted, 'but I'm just not going to freak myself out about it any more. I have to be me. The way Coco had to be Coco. That's just fact, Auntie L. Fact,' he declared firmly. 'She'll come round because she loves me. It might take her a while, but I think in my heart, she'll come round. This is me. This is who I have to be.' He turned to smile at her and for a brief moment, their eyes made contact, before his gaze moved slightly and seemed to look at her face, but not directly into her eyes. As if he was doing something he'd been taught to do but didn't really want to.

'It's OK, Deevs. If you want to look up and all around while you talk, it's fine. It's just me.'

'OK... so,' he began, 'I'm going to stop learning about finance and start studying musical theatre. I'm going to sing better, dance better, go to auditions. Toughen up as a performer. Learn how to handle rejection and get better and better every single day. Commit to the craft,' he said, then added, 'Think about all the thousands of hours Coco spent here, sewing sheets, embroidering napkins, darning and patching old clothes before she started to create her hats, then her jersey tunics and only much later did she move on to lace gowns and those still unmatched jackets made from cashmere-spun tweed. I've got to start the acting and singing equivalent of hemming sheets, until my stitches are immaculate.'

'I am so proud of you,' Lucie told him, trying to hold back the happy tears that his words were provoking. 'Really proud. You go for it, Deva. And like you say, your family will come round.'

'What about you?' he asked. 'What are you going to do next? And was that really your new boyfriend?'

'Ha...' She laughed and felt a little jolt of excitement at the thought of Clark. 'I'm going to be with my dad for the next few... months, hopefully. Then I'm going to launch a new interior design business, totally inspired by the convent... And hopefully, yes, I will be spending some time with Clark. The aim, Deva, is to get out of this safe little cocoon I've built around myself.'

These words made Deva laugh. 'Safe little cocoon... That's exactly it. Exactly! Down with safe little cocoons!'

* * *

Then they drove to the hospital and tracked Pete and Fikru down. Fikru, looking frail and skinny, was lying fully dressed on his hospital bed, while Pete was seated on the plastic chair beside him, his collection of plastic bags at his feet.

At the sight of them, Pete smiled brightly and jumped to his feet.

'Hello, Miss Lucie and Deva!' he exclaimed.

There was enough phone signal in the ward for them to be able to use the internet and find enough phrases in Pete's language to work out that they were planning to leave today. They were going to walk and maybe hitchhike, if they could, with the aim of getting to the north coast and then on to the UK. From what Lucie could make out, they had an uncle in London, who had something to do with cars or garages, and he was going to help them.

'Not France.' Pete was shaking his head. 'Not French, we have no families here.'

'But is Fikru ready to leave?' Lucie asked, looking at the frail boy stretched out over the bed. He didn't look ready to get up and walk about the ward yet, let alone start walking, or hitch-hiking to England.

'Fikru is good,' Pete declared, and Fikru managed a cheerful smile.

And now, the solution seemed obvious to Lucie.

'You and Fikru' – she pointed to Pete and his brother in turn – 'drive in the car with me' – she pointed to herself – 'to Calais.'

When this had filtered through to them, Pete dissolved into smiles of gratitude and explained it in excited terms to Fikru. Fikru managed a smile but was too tired out to do much more.

29

First, Deva had to be put on the train back to Perpignan.

Before he boarded, he handed back the blouse, the tweed jacket and the handbag, as he'd now changed into a t-shirt for travelling.

'Some outfits aren't for every day,' he told her.

'I'm going to give you the dress, the jacket and one of the bags,' Lucie decided.

'Auntie Lucie, you can't!' he protested.

'I can! You have to have the dress you wore when you were singing to the hilltops. It was a very important moment for you...'

'The most important,' Deva said.

'Exactly, so you need to have that one as your inspiration. That dress is your reminder never to let your song stay inside when you need to share it with us all.'

'Oh my God. That's amazing. This whole trip has been amazing. Thank you so much. Can I have a hug?' he asked.

'I was going to ask you the same thing.' She smiled and held out her arms.

'Thank you,' he told her again. 'You're my fairy godmother.'

'Thank you,' she told him. 'Zoe and I loved getting to know you properly. Don't be a stranger, and we will be coming to your first show. So you better let us know where and when it's happening.'

* * *

Back at the hospital, Lucie led the two boys, one still weak and a little dazed, and the other with his shabby rucksack and collection of plastic bags, to her car. They wanted to sit together on the back seat and keep their precious bags, with all their possessions, beside them.

Once she'd made sure they were safely belted in, she put a bag of food and drinks she'd picked up between them.

'Something to eat, some water to drink,' she encouraged. 'We drive for two hours' – she held up two fingers to try and convey her meaning – 'then we stop for a rest. But if you need to stop before, tell me.'

They smiled and nodded, but it was hard to tell if they'd understood much. Nevertheless, she set off, guided by the satnav towards the big toll motorways that would take them directly through France, without any Chanel-themed detours this time, and up towards the north.

She settled into the seat and prepped herself for a long, long drive. It was already two o'clock in the afternoon. Now that the tunnel trains were running again, she wanted to change her ferry ticket for the train and knew that the last train left just before midnight, so if she was going make it in time, she would have to stick to the main motorways, keep her speed up, the breaks short and focus on getting there.

Just before she set off, she checked her phone one last time and saw with a skip of the heart that a new message had come in from her father's carer, Domenica.

> Dear Miss Lucie, I hope you won't be upset, but we are going to move your dad into HQ, as you know he calls it, later today. He has reached a new stage and we can't give him the pain meds he needs any more. He is glad you're not here for this day, as he is saying a long goodbye to his house and his garden and he didn't want you to be sad for him. He is so cheerful still and looking forward to seeing you, Zoe, Ritchie and family when you all get here. Much love to you, Domenica.

Quickly, Lucie replied to Domenica and sent a message full of love to her dad's phone. Her dad was going to the hospice today... weeks ahead of what he had expected. Or maybe weeks ahead of what he had wanted her to expect. Now, her reason to get to Calais in time for that last train was even more urgent.

* * *

She had been on the road for several hours when a call came in from Zoe.

'Hello! How is my engaged daughter?' Lucie greeted her, glad to have something else to think about on this long, featureless stretch through France.

'How are you, Mum? I was thinking of you driving that massive car all on your own. Are you OK?'

'Yes, fine, honestly, don't worry about me. I hated being on the boat, so I'm going to take the tunnel home. Hoping to be on that train by midnight, so gunning it through France. Here's hoping that mechanic repair holds up well.'

'You take care of yourself, Mum. Take all the breaks you need.'

'I will...' She glanced in the mirror at the two young men, both asleep in the back of the car, and decided she wouldn't mention them.

'And how's Clark?' Zoe had to ask, sounding like she was trying not to giggle.

'Oh... well... gone back to his holiday cottage to continue his holiday.'

'Missing him yet?'

'Too soon, Zoe, too soon. But it's all very interesting. I will keep you posted.'

'You better.'

'What about you?' she asked her daughter. 'How are you and Rafi, and has your maternity leave started yet?'

'Another week of waddling around the ward. Then that's it. Me and Rafi are good. Very good...' She could almost hear the little sigh of happiness that came with this.

'House hunting again?'

'Online only, we need this little girl to arrive before we kick into action on that front. Making wedding plans though. I'll tell you all about that.'

'Booking the wedding swing?' Lucie asked, and they both burst into laughter.

'You know, Jacasta did actually post a swing-breaking video with a #noweddingisperfect hashtag and it's had... 66k views so far. So good for her.'

'Yeah, I suppose so,' Lucie agreed. 'One thing...' she began. 'I know you're about to have a baby and about to get married and looking for somewhere to live and all those very big things, but you probably want to know that your grampa is being moved into the hospice today...'

'Oh, Mum, is he?'

And now Lucie found herself struggling to keep her voice level. 'Yes... and I'm going to be there with him every day, once I'm back. And I hope it's OK... but Zoe, could you come up and see us? Just as much as you can? Because you are so strong and so amazing with patients,' Lucie swallowed before adding, 'I don't know if I can do this without you.'

'Yes, of course, Mum, of course. Let's go together for your first visit because that will be hard. Him not being at home and you being all emotional about it. Do you think that will be tomorrow? Afternoon? You'll need some time to go home and rest first.'

'Ummm...' Lucie tried to work out the timings. And yes, she would need to factor in some rest. 'Maybe about 3 or 4 p.m. tomorrow?' she decided. 'I don't know how long we'll stay... how long we'll be able to...'

'Hospices are completely chill. It's all about the patient and their family. We'll be completely looked after, don't worry about it. There will be food, somewhere to rest, sleep, everything you need. Maybe even somewhere to give birth,' she joked.

'What about your work?'

'Let me call them up and do a bit of rota shuffling. To be honest, they're expecting me to drop out at any moment, so I should be able to sort it.'

They ended the call, promising to see each other the next day. And Lucie felt as if a weight had been lifted from her shoulders. Zoe... Zoe was more than fine, she was amazing. And all that mother–daughter tension around Rafi and the baby and what Zoe was doing with her life, it was hard to believe how quickly that had all melted away. They had just needed to spend some time together and really listen to one another. She felt so relieved that what had been strained and difficult between them had eased and, for now, they were totally back on track.

She drove and drove and drove. Only stopping every few hours at service stations to refuel and to take Pete and Fikru with her into the cafés for toilet stops and something to eat and drink. She could see the surprised looks that people at counters and behind tills were giving her when she, all dressed and made up with a posh bag and shades, came in with two tired, shabby young men who didn't speak much and clutched at the precious bags that they didn't even want to leave in the car.

They didn't ask for much, the boys. They seemed to like sugary, milky teas and snack foods. She wondered if weeks of not eating much meant they didn't have an appetite for anything bigger. Often Fikru had to lean on his brother, because he was still so weak. And when she saw that, she didn't even want to think about these two young souls drifting about Calais, falling in with gangs, paying whatever money they might have left to gangsters prepared to put them into the back of lorries, or even worse, pack them onto inflatable dinghies to try and cross the Channel.

They were kids – Pete was only just out of his teens and Fikru didn't look as if he'd left his teens yet. Lucie wondered if she could hand them over to the care of an organisation in Calais, take them somewhere where they could be safe?

30

It was almost 11 p.m. when they entered the outskirts of Calais and the signs directing traffic to the ferries and the Channel train began to appear at the roadside. There were other sights on the side of the road too. Huddles of people with sleeping bags, rucksacks, and carrier bags with their belongings.

Pete and Fikru had been awake for an hour or so and seemed to realise that the end of the drive was approaching for them. They were tidying up the back seat, draining the last of the water from the bottles, checking and re-checking the belongings in their own bags, as they bravely prepared themselves to get out of the car and into the unknown. All Lucie could think about was the boys, younger than Deva, who had quietly slept almost all the way through France, and the horrible stories on the news about smuggler gangs and refrigerated lorries and dinghies...

'The car can stop here?' Pete asked from the back seat, and he pointed to a big supermarket coming up on the side of the road.

She indicated and turned off, then drove into the car park.

The enormous supermarket was still brightly lit and open. Outside it was another huddle of young people who looked as skinny and uncertain as the boys in the back of the car.

Pete tried his best to smile and look cheerful. Maybe he had a sense of how nervous she was for them.

'Very, very thank you very much,' he told her.

'Pete, I don't think this is a safe place. I want to take you to the Red Cross, to a proper camp where people will look after you.'

She wasn't sure if he'd understood, but he just smiled again and repeated his 'very, very thank you'.

Then he spoke to Fikru in their language. Fikru nodded and gathered one of the bags into his hand. And maybe Lucie would have let them leave the car and take their chances in the darkness with all the other refugees seen and unseen around them.

But two things happened. Fikru made just the smallest sniff and wipe of his eyes as he prepared to exit the safety of the car. And a loud and angry scuffle broke out among one group of people in the car park.

Lucie immediately imagined the two of them in a dinghy – frail Fikru, just out of hospital. And she thought about someone robbing whatever was left in their precious plastic bags. And she just couldn't do it.

They were Eritrean... They were escaping war and persecution. They would almost certainly be allowed to claim asylum in the UK. She had googled it during their last café stop. They had an uncle to stay with, but they had no visa to get them into the UK to their uncle.

She thought back to those days of sneaking in and out of nightclubs and getting minor celebrities out of the back of gigs away from fans and photographers. It was always good to have some kind of decoy or distraction, even a towel, a pretence that someone was sick or injured... something to just take people's mind off thinking too much about things.

If she was going to do what she thought she might, she needed a decoy. She had a big car... she'd been on a short trip to France, and right over there was a massive supermarket that was still open. And now a plan, not too complicated, just needing a little bit of nerve, fell almost fully formed into her mind.

Best to just get on with it, she told herself. Plans like this, you didn't want to mull them over too much. You needed to just smile, be bold, and crack on.

'Stay in car. Stay here,' she told the boys as she drove the car to the brightly lit spaces right beside the supermarket entrance. Then she got out of the Jag, shut the door and locked them both inside, after making sure they understood her. 'Please wait, in car, for me.'

Inside the supermarket, she grabbed a trolley and hurried to the shelves of wine. She bundled whichever bottles were nearest into the trolley until she had about forty of them. At the till, she managed to convey to the cashier that she needed some boxes. Her simple idea was to put two boxes of wine in the boot of the Jag and one on the back seat. Then the boys would hide in the back seat footwells, covered by a jacket or two.

The wine was there to give her and whoever was on passport control something to have a tiny chat about. Put their minds at rest that she was just your average Englishwoman stocking up the wine cellar in Calais.

Back at the car, she packed the boxes of bottles into the boot and then onto the seat beside the boys. She tried to explain to the now anxious, wide-eyed boys what she had decided to do.

She used the simplest words. For their benefit and also for

hers. She wanted it to sound completely straightforward. She wanted it to sound as if it would be an easy enough thing to do.

'Pete, you and Fikru will hide in the car. And I will take you to London.'

It didn't seem to register. So, she tried to show them. 'Hide in car.' She put her arms over her head. 'I drive.' She pointed to the steering wheel. 'London, UK.'

It dawned gradually.

A slow spreading of joyful smiles, first on Pete's face as he realised, then on Fikru's as the words were translated.

She was the one feeling anxious now, but she could understand why they were feeling happy. Hiding in a car when the driver knew you were there and you knew who the driver was, was a world away from having to sneak into a lorry or brave an open-sea crossing.

Plan, act, then breeze on through. That's what she had to do now. Just a bit of breezy confidence. Don't overthink it.

She got the boys to move down into the footwells, and she pulled a jacket over each of their heads. Their backpack stayed on the back seat, but she moved the plastic bags to the passenger's seat footwell, so they couldn't move against them and cause any rogue crackling.

Then she tossed her bag and a lightweight sweatshirt over the back seat, aiming to make everything look hurried and casual back there.

All set, she told herself. Time to drive out of the car park and towards the train terminal.

* * *

Just a brief, jumpy drive later and she was there. And because the queues were short, an official appeared at her window, just about scaring the life out of her, and offered to bump her forward onto the earlier train.

'Yes, of course... How handy...' she squeaked, swallowing quickly and trying to get full control over her voice.

And now, before she'd really, definitively confirmed that she was definitely going to do this, she was being guided into the queue. And it was moving smoothly and, oh holy people-smuggler-could-I-end-up-in-jail for this? Here was French passport control. She wound down her window and tried to smile rather than actually die of stress. Honestly, sweat and fear was squirting from her armpits in a way that must be rousing the suspicion of every sniffer dog within a half mile radius.

She held out her passport for inspection and tried not to blurt out: *Bonjour, je suis Lucie. Oui, j'ai du contrebande...* or should it be *de la contrebande*?

Holy freaking God, I am going to jail.

They waved her through. But there was no time to relax, or even breathe, and she hoped the boys realised this too because here was UK passport control straight ahead of her. So, did that mean, if she could just get through this... and possibly the highly trained Alsatians roaming the train, that would be it? She would drive out with no further checks at the other side? She crossed everything and hoped she could just put on this one, very important performance. *Channel Deva*, she thought to herself... and her mind couldn't help producing *Chanel Deva...* Stress joking, she guessed.

There wasn't even a moment to tell the boys to be quiet, so she just hoped and prayed that they would understand.

Now it was time to wind down her window and hand over her passport to the UK official. She felt terrible. This was the worst thing she'd ever done, in her whole adult life. Yes, but it was also one of the very best things she was trying to do.

The man in the booth took her passport and seemed to look at her face, look at his screen, then tap on his keyboard forever. *What if they have cameras at the supermarket car park?* she thought, far too late. *What if they saw the boys in the back when I was loading the car... and now they're checking and wondering... and they're going to do a full search? What kind of trouble could I have got Pete and Fikru into, not to mention myself?*

At this point, as well as breath-holding, there may have been a slight escape of wee due to sheer terror.

'It's my dad's car...' she heard herself say in the most weirdly normal voice ever. 'I didn't think it would make it to the south of France and back but she's managed.'

There was no response and in the silence, she was sure she could hear the merest squeak from the back seat.

'And forty-odd bottles of wine is OK, isn't it? I did check on Google before...' How could she sound so breezy when even more sweat and fear was pumping out of her armpits and her knees were actually trembling?

Would they all go to jail, she wondered. As long as it was in the UK... How else would she see her dad... Would they give her some leave to see him? Compassionate leave from prison – did that exist? Honestly, a whole scenario of her being in prison and pleading to visit him in the hospice had all played out in her mind in those terrible seconds. If they're officially in UK customs territory, it would be a UK jail, wouldn't it?

'Personal consumption?' the guy said with a smile.

What! She suddenly couldn't think of any reply. What was he talking about?

Then she remembered her forty bottles of wine remark, but that felt like a year ago.

'Oh, yes... I do like wine o'clock.' Smile. How was she

managing to joke, when she felt as if a heart attack was imminent? Any. Moment. Now.

Her passport was coming back to her, and now the magical wave through followed. She wound up her window and drove onto the train.

Now... just this forty-five-minute journey to get through. Alsatians... Alsatians. She sat in absolute silence in her seat and could hear nothing from the boys either. All kinds of panicked thoughts ran through her mind... Would there be dogs, trained to sniff through the cars? Would there be heat-seeking devices? She had thought absolutely nothing through. And she knew she would not be able to relax for one moment until this journey was over.

'OK, boys,' she said quietly. 'We are on the train... You can breathe but keep hiding. Hide. Please. Fikru, I really, really hope you're OK. Please tell me quietly if you're not OK.'

'I OK,' came the whisper.

It was the longest forty-five minutes of her entire life. She could see other drivers getting out of their cars, stretching their legs, going to the toilet, relaxing, enjoying life. But she just stayed glued to her seat, having to consciously breathe in and out. Willing herself not to die of fright. Because how would that help anyone?

Don't die, don't die, don't die... she repeated in her head over and over again, frozen in position in the driver's seat, too frightened to do anything, even drink water from a bottle, in case it attracted attention.

Was she helping, doing what she was doing tonight? Was she solving a problem? Adding to a problem? She couldn't answer the big difficult questions. She just knew in her heart she was doing the right thing for her and for Pete and Fikru.

* * *

As she drove off the train and realised there were no further checks at this side and she was going to be able to drive right out of the port and onto the motorway, she suddenly felt a monumental burst of happiness, excitement and fizz.

She found herself laughing with relief.

Once they were out onto the road, she called out to the boys.

'You can come out! Pete, Fikru... it is OK. We are in England.'

There was a stirring of the coats, and the boys began to emerge carefully, looking around as if worried this could be some kind of trick, maybe finding it hard to believe that after all this time of travelling and trying and hoping that this could really be true.

Lucy wondered if she had broken a law... She couldn't be a people smuggler, could she? Because she'd not accepted anything for doing this. And the boys weren't going to be illegal immigrants because they were from Eritrea and were going to apply for refugee status. Plus they were going to stay with their uncle, so they wouldn't be put on one of those barges or in a hostel.

Her googled information had advised her that they had to go straight to the Asylum Screening Unit to register for refugee status, but she already knew it didn't open in Croydon, London until 9 a.m. It was now approaching 1 a.m. and she was exhausted. They must be exhausted too.

'Where are we going, Miss Lucie?' Pete asked her with his clear and trusting voice.

'Everything is OK, Pete. And we are going to my home to sleep,' she replied.

31

TUESDAY

'OK... so, here we are...' Lucie rolled the dusty Jag with all its dents and dings into the hospice car park.

She looked at her daughter. 'I'm a bit nervous,' she confessed.

'You've had a very long day... and it's only three-thirty,' Zoe replied with a smile.

And this was true. Lucie had woken up at 7 a.m., showered and dressed, then woken the sleeping boys – Pete, who'd been encamped in a sleeping bag on her sitting room floor, and Fikru, who was under a duvet on the sofa.

They'd showered too and then eaten the breakfast she'd gone out to the nearby shop to buy. She'd also washed and dried their clothes the night before and bought them UK sim cards for their phones, so they'd been able to call their uncle and tell him that they were in the UK and would come to him as soon as they'd registered in Croydon.

She had so enjoyed watching their happy smiles and laughter when he'd been overjoyed to hear from them and told them he would come and meet them in Croydon this morning.

Then, on her Wi-Fi, the boys had been able to contact their parents back home to say they were safe, in the UK and meeting their uncle. Lucie had left the room to give them privacy for the call – but not before she'd seen the happiness and relief on everyone's faces. And she'd felt relief of her own – the conviction that she'd been brave, and human, and had done a good thing.

So then she, Pete and Fikru had driven to Croydon where she'd parked the Jag up and escorted the boys to the entrance of the big official-looking block. They'd both looked so neat, tidy, clean and young, still carrying their rucksack and plastic bags of worldly possessions. She'd left them in the queue for the front door, fifteen minutes before opening time, in the care of their overjoyed uncle.

'You have my number,' she'd told all three. 'Keep in touch. Let me know how everything is going and if I can help you.'

Their uncle had brought her a bunch of flowers with a little note attached:

Thank you so much, Miss Lucie. You have done more than words can say.

When she'd hugged the boys goodbye, they'd felt slight and skinny in her arms. But in Pete's hug, she had felt his wiry and determined strength.

'You're both going to be OK,' she had told them. 'Promise to keep in touch, OK?'

'We promise.'

Then she'd walked back to the car and driven towards Zoe's address, but had to stop to get herself a large, comforting latte coffee en route. When she drank it in the car, she felt a weird mix of sadness and pride.

Pride in the boys and what she'd done for them. Sadness about the day ahead. She was heading to visit her dad for the first time in the hospice – so sad about all that being in a hospice meant for him.

* * *

'My girls! How amazing to see you, all sun-kissed from your French trip!'

All the enthusiasm was still there in his much smaller, much more faded voice, but it was a shock to see her father and how much change could happen in just a few days. He looked so small and frail now, and not able to do more than raise his hands just a little above the sheets to greet them.

But he was still tanned, still smiling.

'Hello, Gramps.' Zoe leaned over to hug and kiss him first. 'I love what you've done to the place.'

And yes, Lucie took a moment to look around. Two of his favourite big, bright paintings had been hung up, one over his bed and one on the wall opposite, so he could look at it. Then some multi-coloured bunting had been hung around the room and his two bedside tables were filled up with framed favourite family photographs and a big jug of bright flowers. In a particularly dad-like touch, Lucie could see that two shiny new bird feeders had been hung on the cherry tree outside his window, so he could watch the little feathered friends eating and twittering.

He was in a bright blue t-shirt and his hospital bed had an old blanket she recognised from home spread over the bright white sheets.

A kind, welcoming woman had already greeted her and Zoe and shown them round the family areas. The canteen, where food and hot drinks were available whenever needed, and the comfortable sitting room with chairs, sofas, a stack of books, and coffee tables with magazines was all set out waiting for anyone who needed time and space to themselves. There were several little private rooms too with day beds and armchairs. Then they'd been shown in to meet her dad.

'And Lucie.' He'd accepted her hug and kiss. 'Now, tell me all about it. I want to hear everything,' he'd said, but he'd closed his eyes as Zoe began to talk first, sensing that Lucie maybe needed a moment to sit, to settle, to ground her swirling emotions.

Zoe's nursing experience meant she was at home with hospital settings, weak sick people, and she had tuned in immediately to the feeling that her grampa wouldn't want her to acknowledge, or even really notice, that things were different now, things were definitely more serious. She knew just how to keep the mood and the tone upbeat and normal.

'Great trip, glorious weather, lovely wedding,' Zoe began. 'And the big news is that Rafi and I are engaged. If we can fit a little wedding in before the baby, we'll do that,' she added. 'Otherwise, it will be afterwards.'

'Congratulations, my darling, he will be so lucky to have you.'

'Thank you, Gramps.'

And Lucie could almost feel the question about whether her dad would be there for the birth, for the wedding, hanging in the air, all of them afraid to even acknowledge it. When she'd left for France, she'd thought he would certainly be there, that he would still be at home for Ritchie, who was arriving with his family on Thursday. But seeing him now, confined to this bed here, every moment was precious, as she could no longer know how many more moments there would be.

'So, Mum...' Zoe went on, 'she's had quite the adventure – she manhandled the Jag across France with only a few dings and one slight breakdown – no need to worry, all fixed now – and she's been dancing, chatting up a very handsome man and in true Wild Child Lucie style, she smuggled two young refugees into the country in the back of your car. How about that, Gramps? Very good thing you made her go with us.'

Her dad leaned back into his pillow and with something of an effort, he opened his eyes and locked them on Lucie's. Then he smiled and gave a gentle laugh.

'Ha ha ha... Good for you, Lucie,' he managed. 'Delighted to hear it. Very glad to hear the old girl's had an adventure.'

'The car, I hope you mean! Yes, she has.'

'Two refugees?' he asked.

'Lovely boys from Eritrea. But that's a long story and you look as if you could do with a little snooze before we tell you all about that.'

His eyes were closed again.

'I need to keep the strength up to see Ritchie and his family. Don't want to be lying here dozing and dribbling when they arrive.'

'No, Gramps, we know you. You'll rally. Get a second wind.'

'Zoe and I could go and have some lunch in the canteen while you have a snooze and then we'll come back and tell you our adventures,' Lucie suggested. 'Show you some photos too. Miles's bride and so on... The rest of the family.'

'Did Deva have fun? He seemed like a nice chap.'

'Oh, yes,' Lucie replied, meeting Zoe's eyes. 'He had a ball. Sang at the wedding and on the dancefloor afterwards. Star performer.'

'Good... good...'

'OK, we'll go out for a bit and come back once you've snoozed.'

As they gathered up their things and prepared to leave his bedside, his eyes opened, so pale, pale blue, almost crystally in the sunshine of the room.

'There are two things I wanted to tell you,' he said very clearly. 'While I remember... I'm always a bit worried each snooze might be my last and I won't wake up.'

Lucie, feeling stricken, looked at Zoe, unsure what to say.

Zoe sat down again, put her hand on her grampa's and said, 'It's OK, we're right here.'

Lucie sat back down in her chair on the other side, took hold of the frail hand in hers. She couldn't think for too long about how that hand used to look, how it used to grip hers, all those years ago.

'Number one, a wonderful daughter' – he looked straight at Lucie, tears forming in his eyes – 'a wonderful granddaughter' – he looked at Zoe now. 'I'm very lucky. And a wonderful son and his family too. What more could I ask?'

Lucie could feel tears slipping from her eyes but kept her gaze steady and her smile firmly in place.

'Love you, Dad,' she whispered.

'What will survive of us is love,' he added in his tired, whispery voice. 'I think Philip Larkin wrote that. I always thought he was a bit of a miserable old so-and-so, but he got that right. What will survive of us is love.'

Then he smiled, paused, closed his eyes and seemed to regroup for a moment or two.

Opening his eyes again and looking at Zoe this time, he began, 'I never sold the first flat that your grandmother and I owned. Sentimental reasons, I suppose. It's in Vauxhall. Been rented out but the latest renters have left.'

He was straining to get all this out and it was costing obvious effort.

'Don't worry about it, Dad,' Lucie began. 'We'll get everything sorted.'

'No, but...' He looked at Zoe. 'I want Zoe to have it. London, so... good for her. Ground floor and basement, four rooms, a garden, very nice for the baby and the husband. So, no need to go looking for anything. This is coming to you, Zoe.'

Zoe's eyes widened in utter astonishment.

'And Lucie.' His eyes swivelled to her. 'You always loved London. You'll have plenty of money from me, my darling. Maybe move, be with your family. Be the gran. What will survive of us is love.'

Both women held his hands tightly and looked at him with love as his eyes closed and he rested back against the pillow.

'Nap now...' he said.

Lucie and Zoe didn't move, didn't even look at one another until his breathing deepened and his slight grip on their hands loosened.

When they were sure he was asleep, they tiptoed quietly out of his room. On the other side of the door, they held hands.

'Where shall we go?' Lucie whispered, her voice sounding ragged and on the verge of tears.

'One of the quiet spaces,' Zoe whispered back.

'I'm going to need to cry,' Lucie confided.

'Me too...'

32

TWO MONTHS LATER – SEPTEMBER

Lucie had always suspected that the final stages of clearing out her parents' house would be down to her and it would be difficult work.

There was already a For Sale sign next to the gate at the bottom of the garden and although the big pieces of furniture would stay in the house until it was sold, she still had boxes of personal clothing and items to sort through and remove.

Her dad had been there for the first ten days of Ritchie and his family's visit, but then, in the early hours, with Zoe, Ritchie and Lucie by his side, he had died peacefully. Two days after that, Zoe had gone into labour and eleven hours later she'd delivered her daughter, who was named Pippa in honour of her great grampa, Phil.

It had all been an emotional whirlwind – so happy, so sad and bittersweet – Pippa was safely here and absolutely perfect, but Zoe's grampa was gone and the family were as much wrapped up in funeral and house-clearing arrangements as they were in welcoming a brand new baby into the family.

Ritchie had stayed on for the funeral and then packed up

everything that he wanted to take from his parents' home – photographs, two of the paintings he'd always liked, some of their more personal belongings... but not much.

All emotional the night before the flight home, he'd asked Lucie if he was making a mistake not packing up chairs and clothes and books, ornaments, and other possessions from the house.

'Am I going to regret not taking more?' he had asked. 'But I'm not that sentimental about stuff. It doesn't mean that I didn't love them both very much.'

'No, of course not,' she'd told him. 'Look, lots is going to Zoe and I'm going to store many things for a few months while I figure out what I'm doing with it... and what I'm doing next. So any time you change your mind, or remember something you wanted, you just let me know. I will find it.'

It had been properly sad to wave him, his wife and their children off into the taxi the next morning. She promised she would finally come out and visit them in Sydney... even though her head was spinning, her thoughts were all over the place and she had no idea when that would be.

'It's OK,' Ritchie had assured her when he'd hugged her in tight for goodbye. 'It will settle down and we'll see you when you're ready.'

When you're ready... That chimed with someone else's very important words, she remembered.

It was overwhelming in that rush and tangle of when too many major things collide. Her father was gone, her new granddaughter was here. Her brother was briefly around. There was a house sale to supervise and there was a lot of money heading her way. Zeros and zeros and zeros... Enough to need to think about new accounts and different pension funds and talks with a financial adviser.

Honestly, it was overwhelming. And, as she'd always suspected, the money and what to do with it only reminded her even more that her father wasn't here to give her his very good advice.

'Please take your time,' her new adviser, from the firm that her father had used for years, assured her. 'There's no rush. We'll move the funds into safe and sensible places until you can gather your thoughts and make your plans.'

So she was trying to remain calm and restore some routine in the face of it all. She went home to her little flat in the evening, made supper, kept house and tried to sleep well. Then she was back at her father's house during the day, clearing out rooms, boxing up possessions, taking things to auctions or charity shops, or to Zoe and Rafi. Along with their baby, they had moved as soon as they could to the flat in Vauxhall, which was where Lucie's mum and dad had begun their married life all those years ago.

As her dad had promised, it was perfect for a young couple and a new baby. There was a spacious kitchen and sitting room down on the lower garden level and upstairs, on the ground floor, two generous bedrooms. Then just one set of neighbours on the two floors upstairs. Through the kitchen's back doors was a small town garden with a lawn, flowerbed and shrubbery, perfect for sunny days with a baby.

At first, Lucie didn't think she could find the smallest traces of her parents in the flat, because over the decades, everything had been repainted, redecorated and renewed. But one afternoon, when she was sitting at the table in the garden, rocking the sleepy Pippa bundle in her arms, she suddenly realised that the trees, a bright pink cherry and a romantic lilac, planted along the back wall, must be over fifty years old and that her parents had always had a cherry and a lilac in every garden after this one. So there, she thought, with a tear sliding down her face, was proof of them. 'What survives of us is love,' he'd told her. Love and plants, and piles of belongings and a strong desire to feed the birds.

* * *

So here she was today, in the spare bedroom at her father's house, hauling her own boxes out from under the bed. Wondering once again what she was going to do when all this period of sorting and filing and storing and 'Dad-min' was over.

She would move to Vauxhall too, she'd decided. She liked it. It was inner city, a little buzzy, a little gritty. And how lovely for Zoe and Rafi to have a helping hand just a few streets away, someone to land baby Pippa on, someone who could come and babysit when required.

Zoe had been overwhelmed too, not just by the baby and the planning of a wedding, but by inheriting a whole flat. The kind of thing you could only dream about had become real. She and Rafi were able to take proper parent leave together now. And Zoe, who loved her job, and had always been completely proud of it, had nevertheless made the very first mention of going back to uni… and taking that medical degree.

'Not that I'm undermining nursing in any way at all,' she had insisted when she'd first mentioned the plan to her mother. 'But the lines are blurring. Nurses are much more involved in treatment and doctors are getting far more involved in caring. I think I'd make a pretty good GP, or maybe I'll choose geriatrics, or maybe I'll just roll up my sleeves and cure cancer,' she'd joked.

And Lucie was beginning to feel fired up too, seeing all the possibilities that this life-changing amount of money could bring. She would start up the new design business just as she'd planned in France. She would begin small with projects that were genuinely interesting and grow it slowly and steadily. No need to do a Miles and charge off at a hundred miles per hour.

Pulling out the boxes from under the bed, she thought of Chanel, and Deva, of course, and sent him a quick 'how are you doing, favourite nephew?' message.

And the other boys on that memorable trip, Pete and Fikru, they were doing just fine. Their applications for asylum were in, and while they waited, they were staying with their uncle, helping out at his garage, learning more English and mechanics.

She lifted the lid on the old carboard box of nineties nostalgia. One Union Jack mini-dress, good grief! She smiled as she unfolded it. And there was the silver and gold dress worn at *that* Christmas party. The one where the photo of her and Clark had been snapped, all those years ago. She unfolded it too to look at it. Then, before she could give it too much thought, she was taking off her workaday jeans, t-shirt, trainers and socks and pulling on this lovely Italian-made dress, bought all the way back in her twenties, from a much pricier shop than usual, to celebrate Christmas and a pay-rise and having a proper first job.

She wasn't expecting to fit into it; too much time, hormonal upheaval, recent comfort eating and drinking for that. But... the colour and the shape still suited her very well. She wondered if side panels could be added to make it wearable again... not to mention doing some stomach crunches or even buying a pair of the dreaded Spanx... she couldn't help the ripple of laughter as she thought of poor old Miles.

She looked in the mirror and couldn't help thinking that she looked pretty OK in this dress from her twenty-something self. She had a great new haircut from Zoe's trendy hairdresser, plus the kind of decent makeup job that she spent a bit of time doing in the mornings these days, and fancy earrings. Yes, not too shabby at all. A woman who still had a lot of interesting things to do.

She went back to the box and looked for the photo she knew was still in there. When she'd found it, she sat on the bed and looked for a few moments at her much younger face, laughing, smiling, deeply concentrating on him... Clark.

Yes, they had exchanged some messages since France. But she'd not seen him and hadn't expected to. After all, she was the one who'd told him that she would be at her dad's bedside until he was gone and then busy dealing with the aftermath.

But was it time now to get in touch with him?

What did she really want from him?

What did he want from her?

Would it really be possible to pick something up from whatever there had been all those many years ago? Or create something brand new from what they had kindled at the wedding and in that little hotel afterwards?

She was uncertain, phone in her hand, wondering if she dared.

Just then, a reply landed from Deva.

It was a photo of him and his mother. Two things struck her immediately: how happy and smiley they both looked, and the fact that he was wearing Lucie's beautiful Chanel jacket dressed down with a black t-shirt and wide-legged jeans. His arm was around his smiling mother as he hugged her in for a selfie.

Lucie read his words:

Just about to go for my first London show chorus audition. Wish me LUCK!! What doesn't kill you makes you stronger, right, Auntie L? Permission to do something extraordinary, granted! xxx

This was so obviously a sign that she didn't hesitate, immediately scrolling to find Clark's number, and then she typed quickly, realising that there was no danger of stalling, or worrying or overthinking, because this was what she wanted to do.

Clark, it's Lucie. I'm ready.

Just moments after she'd hit send, her phone began to ring, and when she saw his name on the screen, well... after so many things that had come to an end, this felt like the start. And it was very good to be at the start.

33

Pascoe & Friends had been serving London customers since 1995. In all that time, the menu hadn't strayed too far from the original. They still served mussels with fries, a decent steak, a fish pie, along with vegetarian and even vegan dishes for the discerning modern customer.

The online reviews showed that many people came back to the restaurant once or twice a year, even once or twice a decade, and loved the fact that it wasn't so different from how they remembered it.

Lucie hadn't been back since that Christmas party in the late 1990s, when Pascoe's was a premier celebrity haunt and the place to go and eat alongside a smattering of famous faces. When she arrived tonight, almost exactly on time, she could tell it wasn't such a hot, showbiz place as it had been back then, when there was usually a handful of photographers scouting about outside, but it still exuded glamour, still allowed guests to relax as soon as they walked in, secure in the knowledge that they were going to be well looked after and would enjoy an evening of good food and good wine.

As the waiter guided her to the table, her heart did quite genuinely leap to see that Clark was already there.

And he looked just as pleased to see her as she felt to see him once again. As they kissed hello, the connection buzzed between them much more powerfully than she'd expected.

For the first half an hour, the conversation felt a little nervy and almost shy, as they caught up on what had happened since France. But as they began to eat and relax, the warm, much more intimate atmosphere began to build once again. They started to really talk... about back then, when they were working together, of course, and about their families, their businesses, their future plans.

'I've decided I'm going to move back to London and start a new interior design business,' Lucie told him.

Clark's reaction to this was incredibly positive.

'That's very good! I love it – especially because I live in London too.'

She went on. 'I think I liked myself best when I lived in the city. I don't want to slide into being that woman of a certain age going about the suburbs in a car, spending too much time gardening, gossiping and drinking wine. Not that I'm opposed to wine.' She gave him a wink that caused him to lean forward and kiss her on the mouth.

As she kissed him back, she immediately wished that dinner was nearly over and they could take this kissing outside and pay some proper attention to it.

'I still feel like I have a lot to do,' she told him.

'Me too, me too,' he agreed. 'And I love this moving to the city idea... I was toying with the idea of moving out, having more space and more greenery, but you've convinced me it would be the wrong thing to do.'

'Much more fun to be had in town,' she said and they smiled conspiratorially at one another.

'When we were younger... when you were working with me...' he began, and Lucie could feel her heart rate skip a little because she sensed that he was going to say something important about how things were between them back then.

'I always thought we would get together. End up together even, and I was so sorry that it didn't happen. You lit up the office, lit up my working days, and I could not stop thinking about you, Lucie. Even when I should not have been thinking of you. You were full of ideas and creativity and I knew there was such a bright future ahead for you.'

'I should have been with you,' Lucie said but she smiled about it and added, 'our timing was always terrible.'

'No point in regretting what's happened,' he said, his eyes fixed intently on hers. 'I think we should just look forward to being together now and seeing what we can inspire in each other.'

Lucie put her hand over his, and honestly felt a physical crackle of energy between them. The thought of loving him again passionately, like she had done in France, was right there at the forefront of her mind.

'That is pretty interesting,' she said. 'I am completely up for seeing what we can inspire in each other.'

'You look so exactly the way I remember you...' he said, looking almost puzzled. 'Weren't you wearing a dress just like this one at that Christmas party?'

'This is the dress,' she admitted. 'I've worn it for luck.'

'Now that's funny... because this is my trusty 1990s watch' – he pointed to his wrist – 'and I've worn it for luck too. And I am so waxed,' he added, making her laugh, 'Practically bald!'

* * *

If whoever had taken that photo of the two of them all those years ago had just happened to pass their table tonight to snap it again, they would have seen Lucie and Clark, almost three decades later, but looking as if the time and the distance between those photos had been erased.

Once again, their eyes were locked, they were totally captivated and they looked exactly like a couple.

'Time to let the adventure begin...' Clark said.

Lucie smiled right back at him. 'Maybe we should go on a journey. I've inherited this lovely old car...'

ACKNOWLEDGEMENTS

Thank you so much awesome Team Boldwood for all the hard work that goes into making every one of my books better and bolder! Special appreciation for my editor, Emily Ruston, copy-editor, Jennifer Davies, and proofreader, Rose Fox, who have all helped to shape this story for the better.

Thank you also to Boldwood's Nia Beynon, Issy Flynn and Niamh Wallace who all do such great work on the sales, marketing and publicity side. I really do appreciate you all.

I always thank my friends and family for putting up with having a writer in their lives. Moody, on a deadline, and then there is always the worry that our escapades and adventures will end up in a story – heavily disguised! I don't think I've copied much from real life in this one and just to say, I have loved all our holidays, road trips and weddings and hope there are many more to come.

ABOUT THE AUTHOR

Carmen Reid is the bestselling author of numerous women's fiction titles including the Personal Shopper series starring Annie Valentine. She lives in Glasgow with her husband and children.

Sign up to Carmen Reid's mailing list for news, competitions and updates on future books.

Visit Carmen's website: www.carmenreid.com

Follow Carmen on social media:

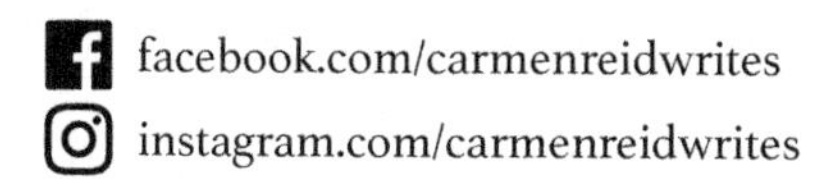
facebook.com/carmenreidwrites
instagram.com/carmenreidwrites

ALSO BY CARMEN REID

Worn Out Wife Seeks New Life

New Family Required

The Woman Who Ran For The Hills

Three in a Bed

Stuck in Second Gear

The Annie Valentine Series

The Personal Shopper

Late Night Shopping

How Not To Shop

Celebrity Shopper

New York Valentine

Shopping With The Enemy

Annie in Paris

BECOME A MEMBER OF
THE
SHELF
CARE
CLUB

Printed in Great Britain
by Amazon

53653906R00165